send pics

lauren mclaughlin

dottir
press

NEW YORK CITY

Published in 2020 by Dottir Press
33 Fifth Avenue
New York, NY 10003

Visit www.dottirpress.com

First printing April 2020
Cover design by Erin Wade
Text design and production by Drew Stevens

Trade Distribution through Consortium Book Sales and Distribution, www.cbsd.com.

Library of Congress Cataloging-in-Publication Data is available for this title.

ISBN 978-1-948340-26-7 (Paperback Edition)
ISBN 978-1-948340-28-1 (Hardcover Edition)

"Don't let anyone rewrite your story."
—ALY RAISMAN, GYMNAST

"This is a steep price to pay for
twenty minutes of action."
—DAN TURNER, FATHER

"What one does when faced with the truth
is more difficult than you'd think."
—WONDER WOMAN, AMAZON QUEEN

JONESVILLE, MASSACHUSETTS
2017

NIKKI

I remember the first time I saw Suze Tilman. Lunch period, this past April. She didn't look like a Jonesville girl. She was alone out in the parking lot, leaning against the hood of her silver Prius, reading an old paperback. *Jaws*, I think. She kept pushing her fine, light brown hair out of her face whenever the wind blew it. She wore a vintage Bob Seger concert T-shirt, baggy 501s, and these old black Chuck Taylors. Anyone else would have looked like a slob in that getup, but she pulled it off. She had beauty to spare, like a Disney princess, but of the alt variety—like if Disney ever made a movie about Frances Bean Cobain. Practically the whole school was staring at her through the floor-to-ceiling windows, wondering who she was and where she came from. I remember turning to my friends, Ani and Lydia, and saying, "There is something *off* about that girl." I meant it as a compliment. Normal people bore me.

It didn't take long for Tarkin Shaw to notice her too. Jonesville High's a jock school, and he's the king jock. He thinks he owns the place and every girl in it, because his parents are rich and he made all-state in wrestling his junior year, like these are major accomplishments. Actually, most girls go giggly and stupid whenever Tarkin comes around, like even being seen with him makes you a minor celebrity. Of course, Suze, being new to the school, didn't know his "status," so when Tarkin went out there to hit on her with his posse of wingmen, all he had going for him were his movie-star looks and I guess what passes for charm. I couldn't hear anything, but I'm sure he pulled out all the stops— flattery, negging, his pathetic attempt at humor. Whatever he was slinging, though, Suze wasn't having it. Never even changed her expression. It was like she was *analyzing* him. But not like an interested girl sizing up a hot guy, more like a scientist inspecting a vial of urine. You could tell, just from her body language, that all she wanted to do was get back to her book. Tarkin was so confused. It was beautiful.

Tarkin and I have a history. But I don't like to talk about it.

After he got the message that his "charm" wasn't working on Suze, he turned tail and jock-walked out of there, flexing his pecs and smirking with his wrestler buddies. By the time they made it back into the cafeteria they were dropping words like "dyke" and "skank." Typical. They say that about me and my friends, too. They say that about any

8

girl who doesn't worship them. By then, Suze had gone back to her book, like the whole incident had no effect on her at all, like it was just some lame Netflix series she wasn't going to bother finishing. I turned to Ani and Lydia, and said: "We need to meet this girl." They agreed.

The three of us went out to the parking lot while Tarkin and his buddies stank-eyed us the whole way. I guess he assumed that since he'd written her off, everyone else had to.

"Hi," I said. "You're new. I'm Nikki."

"Suze," she said, offering her hand.

"Are you English?" Lydia asked.

"No. But I lived there for a while. Hence the accent. I was born here, actually, but I haven't lived here since I was a baby. Been in Munich for the past three years." She nodded toward Tarkin, who was openly glaring at us through the window. "Are all American boys like that one?"

"I wouldn't know," I said. "Are German boys different?"

"Loads." Then she told us about Hans from Munich, who lived next door to her. "He was a bit of a nerd, really. But he had eyes the color of pond water."

"Was he your boyfriend?" I asked.

"More of a friend, actually. But we fooled around sometimes. Now, Piotr." She put her book down on the hood of her car and settled in to talk. "He was this university student from Poland, studying microbiology. He had the most expert hands in the world. Older guys, you know. They're much better at it."

"Really," I said, making a mental note that there might be something to look forward to, romance-wise, beyond Jonesville.

"We're not dating anyone until college," Ani said. "Jonesville boys are revolting."

"Are they?" Suze surveyed the cafeteria crowd. She didn't seem intimidated by the fact that people were staring at her. It was like she expected it. Like people stared at her all the time.

"To be honest," Lydia said. "Most of the girls around here are pretty revolting, too."

"You don't seem revolting," Suze said.

"Oh, we are," I said. "But we're the good kind of revolting."

She cocked her head as she looked at me. Curious, appraising. Sort of the way she looked at Tarkin. Was I a vial of urine, too?

"Want to come for dinner tonight?" she said, finally. "My dad's an appalling cook, but he means well."

SHE WAS RIGHT about the food. It was awful, some kind of lamb-sausage casserole. I had to hold my breath while eating it. But the girls and I stayed until midnight, listening to Suze's stories about Munich and London and Paris and Madrid. She was seventeen, a junior like us, but that's where the similarities ended. Compared to her adventures, life in Jonesville seemed small and dull. Suze had already lived in six different countries and traveled to more than she could count. Her parents were academics: a historian (her mother) and an ethnomusicologist (her father). According to her, they took lots of sabbaticals and only worked when the money was running out. Their main interest was traveling. Nomads, basically. They were only here in boring old Jonesville because her Dad's great-aunt had died, leaving her house empty and available.

I'd never met anyone with a history like Suze's. But the strangest part, for me anyway, was that she was just as fascinated by life in Jonesville as we were by her life on the road. She'd tell us about the sprawling souk in Marrakesh, where the leather factories smelled so bad you had to walk around with orange peels under your nose, and we'd take her to the food court at the Liberty Tree Mall, which smelled like Windex and pizza. Imagine being wowed by a food court. But Suze could create an adventure out of anything. I remember one Saturday a few weeks after that dinner party, she drove to my house at 5:30 a.m., unannounced, because she'd read about this place called the Desert of Maine. "It's a *real* desert," she said breathlessly, practically jumping out of her skin at my front door. "And it's in *Maine*."

"Okay," I said.

But it wasn't just okay to Suze. It was an

emergency. She had to go there. And it had to be now. I'd planned on spending the day doing homework, but this sounded way more fun, so I grabbed a backpack and jumped in her car. We hit Dunkin's for some iced coffee, then drove all the way to Freeport.

As it turns out, the Desert of Maine is not a real desert, just a forty-acre patch of glacial silt that basically grew out of an old farmer's mismanagement of the land. But that didn't dampen the thrill for Suze. She loved every minute of the tour. I think it was the tour guide's thick Maine accent that did it. Afterward, we stopped for lunch at this rustic dive called the Muddy Rudder and shared a lobster roll.

"What if we dropped out of school and moved here?" she said. "We could be waitresses at this very restaurant!" I told her I had plans, like graduating and going to college, and she just laughed and laughed.

"Plans," she said.

Suze didn't believe in plans. She believed in improvisation and serendipity. "After all," she explained, "if everything goes according to plan, how can you ever be surprised?"

I guess she had a point, because I had certainly never planned on meeting her. But before long, we were doing everything together. My little nation of three became a nation of four. Ani, Lydia, and I had been tight since freshman year, which is when things were at their worst for me. Ani and Lydia were the only ones who knew about Tarkin and me. I was nervous about telling Suze, because I figured it would change the way she saw me. But it didn't, and I'll never forget what she said to me afterward. We were in the woods behind her house, sitting on this big, sloping rock she liked. I told her what had happened. She closed her eyes for a minute. Then she looked straight into my face and said, "Do you know what you are, Nikki?" At that point, I felt so wrecked from telling my story, all I could think was, *Yes. I am dirt.* But she said, "You're gold."

"Really?" I said.

"Yes," she said. "You're gold and he's nothing."

And you know what? At that moment, I believed her.

THE WEEKEND

MARCUS

My name is Marcus Daubney. I'm a reporter and a junior at Jonesville High. When I say that I'm a reporter, I don't mean I'm an *aspiring* reporter. I also don't mean I write for the school newspaper, which doesn't even exist at my stupid, jock-worshipping school. I write for the Jonesville *Bugle*, a real paper. Print and digital. My mother once described me as a "born skeptic with an instinctual hatred of falsehood," which I find very flattering. I can't remember a time in my life when I wasn't trying to smoke out the truth. "Journalism's first obligation is to the truth." I read that somewhere and wrote it on a green Post-it, and it's been stuck to my bedroom mirror for seven years. The story I'm about to tell you would make an amazing article, a *career-making* article. Unfortunately, I can never write it. Well, I can write it, but it can never be published. By the time you reach the end of this story, you'll understand why.

I guess I should start at the beginning.

Sunday, September 10, 2017. I've just filed an article to Frank Schnell, my editor at the *Bugle*. It's about the upcoming school-board election, and I feel pretty good about my work. It's been a heated campaign, pitting a loud-mouthed "conventionalist" against a group of angry moms who think more money should be spent on the arts. It's the same fight every year, and the conventionalist always wins. Jonesville is a jock town, always has been. "Reading, writing, and wrestling." It's not our official motto, but it might as well be.

While I wait for feedback from my editor, I text my best pal, DeShawn:

You in the hole?

He texts back:

Yup. Come on over.

So I head outside and hop on my ten-speed. Having spent the last six hours in my bedroom banging away on my laptop, it feels good to be outside on this fine September Sunday, cycling down Cherry Street. Jonesville is just about the most boring place imaginable—an outer suburb of Boston, solidly middle class, with a thin crust of new money that lends the place its piquant aroma of aspiration. But it does autumn very well. The russet trees arching over Cherry Street flicker in the sun, and there's a faint smell of smoke from burning leaves somewhere. If you squint, you can almost imagine you were in a Norman Rockwell painting.

DeShawn lives in a two-story colonial on Elm

Street, anchored by a huge, overgrown maple tree in the front yard. I ride straight up over his front lawn and around to the back, dump my bike by the basement door, and head inside. DeShawn's basement is split in half. One side is an unfinished rec room with a secondhand bumper pool table and an out-of-tune piano slowly moldering from neglect. The other half, "the hole," is DeShawn's domain, a sovereign nation, devoted to robotics and modeling in a variety of materials. Nobody else ever goes there. But I have a passport and can come and go as I please.

The curtains are drawn on the ground-level windows, and DeShawn, lit by a trio of bendy lights, hunches over an unfinished insectoid robot with a soldering iron in one hand. The robot's name is Terence, and he's been working on it for six months.

I don't believe in genius as a concept. I believe in commitment and focus. But if I did believe in genius, DeShawn would be its poster child. Nobody ever taught him how to make these robotic marvels. He taught himself. You want the art on DeShawn? Focus hard because he won't fit into any of your boxes. He's built like an athlete, but don't let that fool you, he's a hard-core nerd. Handsome in his way, with dark skin and a Lenny Kravitz Afro. He's definitely better-looking than me. I'm the kind of guy who fades into the background: average height, average weight, pale, with dirt-brown hair. If you took all the white people in Massachusetts and blended them into a statistical average, you'd get me. DeShawn, on the other hand, is a true original.

"We should be outside," he says, without ever looking up from Terence. "My mom says I need fresh air."

"Yeah, I've just come from there. It's overrated."

My cell phone chirps as I pull up a chair and sit beside him at his workbench. It's a message from Elena DePiero, my colleague at the *Bugle*. Apparently the police were called out last night to a keg party on Brooks Road, and Elena wants to know if I was there. I wasn't, of course. I eschew keg parties. Or they eschew me, depending on your point of view. I'm pretty sure the party she's talking about happened at Tara Budzynski's house. I overheard people talking about it at school on Friday. Tara's a junior, a middling field hockey player, marginally well-liked but not quite *popular*. Definitely not in the upper echelons of Jonesville High society, but reaching, baby, reaching for the stars.

It must be a really slow news day if Elena's trolling high school keg parties in search of a lead. Then again, this is Jonesville. Every day is a slow news day. I tell her I'll dig up whatever I can, then, while DeShawn works on Terence, I hit the usual sites on my phone. Sure enough, there's loads of chatter about who hooked up with whom at Tara's party, who broke up with whom, who got drunk, who got stupid. It's the typical Jonesville bacchanalia, with the requisite pics to back it up: girls flashing their bras, guys chugging beer, other guys passed out, somebody's naked butt, a still life of puke in the flower beds. Someone even captured video of the cops arriving while dozens of kids fled the scene.

"Hey, who's that?" DeShawn asks, pointing to my phone.

On the screen is a poorly lit image featuring an unconscious girl being carried by three other girls across the front lawn, her long hair dragging along the grass.

"Is that Suze Tilman?" he asks.

It's hard to tell. The unconscious girl's face is obscured behind the legs of one of the other girls.

"Well, that one's Nikki Petronzio," he says, pointing to the girl on the left.

I can't see her face, but I recognize Nikki's distinctive hair: long and dark, like Cher from the early days.

"And that's Lydia Moreau," he says, pointing to the little blond pixie on the right. The third girl is hidden behind the others, but I'm guessing it's Ani Chakrabarti, because these girls tend to move as a pack. Which, by deduction, means the girl being carried out of there is almost certainly the illustrious Suze Tilman, the fourth and newest member of their pack.

"I hope she's not hurt," DeShawn says.

"She's probably just drunk."

"Dude, everyone knows that Suze Tilman doesn't drink."

"Really? *Everyone* knows that? *I* didn't know that."

"What's she even doing at that party?" he asks. "Since when do Suze and those girls go to parties?"

"DeShawn, you've never been to a party. How do you know who goes to them?"

He ignores my question. He's too stricken by the photograph. "I'm really worried about her, man."

To be clear, Suze is not a friend of ours. Neither of us has ever spoken to her. We're juniors. She's a senior. She moved here from Munich last year and was immediately co-opted by Nikki and her icy friends. Rumor has it she was born in the States but spent most of her youth moving from one European city to another, which makes her glamorous by Jonesville standards.

She doesn't look so glamorous in this picture.

As a joke, I text the photograph to Elena with the fake headline: *Cool New Girl Who Doesn't Normally Drink Gets Trashed at Kegger.*

A minute later Elena texts back: *Stop the presses.*

Like I said, Jonesville does autumn well, but every day is a slow news day.

NIKKI

Tara Budzynski's party was a joke. The only reason the girls and I were even there was to score some weed. We don't do parties. But Lydia's cousin had utterly failed to score us the weed she'd promised, so we had no choice. We're not stoners or anything, but sometimes you need to get out of your head.

"Shields up," Lydia said as we made our way across Tara's front lawn to her big house. *Shields up* is our motto, our superpower. We watched the *Wonder Woman* movie together this summer, and afterwards we all vowed to be one anothers' Shield—especially in dodgy social situations like the one we were about to enter.

Two sophomore guys were vaping weed on the porch.

"Bingo," Ani muttered.

We stationed ourselves there and let them try to make us laugh, waiting for them to offer us some weed. Meanwhile Suze wandered off to go "check out the scene" inside. She likes to think of herself as an anthropologist of the suburbs, observing the natives in their "natural" habitat, but I figured she'd wind up in the woods behind Tara's house. Suze has a thing for trees. She says it comes from the summer she spent living on the edge of a forest in Poland, which is classic Suze. Who else can say they lived on the edge of a Polish forest? The plan for the night was to get high then hit Singing Beach, look up at the stars, say deep shit. A typical Saturday night for the girls and me.

At some point in the festivities, if you can call them that, someone turned up the music and all the girls at the party ran out onto the porch to grind, flaunting their asses while the boys gathered around to snap pictures and make gross gestures. The girls and I are into exactly none of that, plus we were sufficiently high, so we went looking for Suze to make a clean adios. Suze's car was still parked out front, but Suze herself was MIA. Typical. The girl has a severe case of wanderlust. One time over the summer, she picked me up at dawn and we drove all the way to New York City just so she could buy a bagel from this place called David's. They were okay, I guess. But it seemed like a long way to drive for a *bagel*. That's Suze though. She gets an impulse and she goes with it. She doesn't second-guess herself.

Eventually this little sophomore dude comes out and tells us he saw Suze going down into the basement with Tarkin Shaw.

"I seriously doubt that," I tell him. Suze may be curious about these suburban natives, but she knows well enough to steer clear of Tarkin Shaw.

"I saw what I saw," he tells me. "She was all over him too."

"No," I say. "That's not possible." He must have her confused with someone else.

In any event, she's definitely not out here, so just to be sure we head inside and go down to Tara's basement, which is like sinking into a testosterone swamp. It smells like beer, BO, and Axe body spray. Tarkin's wrestler buddies are playing pool, trying to look tough and super-casual at the same time. Like, sure, they notice us, but they're not going to lower themselves to acknowledge the fact. Very unconvincing. One of them, Russ Minichek, can't take his eyes off of Ani's butt. They're pathetic, all of them, douchebag clones of Tarkin Shaw. I guess he's their alpha douchebag.

"Can we hurry this up?" Ani whispers, trying to back away from Minichek so he'll stop staring at her.

Ani can be ferocious online. But IRL, or in "meatspace," as she calls it, she's pretty timid. Lucky for us Tarkin Shaw himself staggers out of a back room, drunk off his ass and swaying side to side. His blond-tipped hair flops into his eyes and every time he swings it away, he nearly falls over. "Well if it isn't the bitch queen herssssself," he slurs at me.

Bitch queen has been his nickname for me ever since freshman year, which is ironic because neither "bitch" nor "queen" is an insult.

"We're looking for Suze," I tell him coldly.

"Well, she ain't looking for you." He tries to stare

me down, gets real serious, puffing out his chest to intimidate me. And you know what? He *is* intimidating. He's six three and I'm pretty sure he takes steroids. I'm five six if I stretch and I'm not what you'd call physically imposing. But I refuse to let him see how scared I am because that's exactly what he wants. He wants everybody to be scared of him, as well as impressed, amazed, and attracted. In his mind, those things don't even cancel each one other out.

"Is she in there?" I ask, gesturing to the room he just came out of.

"See for yourself."

"Suze?" I call out. But there's no answer.

"See what I mean, bitch queen?" He stands in the doorway, blocking my way. "It's not you she wants."

I take a deep breath, psych myself up, then squeeze past him. He's so drunk he practically falls over. The room I enter is dark and smells like old sweat. It takes a moment for my eyes to adjust. Barbells, dumbbells. It's a weight-lifting room.

And then I see her.

She's unconscious and draped over a red vinyl weight bench, her T-shirt pulled halfway up, showing the bottom of her left boob.

Tarkin stumbles into the room and says, "She threw herself at me."

The words pierce me like a serrated edge. It's not the first time I've heard them and I swear to God I want to smash his face and his stupid blond tips right into that poster of Megan Fox.

But Lydia and Ani rush in before I can do anything stupid. They kneel down on either side of Suze and lift her head off the weight bench. She isn't passed out exactly, just groggy as hell. When her eyes finally focus on me, she smiles like a little girl and tries to say my name. She goes "Ni—Ni—Ni—" When she can't get the word out she giggles, then curls up in Ani's arms.

"Awww," Tarkin says, like this is the cutest thing ever. "Another satisfied customer. Seriously though, you should take her home. That girl is drunk as fuck."

"She doesn't drink, moron." Lydia says.

"Really? She looks pretty drunk to me." He leans in close to me and whispers: "I think she's in love with me. Jealous?"

Having him that close freaks me out. The rank smell of beer on his breath sends me right back in time.

"Nikki?" Lydia says, trying to snap me back to the present.

"*Nikki*?" Tarkin mocks. He throws his arms around me from behind. "Come on, let's make it a party."

"Get the fuck away from her!" Lydia says. Then she leaves Suze with Ani and stalks over to us.

"Yo, calm down," Tarkin says, peeling himself off of me. "There's plenty of the Tarks to go around. Want to hop on?" He thrusts his crotch at her. "I mean if that's alright with the bitch queen here."

Out in the other room, his buddies start yukking

it up, like Tarkin Shaw is some kind of A-list comedian.

"Hey, save some for me," Aaron Paulson shouts, to much snickering.

While I stand frozen like a statue, Lydia's rage begins to grow. She may look like Tinker Bell, but you do not want to piss her off. Her dad is an ex-boxer and he's taught her a thing or two.

"Ooh," Tarkin says, looking down on her. "You gonna fight me?"

Her answer to that is a quick and brutal knee to the nuts.

"FUUUUCKKK!" Tarkin drops to the floor and starts rolling around, moaning about his testicles, going "*Unh, unh, unh,* you stupid bitch!"

"Nikki?" Lydia says, snapping her fingers in my face.

I haven't moved since Tarkin touched me.

"Come on," she says. "Let's go."

We drag Suze off of the weight bench. She's like a rag doll. It takes me under one arm, Ani under the other, and Lydia steadying her from behind to get her up.

"You're a total fucking whore," Tarkin barks at us from the floor. I guess he's talking to Lydia for kicking him. Or maybe to Suze. Or even to me. Who knows? On my way out the door I flick the back of his head with the toe of my sneaker, just enough to make him groan again. I'd like to do more, especially with him being so helpless down there. Sometimes my own anger scares me.

When we get Suze out of the weight room, Tarkin's idiot friends suddenly switch to fucking gentlemen and offer to help us carry her up the stairs, but we're like no thanks, we got this, keep your grope-ass hands to yourself.

By the time we get around to the front of the house, Tara's porch is overflowing. The music is super loud, and as we drag carry Suze across the front lawn toward her car, we hear a siren in the distance.

"Uh oh," Ani says.

Then it's mayhem. Kids start spilling out of the front door, sprinting for their cars, stumbling over the hedges. Eventually we make it to Suze's car and lay her down as gently as we can in the back seat. She's five ten, so it takes some doing getting all her arms and legs in there, like cramming a grasshopper into a Tic Tac box.

"She's our designated driver," Ani says in a panic. "What are we gonna do?"

"Relax," I tell her. "Don't get paranoid."

Ani starts taking deep breaths to calm down, but it doesn't work. She's practically vibrating with anxiety. Weed does that to her sometimes.

Technically, we're all too stoned to drive, but those sirens are getting closer. Ani is way too freaked out to take the wheel, and Lydia is a rage driver in the best of circumstances, so it's on me. I get behind the wheel and try to do things as methodically as possible to override my high. Key. Ignition. Seat pulled forward. Mirror adjusted. Seat

29

belt clicked. Because I'm high, everything seems to be moving way too slowly. I'm convinced the cops are going to wheel up and arrest me right then and there, but somehow, I manage to pull away before they arrive. I weave around all the kids running to their own cars, then about a hundred yards down Brooks Road, right before the turn off to Main Street, the police cruiser glides right on by us.

Ani's in the back seat with Suze's head in her lap. "Let's never do this again," she says. "Let's never go to a party again."

Lydia and I agree. No amount of free weed is worth this.

WHEN WE GET to my place, the three of us carry Suze up the front steps then again up to the second floor, which is no easy feat, especially since we have to keep things quiet or risk waking up my parents. They're not what you'd call cool. They're in the scream-first-ask-questions-later camp. They wouldn't necessarily mind my being at Tara's party. My mom thinks I'm too antisocial for my own good. But they do not know I smoke pot, and they would not approve of Suze being passed out like this. They already think she's "a little strange." I'm hoping to handle this situation on my own. The less my parents know the better.

Once we get Suze into my room, I text her parents from her phone to say:

Crashing at Nikki's

They text back:

Okeydokey, honey bunny. Stay safe. xo.

Parents, I swear to God, no clue.

Suze barely even stirs as we get her tucked in safe and sound in my bed.

"She's not going to choke on her own vomit, is she?" Ani asks me, like I'm an expert in people choking on their own vomit.

"I think you're supposed to put her on her side," Lydia says. "Then prop her up with a pillow. I saw that in *Breaking Bad*."

"Yeah, but that girl died anyway," Ani says.

"Right, because she rolled on her back and choked on her vomit."

To be safe, we prop Suze onto her side with a pillow and watch her sleep for a minute to make sure she's steady. Then Lydia and Ani Uber it home before their parents start getting curious.

Once they leave and I can process what just happened, I realize I'm shaking, and have been ever since Tarkin touched me. We like to say we can protect each other, *Shields up* and all that, but things could have turned out very differently tonight. Never mind getting busted by the cops for smoking pot, the truly scary thing is that we were in Tara's basement outnumbered by wrestlers. The even scarier thing is that I was in an enclosed space with Tarkin Shaw, which is something I swore I would never ever do. How did any of this even happen? How did Suze end up in that weight room? She knows better than to be alone with Tarkin Shaw. Did she go there voluntarily? Was she feeling bold in her role as amateur anthropologist? I want to ask her, but she's fast asleep now and I don't want to wake her.

What a strange and unsettling night. We should have wound up at the beach picking out constellations while snarking on all the doofuses at that party, not carrying our unconscious friend while fleeing the police. Ani's right. We should never do this again.

On the plus side, we did get to watch Lydia drop that shartgibbon with her amazing self-defense moves. I think Wonder Woman would be proud.

I STAY UP for a while and watch Suze sleep. There's something peaceful and reassuring about seeing her there safe and sound. Then, around midnight, I get out this old princess ready bed I haven't used since middle school and go to sleep, too. I wake up a few times to check on her and she seems fine, her belly moving up and down with her breath.

But when I wake up the next morning around eight, she's gone. No note or anything. I call her to make sure she's okay, but she doesn't pick up. When I check in with Lydia and Ani, they haven't heard from her either. This isn't necessarily out of character for Suze. She comes and goes according to her own whims. She once blew off school for three days when an old friend from Munich was in town. She didn't tell any of us where she was and when Principal Everett asked her for a note, she told him, "I didn't take any."

MONDAY

NIKKI

As soon as I dump my stuff in my locker at school, I head right over to Suze's locker in the West Wing. To my relief, she's there, hanging up her coat. I wave to her but she doesn't see me through the scrum of kids between us. When I'm about five feet away from her, weaving around a cluster of freshman girls, she closes her locker door. And you will not believe who's leaning against the locker next to hers.

None other than Tarkin Shaw, Mr. "You're a Total Fucking Whore."

While Suze spins her lock shut, Tarkin leans over and fiddles with the ends of her light brown hair. My first instinct, it goes without saying, is to shove him off of her and get Suze into a delousing shower ASAP. But Suze sees me coming and puts her hands up.

"Nikki," she says. "Nikki, no. Stop."

By now Tarkin has draped himself over her and is running his hands down her bare arms, which is the same move he tried on me in Tara's basement.

"Why is he touching you?" I ask her, my voice brittle. "Why are you *letting* him touch you?"

Tarkin squeezes Suze's shoulders. "See?" he says. "I told you she hates me. She kicked me in the nuts, you know. I should sue her."

"I kicked you in the *head*, dipshit. It was Lydia who kicked you in the nuts. Made you cry like a little bitch, too. Remember that part?"

"Shut the fuck up," he says.

"Or what? Are you going to put on your leotard and wrestle me to the floor? Actually I'm surprised Lydia could even find your nuts. Must have had a magnifying glass."

Tarkin's eyes blaze. His lips get small and white. I recognize the expression because I've seen it before. He wants to hit me. But I know he won't do it, not there in the hallway in front of other people. Hitting a girl would make him look bad.

So instead, he puts his finger under Suze's chin and pulls her face toward his. "Tell her."

"Tell me what? Suze? What's going on?"

"Yeah, we had a long talk," Suze says, not looking at me. "We were wrong about him, Nikki."

"Excuse me?"

"He's not what you think," she says, looking at the floor.

"What are you talking about?"

"Tell her," Tarkin says. "Tell her what you told me."

Suze looks up at him, takes a deep breath, then glances at me for a second before returning her eyes to the floor. "I guess . . . I think we've been unfair."

"To *him*?"

"There's a lot more to him than you think," she says.

"*Thank* you," Tarkin says. "I'm glad somebody sees it."

I lower my gaze to try to catch Suze's eye, but she'll only glance at me. "Are you forgetting Saturday night?" I ask her. "Are you forgetting Tara's party and how we found you passed out in the basement with him?"

"It's not what you think though."

"What is it then? What happened?"

"Um," she says. "Well, I think what happened was—"

"Look at me, Suze."

"Yeah," Tarkin says. "Look at her. She's not gonna hurt you. Go ahead. Tell her."

Suze takes another breath then slowly brings her beautiful brown eyes up to mine. "I think what happened was . . . um . . . I went inside to get a soda while you guys were out on the porch and I put my cup down to check my phone. Then, when I picked it up again it was the wrong cup. It must have had something in it. Maybe vodka? You know how you can't taste that, right?"

"It's a classic rookie mistake," Tarkin says.

"Always label your cup. Right, babe?" He squeezes Suze's shoulders and she giggles nervously.

"Anyway, Tarkin saw me and . . . we got to talking . . . and . . . something just . . . clicked."

I can't believe what I'm hearing. I keep waiting for something to come out of her mouth that remotely resembles Suze. Because this isn't it.

"Please don't make this harder than it needs to be," Suze says.

I grab her wrist and try to pull her away for a private discussion. Tarkin holds onto her with his bulging mutant arms for a second, just to show that he can. Then he lets her go and I drag her a few feet away. "You picked up the wrong cup? Is that what he told you?"

"Nikki, please."

"So it hasn't occurred to you that he spiked your drink?"

"I can hear you," Tarkin shouts. "And it definitely wasn't me."

"Yeah, right," I say. "Because you've never done that to a girl before."

"Nope. Never."

"Liar."

"I'm a target," he says, walking back to us to mansplain. "Girls throw themselves at me all the time. Then, when it doesn't work out or whatever, they're all, *Oh, poor me, it was rape. Tarkin Shaw took advantage of me.*"

My body tenses with rage. I picture slamming

his head into that locker until he stops breathing. I picture squeezing his throat until he turns blue. This isn't the first time I've imagined killing Tarkin Shaw. I've pictured his death in a variety of ways.

"The sad thing is that this happens every day," he says. "But you can't even stand up for yourself because then you're 'blaming the victim.' But you know what? Guys are the real victims of rape."

I shoot Suze an *are you listening* to *this* look, but she just shrugs and I don't know how to read it. Is she saying she agrees with him? Is she saying he's an idiot so it doesn't matter what he says? Suze can be pretty live-and-let-live about things, especially sexual things. Her parents are basically hippies and she was raised to be "sex-positive." I know she's not a virgin. But this is something else. This is Tarkin Shaw—basically the Pol Pot of date rape. And yes, we are studying genocide in AP history this term, and no I do not think the comparison is tasteless.

I try one more time. "Suze, I think the alcohol is still in your system. You're not thinking straight."

"No, Nikki, listen," she says. "I'm sorry. I really am. You've been a good friend and all, especially when I was new here. But maybe it's time we both moved on."

She looks up at Tarkin, who grins smugly. He's eating this up. Not only has he somehow managed to score Suze Tilman, the coolest girl in school. But he gets to do it at my expense. It's like Christmas and summer vacation all rolled into one for him.

How is any of this happening?

While I stand there, shocked to the core and unable to speak or even move, Tarkin puts his arm around Suze and walks her away. Halfway down the hall, he leans in to whisper something to her. Suze looks up at him, smiles, and then rests her head on his shoulder—like she's in love with him! And the two of them walk down the hallway like that together, as if it were the most natural thing in the world.

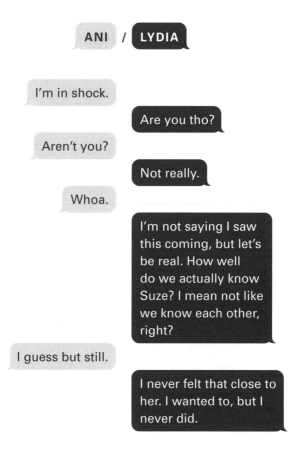

ANI / LYDIA

I'm in shock.

Are you tho?

Aren't you?

Not really.

Whoa.

I'm not saying I saw this coming, but let's be real. How well do we actually know Suze? I mean not like we know each other, right?

I guess but still.

I never felt that close to her. I wanted to, but I never did.

Nikki did tho.

Didn't it seem one-sided tho? Like Suze would blow us off whenever she wanted to "go analog" or hang with her German friends. Then come back and expect us to just be there for her.

I guess.

Remember when we all got tickets to that festival in Boston and she ditched us to go to Virginia instead?

She paid for the ticket though.

But she didn't tell us she was doing it. Nikki was really hurt by that.

I know. But Nikki forgave her.

That's just it though. How many times has Nikki forgiven her or made up excuses for her.

I guess she can be a bit of a flake.

She was strange, Ani, admit it.

Don't talk about her like she's dead.

Well she may as well be, I mean what we're supposed to hang out with Tarkin Shaw and the wrestlers now?

Hard pass.

Exactly.

I just can't wrap my head around it tho. She knows what Tarkin did. Does she think Nikki lied about it?

Why not. People always believe Tarkin. You saw what happened to Amber Laynes when she accused him. It was her reputation that got destroyed. Not his.

Which is so unfair.

Tell me about it.

What I don't get though is that Suze knows all of this.

My mom says sometimes even smart girls go with assholes because of low self-esteem or whatever.

Suze doesn't have low self-esteem though. She's super confident.

Could be an act tho like with bullies and how they act all tough but they're actually hurt inside.

She's not a bully.

It was a metaphor.

No a metaphor is when you compare her to a tree.

OMG stop being so literal. All I'm saying is what do we really know about her? She only moved here six months ago. Maybe she's not who we think she is.

Who is she then?

Someone who turns her back on her friends for one. And after we rescued her drunk ass from that asshole? After we fired up the Shield to drag her out of there, she looks Nikki right in the eye and says, yeah thanks bitches but I'm with the asshole now.

Yeah, I can't believe she defended him. She actually took Tarkin's side.

It's called being an enabler. Don't ask, look it up.

I know what an enabler is.

Yeah Suze Tilman is an enabler, and that's even worse than being a rapist IMO.

Maybe we're being too harsh.

No, Ani, we have standards, there's a difference. Whoops, gotta run. Mrs. Thibedeau just busted me for texting. X

X

DESHAWN

I should probably confess that I've had a crush on Suze Tilman ever since she moved here. And it's not because she's beautiful. It's because she's different. She seems to come from a separate universe. Not Munich, some place even farther away.

I feel like I come from a separate universe, too. And I'm pretty sure my fellow students would agree. They think I'm strange, shy, introverted, off-kilter. They have a hundred different ways of describing what they don't understand. And I don't care. They leave me alone, and I leave them alone. That arrangement works fine. But I've always hoped that at some point Suze's universe and my universe would collide.

Unfortunately, according to Marcus, Suze is with Tarkin Shaw now. At least that's the gossip at school. She got drunk at Tara Budzynski's party and threw herself at him. I don't listen to gossip, but Marcus does. In this case he's hoping to pick up something "newsworthy" from Tara's party, like a drug angle or some arrests. But all anyone wants to talk about is how Tarkin Shaw finally "landed" Suze Tilman, like this was inevitable, like this puts their social universe in order. King of the Jocks with Coolest Girl in School. They don't see. Everyone thinks Tarkin and Suze belong together because they're both good-looking. But Suze's beauty is different from his. Hers comes from within. It's a glow that emanates outward, like a spell. Tarkin looks like he spends hours in front of a mirror, swapping out Hollister shirts and gelling his blond-tipped hair just so. He's always flexing to accentuate his pecs and he's definitely on steroids. You don't bulge like that from doing normal human activities. I should know. I'm pretty strong myself and I don't look anything like that.

Even Marcus doesn't get it. In third period English, he shows me an article he's written with the headline: "Cool New Girl Gets Drunk at Kegger, Throws Self at Jock." It's a joke between him and one of his colleagues at the *Bugle*, because they're always complaining about how nothing newsworthy happens in Jonesville. But I don't find that joke particularly funny.

Also, I don't believe the rumors. After English class, I spot Suze walking alone through the hallway. She looks better than she did in that photograph, which means at least she wasn't hurt at Tara's party. But she doesn't look like her normal self. Usually she breezes through the halls with this luminous smile like she's just seen something interesting and she can't wait to share it with her friends. Now she walks with her head down and she keeps pulling the sleeves of her sweatshirt over her hands.

I follow her around a corner from a safe distance and there's Shaw, hanging with his wrestler buddies by the water fountain. When he spots Suze, he peels away and swaggers over with that cocksure pose, like he's the center of the universe, like no matter who else is around, he's the most interesting and important. Suze smiles at him, but it's not her usual smile. It's lifeless and fake, full of teeth. Not that Shaw notices. He's still looking at his buddies. And his buddies are impressed, which I guess is the point. Everything for him is a performance. It kind of makes me sick. The guy has his arm around *Suze Tilman* and he can't see her at all.

When they head off down the hall together, I decide to keep following them. I don't have a plan. I just know that something seems off here. I stay at a distance, making sure there are at least three other kids between us, because the last thing I want is to make a scene.

When they get to Mrs. Naylor's classroom, Shaw grabs Suze's face and plasters his mouth over hers like he wants to swallow her whole. She kisses him back, sort of, but only with her mouth. Her body angles away like it's trying to escape, like if she could detach her head from her body, she would.

When he finally unsticks his mouth from hers, she giggles weakly then walks away, tugging at her sleeves again. I guess you could mistake that for nervous flirtation—a lot of girls giggle nervously around Tarkin Shaw—but you'd have to work pretty hard to see it that way. To me, she looks traumatized, like she's disgusted by what just happened and she's already trying to erase the memory.

It fools Shaw, though. He eyes her body up and down like he's sizing up his next meal. Total predator. When he heads into the classroom, I make a quick decision and run after Suze. Once I'm right behind her I realize that I have no idea what to say. I've never spoken to her before and I would not describe myself as skilled in the art of conversation, because I don't do small talk. I mean I can talk up a storm with Marcus, but that's different. He doesn't do small talk either. I wonder if Suze does. While I'm thinking about all of this, and making myself more nervous by the second, Suze stops suddenly to look into her backpack and I crash into her.

Our eyes lock. I open my mouth to say something. *Hello, my name is DeShawn Hill and I'm here to help in any way I can,* is what I'm *thinking*, but what I'm saying is nothing. Absolutely nothing. *Less* than nothing. My mouth is open but only air is coming out. Plus, I'm not one hundred percent positive of my own name.

She's even more amazing up close. Her eyes are

dark brown like mine and there's a small gap between her two front teeth.

"I'm DeShawn Hill," I manage to squeak out eventually. I have no idea how much time has passed.

"Wh . . . What do you want?" she stutters.

"Are you . . um . . . I know this is going to sound strange, but are you and Tarkin Shaw, like . . ." I can't even bring myself to say the words.

"Are we what? Are we dating? Is that what you want to know?"

"Um . . ."

I want to know a lot more than that actually. I want to know what she thinks about right before she falls asleep. I want to know why that incandescent smile has disappeared. But my brain has seized up on me and I can't get the words out.

"Yes," she says. "We are. Why?"

"It's just . . ."

"It's just what?"

"You don't seem . . ."

"We don't seem what?"

"You don't seem like you're really into him."

"Fuck," she says. "Really?" Her attention is drawn to something behind me. "Yes," she says quickly. "Everything's fine. He's my boyfriend, okay? Don't talk to me." She turns away and rushes off.

Behind me, I spot Shaw standing in the doorway to Mrs. Naylor's classroom, glowering. *Flexing* and glowering.

AT LUNCH THAT day, I rush to my usual table by the window. Marcus is already there chomping down a turkey sandwich while scribbling into his reporter's notebook. He never goes anywhere without that thing. I tell him about my encounter with Suze in the hallway, but he shrugs it off.

"No drugs, no violence, no broken laws. No story."

He's so full of shit sometimes and this Anderson Cooper routine annoys me.

"No story, huh?" I say. Then I point out that Suze isn't sitting at her usual table with Nikki Petronzio and her other friends. In fact, she doesn't appear to be at lunch at all.

"Hold on," Marcus says, turning to a new page in his notebook. "Girl Skips Lunch. That's a solid lead, buddy. Thanks."

"I'm serious, Marcus. Something is up with her and Shaw."

"It's called dating."

"So why isn't she sitting with him?"

Marcus looks over at Shaw and the wrestlers all the way on the other side of the cafeteria, stuffing giant mouthfuls of chili down their throats.

"Maybe she's on a diet?"

"Look at Nikki Petronzio," I say.

Marcus twists around to have a look.

"She looks upset, right?"

"Yeah," he says. "Word on the street is that Nikki and her friends do not approve of this romance."

"You heard that?"

"I'm a reporter, DeShawn. It's my job to hear things."

"Why don't they approve?"

"I guess they have higher standards. Plus, I think Nikki has some kind of history with Shaw. I don't know the details. It happened their freshman year. We were still in middle school."

"That guy has a history with a lot of girls."

Marcus glares at me then shoves more of his turkey sandwich into his mouth. Tarkin Shaw is a sore spot with him. Ever since the Amber Laynes incident. Marcus was working on the story for the *Bugle*. He had Amber locked down for an on-the-record interview. It was going to be his biggest story yet. But then Amber recanted, leaving Marcus with nothing. He took it personally.

"I think you should investigate," I tell him.

"Amber's history. She lied to the police. Plus, she lives in California now."

"Not Amber. Suze."

Marcus finishes his mouthful then carefully puts his sandwich down so he can look me in the eye. "DeShawn, is this your way of circling around to the fact that you have a gigantic crush on Suze Tilman? Because, buddy, I'm well aware of it. And I get it. I do. She's infinitely crush-worthy. And she'd be lucky to have you."

"This isn't about that."

"Good, because I think it's safe to say she's into jockstraps."

"That's what I'm trying to tell you, Marcus. She's *not* into him. In fact, I think she can't stand him."

"How would you even know that?"

"It's hard to explain. It's like her words were saying one thing, but her eyes were saying something else."

"Wait. You talked to her?"

"Sort of. Yes. I did actually. I talked to her."

"Well, what were her words saying?"

"Don't talk to me."

"And what were her eyes saying?"

"Help."

MARCUS

The thing about DeShawn is that you never know when one of his intuitions will prove correct. As a journalist, I find this annoying. Intuition is not something you can base a story on. When you're a reporter you need proof. DeShawn just *feels* things.

An example: Last year, DeShawn was convinced that this girl in our English class, Maya Geblinger, was, in his words, "right on the edge." I had no idea what he was talking about and, at the time, I assumed it was a crush. But then Maya wound up in the girls' room with her wrists cut, and everyone was shocked. Everyone but DeShawn, that is. He saw it coming, even blamed himself for not finding some way to help her.

She survived. It was a cry for help, or attention, or whatever. Later on, there was talk of an eating disorder. But nobody, other than DeShawn, saw it coming. He's the most empathic person I know. But his empathy isn't soft and amorphous, which is how I usually think of empathy. With DeShawn, it's more like a laser-sharp probe, like something he'd have in his workshop to expose the innards of one of his robotic marvels. Right now, that probe is pointed at Suze Tilman. Personally, I don't see what he's seeing. To me, she's the same beautiful, aloof girl she always was. Only now, she walks around with Tarkin Shaw instead of her frosty girlfriends.

So, what should I do? Trust DeShawn's instincts and go investigate? If there *is* a story here, it goes without saying I want in on it. Tarkin Shaw would be a great scalp, what with him being an all-state wrestler and general alpha male of Jonesville High. Plus, there's the lingering stench of his dust-up with Amber Laynes. Busting that overblown dude-bro would be sweet indeed.

Unfortunately, the mysterious Suze Tilman seems to have ditched school for the day, which means if I *am* going to investigate, I'll have to start elsewhere. The obvious source would be Tarkin Shaw. But he'd probably kick my ass just for looking at him, and I'm not risking my neck unless I'm sure there's a story here. So I set my sights on a less life-threatening source: Suze's three friends, Nikki Petronzio, Anamika Chakrabarti, and Lydia Moreau, otherwise known as the three biggest snobs in the school. To be clear, these girls aren't snobs in the sense of being rich, or super smart, or superior in any measurable way. They're snobs in the sense that they hate everybody. I don't know what's behind that hatred. But I respect it. There's a purity to it.

At the end of the day, I spot Nikki at her locker, bracketed, per usual, by Ani and Lydia, whose haughty presence only amplifies Nikki's baseline unapproachability. This will not be a pleasant conversation. But nobody ever said journalism was supposed to be easy, so I pop a Tic Tac, make sure my fly is up (one must always be professional), then whip up a bit of fake nonchalance and head over.

"Hi Ni—"

"Who are you?" she says.

"I'm . . . um . . . "

Full disclosure here. Nikki Petronzio is disconcertingly sexy. I don't know if it's the high cheekbones, the shiny black hair, or those dark eyes that penetrate with the cold scrutiny of a contract killer, but she does something to me. I'm not saying I like her as a person. I don't know her. Right now, she's leveling those cold eyes at me like I am the stupidest person ever born and I realize I still haven't produced my own name. So, I try again.

"Hi. Um . . . "

"You know what," she says. "I don't need to know your name. I'm good." She turns away and speaks quietly with Ani, while Lydia gives me a quick, dismissive glance.

"I'm Marcus. I'm a reporter for the *Bugle*," I finally spit out. "I mean, I'm a student here, but also a reporter. I just wanted to ask you about Suze Tilman."

Nikki whirls around angrily, practically slicing Ani with her blade-straight hair. "What are you, her new best friend or something?"

Now this is interesting. Clearly, I've hit a nerve.

"I thought *you* were her best friend," I say. "Did I get that wrong?"

"Trust me, you do not want to go down this road. Not today."

But I do. Yes, I very much want to go down this road. This is the road every reporter seeks out. Conflict. Tension. Distress. I whip out my notebook and flip to a blank page. "How do you feel about Suze's relationship with Tarkin Shaw? Are they built to last? Because word on the street is—"

"Uh-oh." Ani says.

I track her gaze to something behind me. And there, materializing out of the ether like a bad smell, is Tarkin Shaw.

I barely have time to register the unpleasant fact that he stands nearly a head taller than me when he grabs me by the shoulders with his giant bear paws and airlifts me two lockers down. He fastens me to the locker door with a fancy wrestling move involving his thigh and my hipbone, while grunting some vaguely obscene in-group slang I'm not cool enough to understand.

It takes a moment to scrape up the courage to say: "Sorry dude, you're not my type."

Stupid, yes. But his junk is pressing into my leg.

In place of a reply, he grabs the hair at the scruff

of my neck and uses it to smash the back of my head against the locker.

"If I get a concussion from this—" I begin, but the sentence goes nowhere because Shaw covers the lower half of my face with his giant paw.

"I don't want you talking *to* Suze Tilman. And I don't want you talking *about* Suze Tilman. And that goes for your little geek boyfriend, too."

As his bulbous thumb digs into my cheek, I can feel him squeezing my jaw to the breaking point. My vision begins to narrow. I'm on the verge of passing out when suddenly everything releases. I slide down the locker gasping for air. When my vision returns, my face is throbbing and Tarkin is lying at my feet, face down.

Holy shit, I think to myself. *Did I do that? Did I acquire superhuman strength in the moment before passing out and use it to knock out Tarkin Shaw?*

Then I see DeShawn, legs wide, hands out in front of him, loose and ready. He's been doing jiu jitsu for only about six months, but when he gets into something, he goes all in.

For one glorious moment, nobody moves. Not Nikki or her friends, not Tarkin Shaw, not anyone watching the scene unfold. The silence in the hallway is as sharp as needles. Sharper even than the pain in my lower jaw.

Eventually, Shaw drags himself to his knees, looks up at DeShawn, who's still holding that ninja pose, and laughs defensively. Rising to his full terrifying height, he shakes himself off and gives DeShawn a thorough looking over. Then, massively overestimating the significance of his size advantage, Shaw reels back and tries—and I do give him credit for trying—to get in a quick sucker punch.

Poor Tarkin Shaw. How could he know that DeShawn Hill has been fighting imaginary Tarkin Shaws all his life? The real one is no match. His fist gets about six inches from DeShawn's face when DeShawn catches it single-handed, twists it behind Tarkin's back and brings him straight back to the floor. All-state wrestler versus jiu jitsu prodigy? Sorry, pal. No contest.

DeShawn *could* dislocate Shaw's shoulder. I know this because DeShawn used to be deeply into karate and he once itemized for me all the different ways he can bring down an assailant, including the various fractures, breaks, contusions, and dislocations associated with each method. But DeShawn does not dislocate Shaw's shoulder, break his wrist, crush his windpipe, or render him unconscious. Instead, he merely holds Shaw on the floor in an uncomfortable, embarrassing, but not injury-causing position. No way would I be that restrained. I'd have the guy begging for mercy.

"Get off me!" Shaw spits through clenched teeth. He's completely under DeShawn's control and furious about it.

And now, Mrs. Wentworth, alerted to the fracas,

trundles over, chubby hands aflutter. She's comically useless. She keeps reaching toward DeShawn then backing away as if he were radioactive. While Nikki, Lydia, and Ani skedaddle, a crowd of curious onlookers forms.

"Can someone please tell me what's going on here?" Mrs. Wentworth demands.

"Sure," I say. "I was having a conversation with Nikki Petronzio when this guy came out of nowhere and slammed me into a locker. Then—I'm not sure how else to describe this part—he started *hugging* me?"

"Shut up!" Tarkin barks from his prone position. He struggles against DeShawn's grip, but to no avail. DeShawn has him thoroughly overpowered.

"I can't say how far he would have gone if it weren't for DeShawn coming to my aid, but he does have a reputation for sexual aggression. As we all know."

"I will *kill* you!" Shaw again, still under DeShawn's control, and mightily pissed off about it.

"Anyway, it was quite intrusive," I continue. "And definitely unwanted."

"Did he strike you?" she asks.

"Not exactly."

"DeShawn," she says. "Let go of him."

"I just want to be sure he's not planning to attack my friend again," DeShawn says.

"Tarkin," Mrs. Wentworth says. "Is this true? Did you assault Marcus?"

"No!" Shaw says. "He's lying."

Mrs. Wentworth glances at the gathered crowd, a mixed bag of nobodies, a few semi-somebodies, and a clutch of stoners who arrived too late to see the inciting incident. "Can anyone offer anything?"

Silence. Some shuffling of feet. A few kids snapping photos, making videos.

"So, no one saw?"

Shaw, to his credit, reads the situation perfectly. The "witnesses" in their lumpen mindlessness are adhering to the age-old tradition of sealed lips. They're not about to snitch. Not on someone as important, and as vaguely dangerous, as Tarkin Shaw. You can almost feel Shaw's confidence growing with each passing second.

"I'm saying this for your own good, man," he tells DeShawn. "Get off of me."

Mrs. Wentworth taps DeShawn on the shoulder. "Let him go."

DeShawn looks at me, sees that I'm safe, and releases his grip. Shaw springs to his feet like a freed jack-in-the-box, aiming to give the impression that the takedown was minor, a prank gone awry, an optical illusion. He was actually in charge the whole time. He was just showing DeShawn mercy, like the tough-but-awesome guy he is. Sure, he *could* have busted a move on DeShawn if he wanted to. But that's not his style.

It's quite a performance actually. But he oversells it, chin pushed out, chest puffed up. You'd have to be an idiot not to see the pathos underneath it all, the humiliation and shame of being taken down by a major nerd. Not once, but twice.

Or you'd have to be any member of the drag-net of losers currently lolling about in the hall-way. Either they're all collectively buying Shaw's performance—despite what they've just witnessed with their very own eyes—or they're so dazzled by Shaw's status, and their own proximity to it, that they've been struck mute.

"We can't have students knocking each oth-er down in the hallway," Mrs. Wentworth says, making sure to include DeShawn in her sweep of condemnation.

"This was between me and Shaw," I explain. "De-Shawn was only trying to protect me."

Under his breath Shaw says, "Pussy."

"What was that, Tarkin?" Mrs. Wentworth, to her credit, is not dazzled by Tarkin Shaw's status.

"Nothing," he says. "I just think, you know, two against one is pretty lame."

"It wasn't a fight," I say. "It was an attack. He jumped me from behind."

"Did you, Tarkin?"

Shaw smirks and shrugs at the same time, a move designed to evade the truth without actually lying.

"He did," I say. "He attacked me because I asked about Suze Tilman. Who can't stand him, by the way, and who's probably about to dump him."

"You're fucking dead!" Shaw reaches straight across Mrs. Wentworth and tries to grab me with his giant mitts.

Mrs. Wentworth, who never had more than the slimmest margin of authority over the situation, goes into full panic mode now, waving those chubby hands in front of her face. Mr. Schroeder and Mrs. Pulaski emerge from the special education room to resolve the situation. But, as it turns out, there's no need. DeShawn is there with a smooth, dancerly switchback of arms and legs. And in a nearly perfect replay, Tarkin Shaw is, once again, facedown on the floor.

That makes three times DeShawn Hill has taken Tarkin Shaw down, in case you're keeping score. Three times.

Three.

"You see, Mrs. Wentworth," I say. "The guy can't keep his hands off of me."

THERE IS NO more violence that day. Shaw, De-Shawn, and I are escorted to the waiting room of the principal's office until Mr. Everett can speak with us personally. DeShawn is a new shade of gray I've never seen before: glossy, with undertones of green. I think the whole encounter has upset his equilibrium in some deep spiritual way. He may be a jiu jitsu prodigy, but he despises violence. If you can figure that one out, you're ahead of me.

Shaw keeps whispering death threats to both of

us, but neither of the two distracted secretaries behind the counter hears anything. They're too busy collating some enormous photocopy project that is spread out on every available surface. Eventually Principal Everett emerges from behind his office door and cheerily "invites" us inside with him.

Our principal is a big talker. He believes, adorably, that there isn't a problem in the world, or at least at Jonesville High, that can't be solved if all parties agree to "talk it out." His office is pockmarked with inspirational plaques (*There's no "I" in team, One's reach should always exceed one's grasp*, etc). I sit between DeShawn and Shaw on a slouchy couch that makes it impossible to sit up straight and look receptive to discipline. Then again, it isn't about discipline with Mr. Everett. It's about "coming to an understanding." This is a hopeless task. Shaw and I are in no mood to "understand" each other and DeShawn has cocooned himself behind an unfocused gaze where he can sub-vocally count backward from one-thousand by sixes.

Our reticence only frustrates Principal Everett, who threatens us all with "black marks" on our "records" if we don't explain ourselves. My record is a moot point. I have no plans for college, at least not right away. College, in my mind, is an expensive waste of time. On this point, my mother actually agrees. She went to Harvard, which is supposedly the best one, and she said it was full of d-bags.

The way forward to a career in journalism, we both agree, is to actually do journalism, which I already am. Quite possibly, my mother arrived at this position only as a matter of convenience, relating to certain financial realities stemming from the divorce. Either way, college is not in my immediate future, all of which makes my "record" irrelevant.

College *is* in DeShawn's future, however. His dream is to go to MIT, where he plans to design and invent all manner of cool stuff. No way in hell am I letting Shaw's steroidal outburst threaten any of that. A black mark of violence on a white wrestling captain's record is probably no big deal. Boys will be boys, and all that. But a black mark of violence on a Black kid's record *is* a big deal. Because that is the shitty, unjust world we live in.

Unfortunately, DeShawn refuses to defend himself or even to answer Principal Everett's questions, so I have to take on the role of defense attorney. My strategy is simple: Tell the plain, unvarnished truth about what happened, since the truth is naturally flattering of DeShawn and makes Shaw look like the oaf he is. But then my natural verbosity gets the better of me, as it so often does. DeShawn isn't merely blameless here. He's a "hero" who showed "epic restraint," whereas Tarkin is an "ubridled force of mindless—if ineffectual—violence." DeShawn's spectacular jiu jitsu skills are not to be taken as "a warning sign of future trouble," but rather, as evidence of his ability to apply himself to a challenging discipline and then to use "the awesome power it confers with a sense of proportional justice." I am eloquent AF.

Principal Everett tries repeatedly to get confirmation from DeShawn, but there's no reaching him. He's locked in. He's midway through the five-hundreds and he's not coming out until he hits zero. When he turns inward, there's no getting him out. Shaw, for his part, does a lot of huffing, snorting, and eye-rolling, unwittingly nailing the role I've written for him, i.e., the donkey-brained thug. When pressed, he sticks to his fairy-tale about being attacked in a two-against-one scenario. For him, it doesn't seem to be about dodging punishment so much as salvaging his reputation as a tough guy. I almost pity him.

Except that I don't.

"Consider this a warning," Mr. Everett says. "I'll be informing your parents about what happened."

"Good," Shaw says, glaring at me.

"Is that supposed to be a threat?" I ask him. "What are your parents going to do, *ground* me?"

Shaw's face goes hard as he stares me down. "You better watch yourself," he says. Then he stands up and says to Principal Everett, "Are we done here? Because I've got someplace to be."

I fully expect Everett to *request* that Tarkin sit down until he's dismissed. But he just nods, tells us we can all leave, then starts flipping through some papers on his desk. Shaw smolders at me all the way out the door then runs off, jock-style, his hands clenched into fists.

I'm not worried about the phone call to my mother. She'll totally see my point of view on this. She knows I'm not the type to pick fights. And DeShawn's parents are reasonable. I doubt they'll punish him for standing up for his best friend. If anything, his parents will blame me. DeShawn's mom isn't crazy about me as it is. I'm tolerated, but only because my lackadaisical attitude toward school has failed to rub off on her brilliant son.

I ride home with DeShawn and deposit him in the hole. He has a pewter fire truck to finish for an Etsy client in California and he wants to "disappear" for a while so he can realign his universe. I understand. DeShawn's universe is a delicate structure.

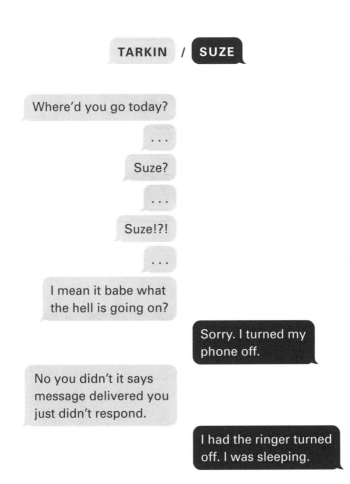

TARKIN / SUZE

Where'd you go today?

. . .

Suze?

. . .

Suze!?!

. . .

I mean it babe what the hell is going on?

Sorry. I turned my phone off.

No you didn't it says message delivered you just didn't respond.

I had the ringer turned off. I was sleeping.

69

Why?

Sick. Went home early.

So is it true?

Is what true?

That your dumping me?

What are you talking about?

That's what that geek said.

What geek?

Marcus Daubney. He said you can't stand me and that your planning to dump me. Have you been talking to him and his friend?

I don't even know who you're talking about.

Don't lie I saw you talking to his friend in the hallway.

That weirdo DeShawn Hill.

Oh that guy.

Yeah that guy. What did he say to you?

Nothing. He just bumped into me.

So he didn't say anything?

No.

Why do I feel like you're lying to me?

Because you're paranoid.

Suze I warned you.

Relax, I'm joking.

Don't joke with me. I told you I hate that.

Sorry.

You're not funny. Only ugly girls are funny.

Right. I forgot.

And you're not ugly.

Stop it. You're making me blush.

That weaselly one is a reporter you know. He writes for the Bugle?

What's the Bugle?

It's our town newspaper. Have you told him anything?

No.

Good cause that would be really bad.

For you.

I know.

So why did he say that?

What?

Don't make me say it again.

I don't have any idea what he said or why he said it.

I wasn't there.

And I don't know him.

His friend the black kid is a total freak.

Okay.

What you don't think so?

I don't know him.

But yeah I guess he does seem a little strange.

A little strange? He attacked me, I had to kick his ass.

Now everyone's gonna think I'm racist like that's fair.

Did you hurt him?

That's what your worried about, if I hurt him?

what about me

he jumped me from behind.

. . .

Hello? Are you there?
I said he jumped me.

Yeah, sorry. I'm here.
Did he hurt you?

No. I can take
care of myself.

Did you get in trouble?

Yeah right. Like
Everett's gonna do
anything to me.

He knows better
than that.

So it's all okay then.

Not really.

Why?

Because they know
too much.

Who?

Ebony and Ivory.

Do you have to say
things like that?

What are you a social
justice warrior now?

One's black one's white who cares?

. . .

Suze!

How could they know anything? I haven't said a word.

Not even to Nikki? They were talking to her.

Really?

Yeah. Does she know?

I told you we're not speaking.

Good. Your way too good for her.

I guess.

Also I don't care what she told you.

She threw herself at me freshman year.

You should have seen her, she was so desperate now she acts like such a bitch.

She has some issues . . .

How could you be friends with her?

Questionable judgment.

I was new in town. Cut me some slack.

What about Lydia and Ani?

Same.

NO I mean have you told them anything.

You should know. You put spyware on my phone.

You love it. Don't lie.

You should have more faith in people.

And you should come prove yourself to me.

That sounds incredibly juvenile.

Don't be such a bitch.

I'm only teasing. You big lug.

I told you not to joke with me.

Come over tonight.

I can't.

You can.

I told you I'm sick. Female probs.

Bullshit you didn't have female probs when I saw you this morning.

That's how it works, Einstein.

Are you making fun of me again?

;)

Oh your so gonna get it, come at 8 my parents are out late.

Not tonight. Sorry.

Yes tonight and don't be late I mean it.

. . .

You know I mean it, Suze.

NIKKI

I turned my phone off after a full hour of messages and calls from Lydia and Ani, trying to pull me out of my funk. But sometimes the funk is where you need to be. So that's where I am. I'm in the funk, at Wingaersheek Beach, sitting on the rocks while the tide comes in. I have about half an hour before I get stranded here. When things turn to shit, this is where I come. This is *my* rock, *my* shoreline, *my* horizon to stare at. Freshman year, when things were at their worst, I used to ride my bike out here and sit until dinnertime. I'd tell my parents I was at the library, because I knew they wouldn't understand why I spent so much time sitting on a rock by myself. It's not like I ever actually figure things out when I come here. The rocks and the foam and the straight-line horizon never have any kind of advice or insight. I come here to feel small. Being here reminds me that, in the scheme of things, my troubles are miniscule. Right now, between the horizon and me, some little fish is losing its life to a bigger fish. And on and on and on.

Below me, the water circles all the way around my rock. It's time to head back or risk getting stranded. So I climb down, carrying my sneakers, and let my bare feet sink into the soft, wet sand. When I look across the beach, Ani and Lydia are coming over the boardwalk.

"I told you she'd be here," Ani says.

Lydia reaches me first and throws her arms around me. "Has the traitor formerly known as Suze Tilman called?"

"I shut my phone off."

"Good." Lydia takes out her own phone and shuts it off too. "Let's all go analog. Give her a taste of her own medicine."

"Hey guys?" Ani says, looking at her phone. "I have a missed call from Suze's *mom*."

"Really?"

"Should I call back?"

"No," Lydia says. She takes Ani's phone, shuts it off, and gives it back to her. "Suze made her choice. We don't need to talk to her or her parents."

"But why would her Mom be calling?"

"Maybe Suze ran off with Tarkin," Lydia says. "Maybe we'll never hear from her again. Fine by me."

Ani looks at me, assuming I'll be the voice of reason here. Lydia can be hotheaded and it's usually on me to calm her down. But I'm with Lydia on this one. What Suze did to me this morning is unforgiveable. She made me feel something I haven't felt since freshman year: discounted. She reminded me that the truth doesn't matter. That Tarkin Shaw can do whatever he wants, then make up a story to cover his ass and nobody will challenge him on it. That's why I never told anyone, except Ani, Lydia, and Suze. I knew people would blame it all on me, or claim I was exaggerating, which is exactly what Suze did this morning. And all that talk about how I'm gold and Tarkin Shaw is nothing? Bullshit. He's not nothing. He's everything. And I'm not gold. I'm collateral damage. Trash on the discard pile.

I'm about to say, "Shields up," ready to block out the rest of the world. But then I remember that Suze came up with it. We were in the parking lot of the multiplex after seeing *Wonder Woman*, and she was going on and on about how amazing it would be if women joined together to maximize their power, because women's power almost never comes from hatred or violence. It comes from love. I wonder if she remembers that.

"Fuck her," I say. "And her mother."

MARCUS

Before dinner on Monday night, I cycle over to the *Bugle*'s office on the outskirts of Jonesville for a chat with Elena DePiero. The *Bugle* occupies a cramped storefront between a nail salon and a sex-toy shop in a strip mall on the Danvers border, journalism having seen better days and all. I could easily have this chat over the phone, but here's the art on Elena: twenty-eight, dark-eyed, with wild black hair and a body I am woefully underqualified to lust after. Also, she's very much my type: mean. Elena has a generalized contempt for humanity coupled with a very small soft spot for me. I have been pouring ridiculous amounts of hope into that soft spot. I figure I have another five years to go before the age difference stops mattering, and I'm willing to wait it out.

On my way to Elena's desk in the back, I pass by the office of the editor-in-chief, Frank Schnell (balding, fighting it, losing). I tap on the glass to say hello, but he's deep into a painful phone conversation and halfway through a bottle of Pepto

Bismol. Schnell hasn't smiled once in all the time I've known him. He's a living, breathing advertisement for avoiding middle age at all costs. He's been on me for months to write a weekly column for the online edition about "what teens are up to these days." The request comes directly from "corporate" and has gone exactly nowhere because I am not a *blogger*.

When I get to Elena's desk, she's banging away on her laptop like it needs to be punished. When she sees me, she holds up a finger then goes back to her laptop to finish whatever she's writing. Three minutes later, I'm still standing there. The office is otherwise empty. Most of the "reporters" work from home. Hacks, mostly. You get what you pay for, and this place doesn't pay much. Eventually, Elena stops typing and leans back in her wobbly chair, which shrieks like a baby dinosaur. "What can I do for my favorite junior reporter?"

"Please don't call me that."

"How can I stop when I know how much it upsets you? You're troubled. What is it? No, don't tell me. You're pissed that Schnell isn't giving you the good assignments. You still believe there *are* good assignments in this one-horse town."

"Actually—"

She stands up. "Walk and talk. I've got to be somewhere five minutes ago." She rummages around her cluttered desk in search of her missing phone. When she can't find it, I calmly take mine out and call hers. It chirps from beneath a sloping pile of manila folders. "Let's go," she says, sliding into her trench coat.

As I follow her through the newsroom, Schnell jumps off his call and stalks after us. "Marcus, we need to talk."

"Is it about the *blog*."

"It's not a *blog*. It's a weekly column focusing on teen issues."

"Don't do it, Marcus," Elena says, leaning in confidentially.

"I want to do hard news," I remind Schnell.

"Great," he says. "Why don't you go dig me up some hard news at Jonesville High?"

"So you can put it in your *blog*?"

"So we can keep corporate happy."

Elena snorts. "Teen clickbait to sell vitamin water and e-cigs."

"Which is why my answer remains no."

"Good boy," Elena says as she leads me out the door.

"Forgive me for trying to keep this goddamn newspaper afloat!" Schnell yells after us.

OUT IN THE strip mall parking lot, Elena digs around in her bag for an e-cig, an irony I am willing to overlook. At least she's not smoking the real ones. Although I'd overlook that too.

"Is the paper really in trouble?" I ask.

"It's always in trouble," she says. "Nobody wants

to pay for anything. People expect shit for free." She takes a drag off of her e-cig. "But as long as there are kids around willing to work for *experience*—"

"I get paid. I'm not working for free."

"Congratulations. Let's form a union and demand higher wages."

I laugh. Schnell would fire both of us and put out the paper with a bunch of hobbyists. No one in Jonesville would even notice.

Elena heads to her ugly brown Nissan, a many-dinged beater from the dark ages, crying out for a paint job that Elena can't afford on her paltry salary. "So, what's so important that you came all the way down here to talk to me?"

"Right," I say, following her. "What do you know about the Shaws?"

"Darren Shaw works at Krieger, Shaw & Associates, Boston law firm, corporate stuff. He's a big muckety-muck at the polo club. Friends in the police force. Tight with local pols. I think he was in a fraternity with Tim Cochrane."

"Essex county DA?" I ask. See? I can keep up with the local VIPs.

Elena nods while pulling on her e-cig. "Mrs. Shaw is some kind of socialite, comes from an old Mayflower family. The Shaws are the reason Hagopian is going to win that school-board election, by the way. Well, them and their rich friends. Why? You got something on him? Oh, wait, is it about the son? You got another joke article you want to run by me? Because you know how much I appreciate having my time wasted."

"Sorry about that. I was feeling petulant."

"Yeah, well, if you want to go up against one of the Shaw boys, you better have your ducks in a row. There are two of them, right? Mason and Tarkin? Jesus, what kind of names are those? Who names their kid *Tarkin*? Actually, Marcus is no mouthful of sugar either."

"Elena is pure poetry."

"Knock my Sicilian heritage at your peril. So what's the deal? You're not still feeling burned over that Amber Laynes story, are you?"

When I don't come back with a sarcastic riposte, she takes a breath and prepares to "set me straight."

"You need to let that go. She recanted. We had a girl like that in my school too. Had the whole town searching for a predator in a Pontiac, some middle-aged guy who grabbed her off the street. Turned out he didn't exist. It was just some dirtbag from the next town over she was banging on the sly. She got herself knocked up and invented the rape story to cover for herself."

"That's amazing that she got *herself* knocked up. She must have been truly gifted."

"You know what I meant. Shit like that makes women look bad."

"But how do you know which story was true? I mean, which one do you believe?"

"Believe no one," she says. "Get proof. Everything else is bullshit. So is that what this is all about? Payback for Amber Laynes?"

"No, no, it's nothing like that."

I'm actually thinking about the way Shaw spoke with Principal Everett today, the cocksure way he dismissed Everett's threats, like Everett had no authority over him. I'm not saying I have much respect for Everett's authority either, or for anyone's authority at Jonesville High, but Shaw was flat-out condescending, like Everett worked for him. Only thing is, I don't want to tell Elena my reasons for being in the principal's office in the first place, because that is not a flattering tale. "He just seems like an overbearing jerk," I tell her. "Like he owns the school."

"Well he did make all-state as a junior."

"I didn't realize you were such a sports fan."

"Yeah right," she scoffs. "But I wrote the article on him." She liberates her luscious hair from the collar of her trench coat, a maddeningly sexy habit that makes me want to melt into a puddle she can walk through. "And around here, high school sports is news." She slides behind the wheel and revs the engine, which produces a dry, hacking cough. "You sure you don't have something on one of the Shaw kids?"

"Nope. Just digging, seeing what's out there. Why? You have something against them?"

"Not really. I just hate rich people." She flashes

me a wicked smile. "But we don't use journalism for personal vendettas, now do we."

"No, we do not. That would be a violation of the fourth estate."

"That's my boy." She pulls the door closed with a mighty screech, then peels out of the strip mall parking lot with just enough attitude to draw scowls from the pretty ladies in the nail salon next door.

DESHAWN

When Principal Everett calls my house after dinner on Monday night, it does not go over well. My parents have never gotten a call from school before because I've never gotten into trouble. I try to explain to them that I was only defending Marcus, who can hardly be expected to defend himself against Tarkin Shaw. But this only makes things worse. My mom thinks I should "put some distance" between myself and Marcus because he's not "the right kind of friend." She thinks he's snarky and a troublemaker and way too impressed with himself. All of these things are true, but they're not the whole story. Marcus is a lot of things. He's decent and principled. He's kind and insightful and a great listener. But my mom doesn't see any of that, so she doesn't get that he'd do the exact same thing for me—if he was strong and able to fight and didn't go limp when Tarkin picked him up and pinned him to that locker. Marcus is a lot of things, but a fighter is not one of them. He's not trained in martial arts like me. But he did defend me in Principal Everett's office. I guess, in a way, talking is his martial art.

I don't know how to make my parents understand any of this though. They're too wrapped up in the fact that Principal Everett is "concerned" about me. So after dinner I go back to the hole to work on Terence. It feels good to disappear into my work again. Here in my workshop, things make sense. If a circuit's dead I know how to fix it. If a wheelbase is out of balance, I can tweak that. I've got my lighting set up just right—one on the left, one on the right, and a softer one from above so I can see everything I do. I've got Earl Sweatshirt playing on my Anker speaker, and a cup of lukewarm cinnamon tea that I make mostly for the smell. About half an hour into my work on Terence's right arm sensor, my mom comes down the stairs to tell me I have a visitor.

"Visitor?" I say. The only visitor I ever have is Marcus and he always texts first to make sure I'm around, then just lets himself in through the basement door out back.

"It's a girl," my mom says.

A girl? Why would a girl be here?

I can hear my dad upstairs making some kind of small talk with . . . I listen carefully. Yes, it sounds like a girl.

A second or two later, I hear footsteps descending the stairs, then Suze Tilman pokes her head into view. "Hi," she says with a little wave.

I know I should wave back, or say hi, or *something*, but I can't seem to move. Hovering there on my basement steps in a bright blue cardigan, she reminds me of a swallowtail butterfly. I worry if I move or say anything she'll fly away.

"You're the only Hills in Jonesville," she says. "I hope you don't mind that I tracked you down."

She *tracked me down*?

"DeShawn?" my mother prods, because I'm still not able to produce sound. "You're welcome to receive your guest upstairs in the living room if you'd prefer."

"No," I say, standing up. "Down here's fine."

My mom smiles politely at Suze then heads back upstairs, her eyes trailing on mine for an extra second or two, like she's hoping I'll be able to explain this unprecedented event to her. Fat chance of that.

"I hope this is okay," Suze says, slowly descending the stairs. "Can I come into your"—she looks around—"space?"

I nod dumbly. I wish I had Marcus in my ear right now. He'd know what to say. He'd say something witty. No. If Marcus were here he'd tell me *just be yourself.*

Who am I again?

Suze wanders around my workshop, taking in the pewter fire truck I've almost finished, a plastic tray with spare gear parts on it. She looks over at Terence on the workspace next to me.

"What exactly is this place?"

"It's my workshop."

"You *make* things here?"

I nod.

"What sort of things?"

"Robots mostly, some plastic and resin models. Soft metals. That fire truck is a custom job." She has a look at it and nods appreciatively. She has a beautifully shaped head. When her hair falls into her face it accentuates the gentle curve of her cheek.

"Do you want some tea?" I ask, then cringe. Is that a stereotype? Am I assuming she wants tea because of her English accent? Does everyone do that? She must hate that.

"Do you have anything herbal?" she asks. "I don't do caffeine."

"Cinnamon?"

"Cinnamon sounds lovely," she says.

I go over to the kettle while surreptitiously sniffing my shirt to make sure I don't smell. I'm definitely sweating, but I did shower this morning. What did we have for dinner though? Shit, spaghetti Bolognese. I hope I don't reek of garlic.

"I heard what happened at school," she says, while fiddling with Terence. That's fine. If she breaks him I'll just rebuild. No problem. Resist the urge to ask her to be careful with my extremely fragile unfinished robot.

"The fight?" she says. "With Tarkin Shaw? You're not hurt, are you?"

"Nope." I drop a teabag into a purple mug my sister made for me at arts camp. I wish I had something more dignified, like a cup and saucer. Am I being stereotypical again? She's not even English. She's American by birth. Do the English even drink tea from cups and saucers? Or is that just in movies?

"Because Tarkin told me he beat you up."

What I'm thinking is *Tarkin Shaw beating* me *up? Hah. His reflexes are a joke. He couldn't get close enough to hurt me.* But that would probably sound conceited, so instead I just say, "No, I'm fine. It was no big deal."

"What about your friend?" she asks. "Whoops." Her hand slips, and Terence buzzes to life and starts jerking its damaged arm back and forth.

"Sorry," she says, cringing.

I come over and turn it off. Calmly, not making a big deal out of it.

"I probably shouldn't touch anything, should I?" she says.

"No, it's fine. That's a work in progress." I go back to the kettle, which is hissing now.

"So your friend? Is he . . . ?"

"Marcus? He's fine."

I pour the water into her mug then bring it over to her two-handed so she can take it by the handle without burning her hands. *My* hands, meanwhile, are on fire, but that's fine.

"Um . . . here." I roll over my good chair, a

Herman Miller knockoff I got on Craigslist. She's even graceful when she sits down, settling with an economy of movement I admire. I clear some space on the workbench near Terence so she can put the mug down. Then I pull up a wooden stool and sit nearby, not too close. I don't want to crowd her. Also, I can't rule out garlic breath.

"I'm glad you're both okay," she says. "Did you get in trouble?"

"Not really. Everett called my parents but they understand." This is a lie. They can't comprehend why I would possibly need to use jiu jitsu on a fellow student. "I was just protecting Marcus."

"Tarkin said your friend was . . . asking about me? And that he's a reporter?"

"Oh yeah. But no, he wasn't . . . I mean he's not reporting on anything. He was just . . ."

Do I tell her the truth? That Marcus was asking Nikki about her because I asked him to?

"He was just what?" she says.

Tell her the truth. I think that's what Marcus would say. *Tell her the truth and be yourself.*

She smells like flowers and spice. Like Christmas and meadows mixed together.

"Can I ask you something, DeShawn?" she says.

And the sound of my name in her voice somehow mixes with that smell to become almost magical. I think I might pass out.

"At school today, were you following me?" When I don't answer right away, she says, "I'm not upset

94

about it. It's just . . ." She tries to take a sip of her tea but it's too hot. "The reason Tarkin got so mad was because he thinks you and your friend know something."

"What does he think we know?"

"So you don't?"

All I *know* is that this exquisite being does not belong with that knuckle-dragging ape-boy. And if she keeps looking at me I'm going to faint.

She sighs deeply, then stands up and walks a few feet away. When she turns around she's tugging on the sleeves of her blue cardigan the same way she did with her sweatshirt at school today. It's a nervous habit that's totally enchanting, like everything she does. "I don't know what to do," she says. "My friends have abandoned me. Which I don't even blame them for, but—"

"You mean Nikki?"

"And Ani and Lydia."

"What do you mean *abandoned*?"

"I mean they won't talk to me."

"Why?"

"Because I looked Nikki right in the eye and told her I was dating Tarkin Shaw. With Tarkin standing right there. They have . . . a past."

"He's bad news," I blurt out. "I'm sorry. But it's true. Nikki's right. You should stay away from him."

"I know. I've been trying to reach them all day. But I can't use my phone because Tarkin put spyware on it."

"He put *spyware* on your phone?"

"Yeah."

"Why?"

"So he can track my movements, my texts, my phone calls. I tried calling them with my mum's phone but they wouldn't answer."

"Why not?"

"Because they think I'm really dating him."

"You're not?"

"No."

I knew it! I knew there was something off about them at school that day.

"I thought I could just ride it out for a few days. Let him have his fun. Parade me around or whatever. I thought that's all he wanted, but . . ." She looks down, letting her long wheat-colored hair fall into her face. "It's gone too far." She takes a deep troubled breath then looks up at me nervously. "Look, I'm sorry to barge in on you like this, but I didn't know where else to go. I don't really know anyone but Nikki and the girls. And I thought . . ." She sits back down in the fancy chair and wheels a little bit closer to me. "The way you looked at me today in the hallway, I thought maybe I could trust you."

"You can." I scoot my chair a little bit closer to her. "You can definitely trust me."

"Really?"

"Yes." It comes out like breath.

"If I tell you what's really going on, will you help me?"

"Yes," I say before she even gets to the word "me."

"Okay." She tries to have a sip of her tea but it's still too hot.

"I can put some cold water in that."

"No." She holds the mug under her nose. "I like the smell. It's soothing."

I like that smell too, but right now it's mixing with her smell of Christmas and spring meadows and I wouldn't call it soothing. I'd call it stirring.

"Do you know about Tara Budzynski's party?" she asks.

"I heard some things."

"Did you hear that I got drunk and threw myself at Tarkin?"

"I don't really pay attention to what people say."

"But you heard that?"

"Yeah."

"Well, that's not what happened."

Of course it's not. That could never happen. No way would the universe, which is sometimes mysterious but fundamentally good, allow such a thing to happen. But as soon as I think this, a feeling of dread overcomes me. *Something* happened at Tara Budzynski's party. And the look on her face tells me it wasn't good.

"What happened was . . ." Her eyes flick up to the ceiling. "Okay, so Nikki, Ani, and Lydia were on the porch getting high while I went inside to get a soda. I swear I only put my cup down for a few seconds. But the next thing I remember is waking up in Nikki's bedroom the morning after."

"What?" I think she skipped something. Like maybe everything?

"I don't even know how I got there," she says. "Maybe Nikki drove me. But when I woke up, I felt so sick I grabbed my car keys on Nikki's dresser and drove myself home. I went straight to bed and passed out. Then around eleven o'clock, I get this text from a number I've never seen. It says *call me when your up*. Then another one that says *p.s. thanks for the pics*. So I text back *who is this? What pics?* And they write back *you're so cute check ur phone*. I thought maybe it was Nikki with a new phone number or something. So I checked my pictures file and there were fifty-seven pictures I've never seen before. I clicked on the first one and I thought it was from a porn site, a screenshot. Some girl with her head thrown back, boobs out, sprawled across a red vinyl bench. You couldn't quite see the face. There were free weights in the background, a blue towel hanging from a hook, a poster of Megan Fox. And this." She pulls something out of the top of her blue cardigan, a small yin and yang pendant hanging from a gold chain.

"What?" I whisper.

"*I* was the girl in the picture."

She shakes the yin and yang pendant to illustrate what she's saying, but I still don't understand.

"I was the girl in *all* of the pictures," she says.

I nod, because I feel like I should probably understand what she's saying, but I still don't get it. How could she be the girl in the pictures?

"So I called the number and when he picked up he wouldn't tell me who he was. He wanted me to guess, thought it was a right laugh too. I recognized the laugh though. It's very distinctive."

"Tarkin?" I say.

She nods.

"I know that laugh," I say.

"It's gross, isn't it?"

"Yeah. It sounds like a wet burp, or . . . no, no, like a bag of trash flopping into a barrel of slime."

"That's an excellent way of describing it."

"Hold on," I say. "You're saying it was Shaw who . . ."

"Took the pictures. Yes."

Oh my God. I get it now. She was the girl in the pictures because he took them. Tarkin Shaw took pictures of her. Naked! But wait.

"How did he . . ."

"He must have slipped something into my drink when I wasn't looking," she says.

"At the party?"

"Yes."

"Like . . . ?" My brain is still struggling to catch up with what she's telling me, but I'm getting closer. At least I think I am. "Like alcohol?"

"Stronger. Probably roofies. Whatever it was, it wiped out my memory. I don't even remember being in that room with him. I don't remember talking to him at all. I *wouldn't* talk to him. Nikki's my best friend. And he's . . . well, let's just say he's toxic. To me and my friends."

"Are you sure it's you in the pictures?" I ask. "Couldn't he have photoshopped your head on someone else's body? People do that."

"I know. But I recognize my body. And the necklace. It's definitely me."

"And you're sure it's Tarkin who took them?"

"Well he's using them to blackmail me, so . . ."

"He's what?"

"He's blackmailing me, DeShawn." She leans forward, and now her face is so close to mine I can see the tiny flecks of gold in her brown eyes. "He's using the pictures to blackmail me into being his girlfriend. Do you understand?"

I desperately want to understand, because I know she needs my help. But she's so close and her scent is so enveloping, I can barely sit up straight, never mind think this through.

Think, DeShawn. You're smart. You're gifted with the power of reason. You design robots for fun. What is she telling you here? Blackmail. Nude photographs. Roofies. You can do this. Yes. It all fits with what I observed at school today. And everyone knows what an asshole Tarkin Shaw is. But what seventeen-year-old kid commits blackmail to get a girlfriend?

"I've upset you," she says.

"No. You haven't. I'm sorry. I'm just trying to process all of this. I'm not usually so slow."

"I'm sorry to dump this on you."

"Don't be."

She leans back in her chair then has a sip of cinnamon tea, lets it warm her, calm her. I have to come up with something. A solution. An answer.

"The police," I say. "Let's call the police."

"No. We can't tell anyone."

"But—"

"It won't matter anyway," she says. "The drugs won't be in my system anymore. I Googled it. There's no way to prove what he did."

"You could show them the pictures."

"I erased them."

"Oh. So they're gone then."

"*My* copies are gone. He still has them. And if I don't do what he says, he'll upload them."

"Where?"

"Does it matter? He's got me, DeShawn. I'm trapped."

"So, what, you're supposed to keep dating him forever? Is that his plan?"

"I don't know what his plan is." She puts the purple mug down then stands up and starts pacing again. "At first I think he just wanted to be seen with me. It was all a show. To prove he could get me. And to make me dump Nikki in front of him. He has a . . . vendetta against her."

"Why?"

101

"I can't really talk about that."

"Oh."

"Sworn to secrecy. Sorry."

Marcus mentioned some history between Nikki and Shaw too. I wonder what it is. The guy keeps getting worse. And I thought he was bad to begin with.

"The thing is, I had it sort of under control," she says. "Until your friend came along and told him I was about to dump him."

"You mean Marcus?"

"Yes, Marcus. The reporter. He told Tarkin I couldn't stand him, right? You were there."

"Yeah."

"So he really said that?"

I nod. He did. He said a lot of things.

"Well that's great," she says. "He *humiliated* Tarkin in front of other people."

It's true. Marcus made Shaw look like a fool. Then I came along and finished him off.

"Now it's all different," she says. "Now, being seen with me isn't enough. He wants proof."

"Proof of what?"

"Proof that I *can* stand him." She stops pacing and looks at me. "You understand?"

I don't right away.

Something crunches and when I look down I realize I've been fiddling with Terence's leg. It's snapped off and now it goes skittering under the workbench. I reach down and find it, roll it back and forth between my fingers. Suze is sitting in that chair again. She scoots it close to mine. "He's expecting me tonight," she says.

That's when I understand what she means about proof.

"Eight o'clock," she says. "That's when he wants me."

I look at my phone on the workbench. It's twelve past seven.

FROM THE SECRET DIARY
OF TARKIN SHAW

If your reading this, your fucking dead, that means you, Mason, you little shit. I don't care if you are my little brother.

Okay so tonight's the night. And it's about fucking time too. Suze Tilman has been running this game on me ever since she showed up in Jonesville, acting all superior, pretending like she's not interested. Yeah right. Like there's anyone else at Jonesville High she'd rather be with. Get real. The girl is mine for the taking. All the guys know it.

There are two kinds of girls in this world. Cut-rate skanks that throw their shit in your face and ice bitches that make you come after them. Everybody's got their game. You gotta let 'em play it too. And play it right back, be the bad guy, be aggressive, be the predator or whatever. Don't believe what they say after the fact. Make them fight you off. They love that shit. I don't usually go for the stuck-up ice queens like Suze Tilman because their too much work, especially when I've got all this low-hanging fruit to take care of. But sometimes a guy wants more. Everybody thinks I'm all about the fuck and chuck, but I can do relationships too. I'm not just a sex hound. That's a total stereotype, like just because I'm built like a sex machine people assume that's all there is to me. Well I have feelings too. I don't go flashing them around like a little bitch, the way that punkass reporter and his psycho boyfriend did at school today. Christ, I thought they were gonna start humping each other in the hallway. But I do have feelings, and for the first time in my life there's actually a girl who's worthy of them. Not like these Jonesville skanks. Suze is pure class. I feel like I could really talk to her, like actually share stuff. I know she looks like a supermodel, and believe me, I plan to get all the way up in that, but I don't just want her body. Shit, I could have had that five times to Sunday if that's all I wanted. The girl was laid out on that weight bench like a friggin' buffet. Took every ounce of willpower not to jump on that. But I restrained myself. Because a girl like Suze deserves that. I don't just want to fuck her. I want to own her. I swear to God, Mason, if I catch you reading this I don't care if you are my brother, you're a dead man.

MARCUS

At 8:07 p.m., DeShawn shows up at my front door out of breath, his bike lying at the bottom of our front steps. My mom, who is DeShawn's Number One Fan, pulls out all the stops to try to get him inside—homemade brownies, leftover pork chops, barbecue-flavor potato chips—but he's having none of it.

"I'll have him back by eleven," he tells her, still panting. He must have raced all the way over here.

"I hope there's no more jiu jitsu planned," Mom says.

DeShawn looks mortified, but my mother smiles. "I know you'd never hurt anyone unless you had to, DeShawn."

"Maybe you could remind my mother of that?"

"How is your mom?"

"Disapproving."

"I'll give her a call."

"It won't help," I say. "It's *me* she disapproves of."

"Anyway," DeShawn says, cutting this conversation short before it winds into uncomfortable territory. "We really have to go, Mrs. Daubney. We won't be out late. I promise."

He drags me down the front steps and over to my bike, underneath the basketball net in the driveway.

"What's going on?" I ask under my breath, while my mom eavesdrops unsubtly from the top of our steps.

"I'll explain to you on the way."

"On the way where?"

"Tarkin Shaw's house," he says. Then he jumps on his bike and speeds out of the driveway before I can object.

It's not until the end of my street that I finally catch up with him to ask, "Are you crazy?"

In lieu of a reply, he races across Main Street, assuming I'll follow. Which I do. About a quarter of a mile down the road, he turns left onto Cherry Street. There are no cars so I pull up to ride side by side with him and demand an explanation. He has one, all right. And it's a doozy.

"Wait," I say between breaths. "Are you telling me he's *blackmailing* her with nudes?"

"Yeah," he says, easily. DeShawn is way more fit than I am. This mad pace barely registers for him. "He drugged her first and took the pictures himself."

"Holy shit," I say.

In my head I'm already writing the story.

"All-State Wrestler Roofies Girl for Nudes"

"Varsity Hero by Day, Pornographer by Night"

**"High School Sex Predator Nabbed
for Blackmail"**

I COULD GO ON. I *will* go on. This could be the break I've been waiting for. The hard news story that will make my name. With the added side benefit of taking down that smug varsity shithead once and for all. Thoughts of my pending triumph give me precisely the adrenaline boost I need to keep up with DeShawn, who is now in a full sprint down Cherry Street like he's Lance goddamn Armstrong.

But wait a minute. Elena's voice enters my head to throw cold water on my excitement. All we have is Suze Tilman's account. What will Shaw say? Surely, he's not going to validate Suze's claims. He's not going to admit he's blackmailing her. If I've learned anything from my dealings in the news biz, it's that there's always another side.

"DeShawn?" I say.

"Keep up, buddy. We've gotta get there quick."

I pull up alongside him, my breath ragged. "You said there are fifty pictures of her?"

"Fifty-seven," he corrects.

"And you're sure Suze didn't . . . you know."

He shoots me a dirty look. "Didn't what?"

"This happened at Tara's party, right? Booze

was flowing. Drugs. Pot. You said her own friends were high, right?"

"Yeah. So?"

"And you said the pictures were on *her* phone?"

"Yeah."

"Why would Shaw take them with her phone?"

"He took them with her phone then sent them to his own."

"Why?"

DeShawn slams on his brakes. I slow to a stop about twenty yards ahead and wait for him to catch up with me. But he doesn't. He just stays where he is, glaring at me so I walk my bike back to him.

"Dude," I say. "Are you telling me you haven't asked yourself any of these things?"

"You think Suze Tilman took those pictures her*self*?"

"Girls do that shit all the time."

"Not Suze."

"How do you know? You don't even know her."

"You know what he wants from her tonight, right?" he asks.

"Look, DeShawn, all I'm saying—"

"Do you?"

Of course I know what he wants from her. He wants to have sex with her. He probably wants to have sex with her then brag to the whole school about it afterward. He may even want to video the whole thing. Which is gross and contemptible, but it doesn't change the fact that we don't know for sure how these pictures came into existence. All we have is Suze Tilman's word for it. And, to quote Elena DePiero: "Believe no one. Get proof."

"Do you know why he wants that?" DeShawn asks.

"What? Sex with Suze Tilman?" Does anyone need a reason to want sex with Suze Tilman?

"It's because of what *you* said to him at school today."

"What *I* said?"

"Yeah. About how she can't stand him, and how she's about to dump him."

"DeShawn, you're the one who told me that."

"I never told you to share it with Shaw."

"So this is my fault?"

"It's *our* fault. And we're going to fix it."

With that, he jumps back on his bike and sprints down Cherry Street.

"Wait!" I shout, but he doesn't slow down. He doesn't even look back at me. I climb on my bike and do my best to catch him.

As we turn onto Cedar Street, I beg him to slow down so I don't actually pass out before we get there.

"What's the plan?" I ask him. "I mean what are we supposed to do once we get there?"

"We're going to delete the photos," he says.

"How?"

"Suze is going to distract him, while we sneak into his bedroom and get his laptop."

"Sneak into his bedroom? How are we supposed to do that without being seen?"

"Suze did some reconnaissance today when she ditched school. His house is huge. Three floors. Assuming his room is on one of the top floors, she'll keep him away from the staircase so we can get up there unseen."

"So you guys planned this all out?" Yesterday Suze was a stranger to DeShawn, a cool, beautiful stranger he wouldn't dare talk to. Today she's his trusted co-conspirator, hatching SEAL team-level missions together?

"In the hole."

"In the hole?" No one ever goes to the hole except me. DeShawn's parents rarely get past the middle of the staircase.

"Is there a problem?" DeShawn asks.

"No. No problem at all, DeShawn. This is an amazing plan you've put together. I mean, what could possibly go wrong?"

"Your negativity is not exactly helping."

"Well, give me a sec, buddy. Five minutes ago I was flossing my teeth. Now you're asking me to break into a guy's house. A guy who tried to crush my face, by the way."

"We're not breaking in," he says. "Suze is going to make sure the back door is unlocked for us."

"How?"

"I don't know. She'll figure it out."

She'll figure it out. Sure. Why not. I bet that's

exactly how the SEALs work. What a great plan.

"Okay," I say. "So let's assume we get inside. Let's say we make it upstairs without being discovered. Then what?"

"We find his room and—"

"How do we know which room is his?"

"We'll figure it out."

"How?"

"We just will. Then we find his laptop and delete the pictures."

"What if it's password-protected?"

"Hopefully it won't be."

"*Hopefully*? You're basing this on *hopefully*?"

"I'm basing this on the fact that it's the best we can do."

He veers right and I follow him onto Walnut Street, which is where the rich section of Jonesville begins. The lawns expand. The houses heave up into mansions.

"Hey DeShawn," I say. "Where are her friends in all of this? Why aren't they breaking in to Shaw's house?"

"They don't know about any of this," he says. "They think she's really dating him. That was part of the deal. She had to dump Nikki in public."

"Why?"

"According to Suze, he has a vendetta against her."

Now that *is* interesting. I knew there was *some-*

thing between Nikki and Shaw. I just don't know the details. But I will. I'll dig them up, and the career-making article I'm writing in my head will have another exciting dimension: backstory.

THE SHAWS LIVE in Cedar Vale, a "luxury gated community" built on the site of a former pasture. I remember when they started digging it up five years ago. Everyone was so impressed with the idea, because they thought it would make Jonesville into something special, like Manchester or Marblehead. But the developers ran out of money before they finished, so now it consists of four lonely houses flicked randomly over a square half mile, like a mild case of acne on the smooth face of the pasture. Also, there are no actual cedar trees in the vicinity, which is something they probably should have thought about when they came up with the name. They should have called it Unfinished McMansionville for Graspy Suburbanites.

DeShawn and I ride our bikes up to two stone pillars, which I guess would have held up the gate for this "luxury gated community" if they'd ever finished it. There being no actual gate, we ride right on through, up and over a low hill until DeShawn stops his bike and points at a four-foot-high stone slab sticking out of a grassy hill. It's lit by its own floodlights and reads: SHAW.

"Oh, now that is classy," I say.

It looks like a tombstone. Above it sits the Shaws'

house itself, a gargantuan mishmash of architectural themes—vaguely colonial in keeping with the rest of Jonesville, but with Greek columns setting off an unusably narrow porch, and incongruous fake stone accents here and there to confuse the eye. The whole place screams new money. I don't mean to be a snob or anything. My family has neither new money nor old, but the Shaw castle is almost poignant in its efforts to impress.

I can't help but think back to my conversation with Elena DePiero about what socially important muckety-mucks Tarkin's parents are. Friends with Timothy Cochrane, the district attorney; members of Abingdale Hunt Club, this super-exclusive country club that has polo matches every Sunday. I've snuck in a few times to steal canapés from posh tailgate picnics there. Polo matches are a who's who of local VIPs. I wonder if these pillars of the community know what Tarkin's been up to. Imagine their horror when I expose it all in the *Bugle*.

No, forget the *Bugle*. I bet a story about Tarkin Shaw, young squire and amateur pornographer, makes it to the *Globe*. All the Greek columns in the world won't salvage a reputation after something like that.

I can't wait.

I follow DeShawn up the zigzagging driveway. The house itself is only about twenty yards away, but the driveway winds around that big stone name tag so we can appreciate it from a variety of angles. What a treat. I guess a regular straight driveway would be too working-class for these Jonesville aristocrats.

They do make it easy to hate them.

We ride our bikes over to the side yard and ditch them in a stand of pine trees. Then we hunker down behind the trees so no one in Shaw's house can see us. The plan, such as it is, calls for us to wait for a text from Suze.

"Do they have a dog?" I ask.

"Suze says she saw two cats, but no dog."

"Good, because a dog basically makes sneaking in impossible."

"There's no dog."

"Where are the parents?"

"At a concert in Boston."

"What about Shaw's brother, Mason? Is he home?"

"Unknown."

This is the problem with their so-called plan. There are too many unknowns, all of which I start silently checking off: What if Shaw made copies of the pictures? What if he's already shared them with his friends? What if Suze can't keep him "distracted" long enough for us to get upstairs? What if his laptop is password-protected?

I hug my shoulders against the cold.

"You should have worn a coat," he says. "Here." He takes off his hoodie and hands it to me.

"Now you'll be cold."

"I'm wearing layers," he says, pulling out his collar to reveal a thermal undershirt under his white button-down.

I put his hoodie on and zip it up.

"Why didn't she go to the police?" I ask.

"Because he told her if she did that, he'd upload the pictures."

"Wouldn't that incriminate him?"

"Maybe. But they'd still be out there."

True. I guess, in the scheme of things, busting Tarkin Shaw for roofying and blackmail isn't worth having the whole world see you naked. I mean, I'd be okay with it. But that's me. And nobody's lining up to see naked pictures of Marcus Daubney, whereas you could sell tickets to see Suze Tilman naked.

"She told me they look like they could be consensual," DeShawn says. "That he angled the phone so that it looked like it was in her hand."

"Why?"

"Well, think about it," he says.

"I am thinking about it. I don't—oh." Now I get it. If she *did* go to the police, Shaw could just say she took the pictures herself. Guys ask girls for pics all the time. And, for some reason, girls send them. "That's pretty smart actually."

"Yeah," DeShawn says. "He's not as dumb as he seems. Hold on." He pulls his vibrating phone out of his front pocket and I huddle in for a look.

Back door's open. Mason's upstairs in his room playing video games. Move fast and don't forget to slam the door when you leave.

"Why are we slamming the door when we leave?" I ask.

"To draw Shaw outside."

"After us?"

"Yeah, then while he's chasing us out the back, she'll take his phone and sneak out the front door."

"Then what do we do?"

"We ride away. Come on. We gotta move."

He sprints for the back door and I follow on his heels, my doubts about this so-called plan growing by the second. What if Shaw catches us during our escape? My God, what will he do to us if he knows what we're up to?

"Look," DeShawn says, pointing to the second floor where a window glows with a flickering blue light.

"Mason?" I ask.

The faint crash and screech of a video game leaks through his closed window.

DeShawn reaches for the doorknob, but I put my hand on his to stop him. "What if this doesn't work? What if Shaw sees us?"

"Don't worry about that."

"How can I not worry about that? He could have killed me today."

"No he couldn't have."

He stares me down and I know what he's thinking, though he's too modest to say it. Shaw couldn't have killed me today because DeShawn would have prevented it.

"So is that our backup plan?" I ask. "If he spots us sneaking around his house, you'll beat him up?"

"All I know is we are going in there and we are deleting those photos. By any means necessary."

"You're quoting Malcolm X now?"

"You got a problem with that?"

"Whoa, buddy. It's me, Marcus. Remember? I'm on your side here."

"I know. I know. But your doubts are kind of bumming me out. I need you on board with this. I can't do it without you."

I hate when he does that. But he's right. He does need me. Who else can he turn to in his time of need? Who else is going to come along with him on this harebrained scheme? Nobody, that's who. Enabling each other's stupid ideas is the bedrock of our friendship. I speak from experience. Once, in pursuit of a story, I got DeShawn to help me plant a bug in Principal Everett's office. Sadly, it amounted to nothing. Still, DeShawn was right there with me the whole way. So I know I have to be here for him. And, despite my doubts about the soundness of this "plan," I have to admit that it's probably the right thing to do. If Shaw is making Suze prove herself because of my big mouth, I'd be a monster not to help her out. Sometimes, when I can't tease out the morality of a particular conundrum, I ask myself, *What would DeShawn do?* Deep at the core of his being, in the same place where I store my relentless curiosity and skepticism, he stores his empathy. It's his superpower. It's hard being his friend. There are no shortcuts, no work-arounds. There's right and wrong, and if you can see that, you have to act on it.

"I really hate you sometimes," I tell him.

"I know," he says. "And it's Jean-Paul Sartre who first used that phrase. Malcolm borrowed it."

Of course he'd know that.

We enter through the back door like two stealthy cat burglars, although I'm sure that's just wishful thinking. I've never burgled a thing. I've never even shoplifted so much as a candy bar. There's music in the distance, a thumping baseline. Hip hop, gangster-style, a favorite of deranged white assholes everywhere. At the very least it'll help cover our footsteps.

We make our way through the kitchen, a hangar-sized cavern bigger than my entire house and full of commercial-grade stainless-steel bullshit. I have half a mind to steal their Vitamix as payment for my efforts tonight. But that would be unprofessional, if not for a burglar, then for a reporter. Can I use these details in the final story?

Tarkin Shaw, whose family's kitchen is worth more than the median house price in Jonesville . . .

119

No. That puts me here at the scene of the crime. Eyes on the prize, Daubney. Delete the photos, escape with your life, *then* write the story.

Once through the kitchen, we enter an even bigger living room three stories high with a skylight way the hell up there. The couch and chairs are so far away from each other it's hard to imagine what the purpose of the room is. It looks like a furniture warehouse after a big sale. There's another room to the right, but it's dark, a dining room maybe, or a TV room. Rich people. They have different rooms for every activity.

The music comes from another room behind some French doors masked by sheer white curtains. I can just make out Tarkin's silhouette on the other side, those hulking shoulders and foot-sized hands. A smaller shape—Suze presumably—sits on a couch across from him. They're talking I guess, but I can't hear anything over the music. DeShawn pauses to look at their silhouettes and I can tell from his body language that he wants to go in there and rescue her. And I don't blame him.

But that is not the plan.

He turns away from Suze and Shaw and leads me up the stairs to our right. The carpeting is so thick it muffles our footsteps, so plush you could lie down and have a nap on it. When we get to the second floor, the sound of screaming and gunshots grows, masking our movements even more. The Shaws' house is a burglar's paradise.

We peek into all the rooms until we find one festooned with dirty laundry—socks, T-shirts, jeans, sweatshirts—a Hollister ad detonated. A Pepe the Frog bedspread lies diagonally across the unmade bed and a black-and-gold wrestling singlet hangs over a desk chair. It's the varsity one, which means this must be Shaw's room. Shaw's brother, Mason, is on the JV team. When we go inside and shut the door, the smell hits me like a punch in the gut. Feet, plus death, plus BO.

"Let's just get this done," DeShawn says, trying not to breathe through his nose.

I pull my T-shirt over my nose and start looking around the room. There's a huge pile of T-shirts on a dark wood desk.

"What's that?" DeShawn says, pointing to the T-shirts. "No. Underneath the shirts."

Using the minimum amount of skin contact, I peel off a few extremely pungent T-shirts to reveal a printer.

"Printers have memories," he says. "If he printed any pictures they could be stored there."

He takes out a mini screwdriver set from his pocket and throws it to me. "Need to remove the hard drive," he says.

"Okay," I say. I guess I have to learn how to do that now. I take out my phone and google the model, a Brother LaserJet, then follow the instructions to find the hard drive. It's held in place by four small screws.

Meanwhile DeShawn unearths Tarkin's laptop on the bedside table underneath a pile of crumpled tissues. He sets it on the bedspread, right on Pepe the Frog's dumb face, and opens it.

"I don't want to look," he says.

I pull out the printer's hard drive then join him on the edge of Shaw's bed. Right there on the desktop is a folder titled, conveniently, "Suze."

"Delete it," DeShawn says. "Don't open the folder. Just delete it."

"What if these aren't the pictures though?"

"What else would it be?"

"I don't know. Love letters?"

He thinks about this. "Okay, you look," he says. "But don't stare."

I open the folder revealing a grid of tiny thumbnails, about fifty of them, with just enough miniature details to make out what they are—wheat-colored hair, golden skin, white tan lines.

"We need to make a copy first," I say.

"What?"

"Let's WeTransfer them to my email."

"Are you crazy?"

"We can still delete them from his computer, but this way I'll have a copy."

"What do you need a copy for?"

I look at him like *Duh. What do you think I need a copy for?* But he keeps staring back like he doesn't get it. So I spell it out for him: "It's evidence."

"She's not going to the police."

"I know, but—"

"Oh wait a minute," he says. "No, Marcus. Just no."

"What?"

"You want to write about it."

"Well somebody has to."

"No. Nobody's writing anything. She wants these pictures destroyed."

"But—"

Before I can even make my case, DeShawn nudges me out of the way, collapses the folder, then drags it to the trash.

"DeShawn, please—"

A few more clicks and he's emptied the trash. When it makes that crumpled paper sound, something inside of me dies.

"This means he gets away with it," I tell him, almost hissing.

"No, it means Suze is free," he says.

"You are an enemy of the fourth estate."

DeShawn shrugs. He's usually supportive of my journalistic ambitions, and I can't say it doesn't hurt that he's so dismissive right now. But this is his show, his mission, and its focus is narrow: rescue Suze Tilman. All other priorities be damned. While I sit numbly on the bed, he peruses Tarkin's desktop, which is covered in folders, a lot of them full of photos. "Summer Jam," "Victory Central," "fuck and chuck." I can only imagine what's in that last one. Shaw seems to have kept a photographic record of every facet of his assholery. DeShawn gleefully deletes them all.

We check the browser history for uploads. There aren't any since Tara's party, when he took the pictures, which is good news. Unsurprisingly, his browser history consists primarily of porn sites. Tarkin Shaw is a true connoisseur of that august art form. To be one hundred percent sure the photos are eliminated, DeShawn unscrews the casing, opens the laptop and removes the hard drive.

"Go big or go home," he whispers.

"We are now felons."

"Only if we get caught. Let's toss the room."

Toss the room? Who is he, Al Capone? What does DeShawn know about tossing a room? He's a sixteen-year-old math nerd. He's never tossed a room.

But I stand corrected because right now, De-Shawn is tearing through Shaw's bookshelves, searching for backups, thumb drives, printouts, basically any other way for the photographs to be leaked into the wild. And since I'm a good friend, I join in the ransacking party. The place was a mess when we arrived so I'm not sure you'd even notice our work. We only manage to find one small thumb drive jammed between two old yellowed paperbacks. DeShawn pockets it. We do find some rather disturbing items, like a half-melted G.I. Joe and a stash of inkjet prints stuffed between last year's yearbook and an old biology book I remember from middle school. I guess Shaw never returned it. The print quality of the photos is bad—he used regular copy paper instead of photo paper—but it's good enough to see what the pictures are of: naked girls. Lots of naked girls. The one on the top of the stack is Marcela DesJardins, a junior in my history class. DeShawn grabs the whole pile out of my hands and shoves them into his backpack.

"That picture was definitely consensual," I say. "She was holding the camera and standing in front of a mirror."

"Doesn't mean she wanted you to see it."

"The disturbing thing is that she wanted Shaw to see it."

"You don't know that."

"What are you planning to do with those?"

"Burn them."

"But they're evidence."

"Of what? You're not writing about this, Marcus."

"That picture has nothing to do with Suze."

"So how are you going to explain how you got it? Are reporters allowed to break into people's houses and steal shit?"

"I just think—"

"Shh . . ."

Footsteps approach down the hallway. DeShawn and I freeze. Shaw's room is big, three times the size of my bedroom, but there's no obvious place to hide. DeShawn tries to squeeze into the closet, but he winds up tripping over a pile of shoes, which makes a calamitous noise. Who-ever is out there has to have heard it. When the doorknob starts to turn, I'm still standing in the middle of the room. I dive over the bed and start sliding underneath it, coming face to face with a smooshed Nike. The door opens but all I can see are the legs and feet. Faded jeans and black Chuck Taylors.

DeShawn emerges from the closet. "Suze!"

She puts her finger to her lips and gently press-es the door closed. "What have you found?" she whispers.

He shows her the hard drives we liberated from the laptop and printer, along with the small dusty thumb drive.

"Where's Shaw?" I ask.

"He's out."

"He left?" I ask.

"No." She takes out a plastic baggie from the front pocket of her jeans. Inside are half a doz-en small white pills. "I think he tried to roofie me again."

I take the plastic bag and examine them. They look like little white aspirin.

"He kept looking at this wooden box on his tro-phy shelf," she explains. "Like it was making him nervous. The corner of that bag was sticking out of it. I pretended not to notice. But I didn't drink the soda he gave me."

"You think he put these in your drink?" I ask.

"I didn't want to risk it. I spilled it and asked him for another one. While he was out of the room, I got those from the box."

"What makes you think they're roofies?" I ask.

"Because I crushed up a bunch of them and put them in his beer."

"Did he drink it?" DeShawn asks.

She nods.

"And then what?" I ask.

"And then it got weird."

"Weird, how?" I ask.

She doesn't answer.

"Did he do something to you?" DeShawn asks very gently.

"Please don't ask me that."

"But—" I say.

She holds up her hand to cut me off.

I look to DeShawn for help here, but he says, "It's okay, Suze. You're safe now. Can you just tell us where he is?"

"He's in the study. He passed out. Eventually."

"Are you hurt?" DeShawn asks. He reaches for her hand, and for a second she looks like she's going to take it, but then she backs away.

"I'll be okay," she says quietly.

I can't quite figure out the dynamic between them. They were strangers this morning and yet she came to him for help. And DeShawn seems willing to do absolutely anything to protect her. Whatever this is, it feels way beyond a crush.

"We need to keep looking," she says. "We need to make sure there are no backups."

I'm pretty certain there are none, but to ease her mind, we go back to "tossing" the room. By the time we've finished searching, there isn't a single spot left for a thumb drive, external, or anything. The place is thoroughly trashed.

"What about wireless backups?" she asks. "Did you check that before you removed the hard drive?"

DeShawn nods. "There was nothing."

"Google Drive? iCloud?"

"Nope."

"What about his browser history? Were there any uploads?"

"None," he says.

I'm sort of amazed that DeShawn was able to pull this off. I've never thought of him as a major hacker, or whatever you'd call this. I mean sure he's generally brilliant, but the thoroughness of this mission, combined with the speediness of the planning is kind of taking my breath away.

"Did you get his phone?" DeShawn asks Suze. "We need to check that."

She pulls it out of her jeans pocket. "I YouTubed how to check if anything's been uploaded from a cell phone and it looks like it hasn't been."

"That's great," DeShawn says. "That's really good news."

"You guys are like spies," I say.

Suze doesn't seem flattered by the compliment.

Also, she doesn't look at me the same way she looks at DeShawn. There's no warmth in her eyes. I don't think she trusts me. Maybe she's mad because I insulted Shaw, which, one could argue, is why we're in this mess.

"We should go," she says.

She opens the door and we follow her down the hallway, gliding quietly over the thick muffling carpet, past Mason's room with its shooting and screaming. Downstairs, the living room is still dark, except for the yellowish light from that other room, where a heavy bass beat thumps away.

"In there?" I ask, motioning with my head.

Suze nods. The French doors are open slightly. DeShawn hangs back with Suze while I head over by myself and look into the room. It's a trophy room, or a study, or a combination of the two. There are framed photos of Shaw and his brother Mason, other photos of their father with local VIPs—priests, cardinals, politicians. There's Tim Cochrane, the DA, with his arm around Mr. Shaw. And, of course, there are Shaw's trophies and plaques. First place, second place. MVP. I don't see Shaw himself right away, but then I spot his leg dangling off the side of a brown leather couch with something tangled around his ankle. It takes me a second to figure out what it is. White boxer briefs. He's naked.

I look back at Suze queryingly. She's gripping DeShawn's arm now.

"Let's just get out of here," she says.

DESHAWN

A minute later, Marcus and I are cycling between the stone columns of Cedar Vale behind Suze's Prius. We keep pace with her as far as Cherry Street, but as soon as she hits Main Street, she speeds up and takes off. The plan is to meet up at Chebacco Bridge, which crosses an inlet of the Essex River. Kids used to dive off of it until a few summers ago, when a middle schooler broke his neck. No one goes there any more.

When Marcus and I finally arrive, Suze's car is parked in the soft shoulder under some pine trees. Suze herself is on the bridge leaning over the railing, staring at the water, her long hair hiding her face. When she hears us coming, she takes Tarkin's cell phone from her pocket, drops it to the ground and stomps it with the heel of her sneaker. The glass front shatters, but the phone itself skitters over to me. We look at each other for a second. Then I stomp it until the case breaks open.

After that, I drop the laptop's hard drive to the ground and Marcus adds the printer's hard drive.

Together the three of us stomp those motherfuckers to smithereens. I'm not a violent person by nature, but I can't help but see Shaw's face down there. And I think Suze probably feels the same way.

When there's nothing left but wire, shattered glass, bent metal, and shards of plastic, Suze picks up the biggest pieces and flings them over the railing into the river. I kick the rest of the debris under the railing and we all lean over to watch it drift away, as harmless as seaweed. No one says anything. Suze is too shaken. Marcus seems frightened of Suze, like he's worried anything he says will upset her. And I just want to make sure Suze feels safe now. I want to take her hand and let her know that I'll be there for her, no matter what. I won't let Tarkin Shaw hurt her ever again. But I think I know what she's feeling right now. To be with people, and not be with them. To be alone in a crowd. That's how I usually live.

NIKKI

I'm dead asleep when a noise outside wakes me. It takes a few seconds for my eyes to adjust to the darkness and I half expect to find someone standing in my doorway. Instinctually, my body tenses. Then I hear a *ping* at the window and I realize whoever it is isn't in my doorway, they're outside. I slide off the bed, crawl over, and peek through the curtains. I can see a shape down there, but I can't make out who it is. Then the voice, a loud whisper.

"Nikki!"

She steps back just enough to catch the light from the streetlamp on Maple Street. It's Suze.

"Can I come up?" she says.

I check the time. It's 1:17 a.m.

"Please, Nikki," she whispers. "I can explain. I swear."

I stare down at her, still angry. I don't want an explanation. An explanation will involve the name Tarkin Shaw and I don't want to hear that name. I think I've earned the right not to hear that name. I start to turn away from the window when something stops me. I don't know if it's morbid curiosity or the need to let her drive this friendship firmly into the ground. But I know if I let her go now, I won't be able to sleep anyway. I'll lie there staring at the ceiling, wondering what her explanation could possibly be.

"Back door," I say, then I throw on a sweatshirt and go downstairs to meet her.

She's waiting for me at the foot of the back steps, hugging herself for warmth. "You didn't really believe I was dating him," she says, shivering. "Did you?"

I stare at her, speechless.

"Nikki, I'm freezing."

I take her inside to the TV room, turn on a lamp, and close the door so my parents can't hear us. Whatever this is, I don't need them waking up and finding out. I never told them what happened between Tarkin and me freshman year. I've never mentioned his name in this house. The few times they've brought him up, I've changed the subject. *Did you hear Tarkin made the varsity team? As a freshman? Isn't it great that Tarkin made all-state this year? Didn't you guys used to be friends?* Yeah, sure, whatever, Mom and Dad. Pass the peas, can we talk about something else?

Suze sits on the edge of the blue plaid sofa, bouncing her knee nervously. She looks charged up, like she just robbed a bank or something. When she opens her mouth to begin explaining herself though, she doubles over and starts sobbing instead.

It takes her three deep breaths to collect herself. Then she sits up straight, wipes her eyes, and pushes the hair out of her face. She's always doing that with her hair and it drives me crazy. I hand her a hair band from the pocket of my sweatshirt and she whips it up into a messy knot.

Then she unloads the story. And as she lays it down for me, detail by hideous detail, I can feel something shifting inside me, something waking up. All the work I've done burying Tarkin Shaw and that awful night crumbles, and there he is, squinting dumbly in the sunlight with that snide grin on his chiseled, steroid-poisoned face. I try to push him away, but he won't go. Grinning. Laughing. Flexing his pecs. Looming over me. Six foot four and totally unstoppable.

"Nikki?" Suze says weakly.

I've closed my eyes. When I open them, she's staring at me, and I realize I've disappeared into the nightmare inside of me when I need to be here for hers.

"I had to make it seem real," she says. "But I hoped . . ."

She hoped I'd see through it. She hoped I'd know that she would never dump me for Tarkin Shaw.

"I tried calling you," she says.

But I turned off my phone. We all did.

"Was that you calling from your mother's phone?" I ask.

She nods. "He put spyware on mine."

"He what?" I say hoarsely.

"Yeah," she says. "That's why I called you from my mum's."

And we'd ignored the call. *The traitor formerly known as Suze Tilman*, Lydia had said. *Let's all go analog. Give her a taste of her own medicine.* And I'd agreed. I'd gone along with it. I'd been so mad at her, so hurt, so betrayed, I hadn't seen his fingerprints on this.

I open my mouth to apologize but I can't do it. It's not enough. It doesn't even come close.

Sensing my shame, she whispers, "It's okay."

"No. It's not okay. Don't you dare forgive me for this."

"Nikki, please, I don't want to be mad. I really need you right now."

"I can't believe we fell for it. I can't believe *I* fell for it."

"It would have been worse if you didn't."

"Why?"

"Because he would have published the pictures. You didn't see them, Nikki. He got me completely naked."

My stomach darkens as I recall the way she was splayed out on that weight bench, her T-shirt hastily thrown back on, her hair messed up. How did I not piece that together at the time? It seems so obvious now. How did I miss it?

"And they look like selfies," she says. "He positioned the camera so it looks like I took them."

I can feel myself shutting down. It's that protective instinct. You grow a shell and disappear inside. If nothing can reach you, nothing can hurt you.

"Like I would do that," she says, her eyes dazed. "Like I'd throw my head back and pose naked for him. It's like he's erased who I am and turned me into . . . someone else."

"They're gone, though." My voice is robotic. "You deleted them, right?"

She nods. "Yeah, they found them."

By "they" she means Marcus Daubney and De-Shawn Hill, the two juniors she turned to because we weren't there for her. The strangers she went to because her friends, her goddamn Shield, were too busy sniping about her behind her back.

Fuck her and her mother. That's what I'd said. And I'd meant it too.

"Nikki?" she says. "I roofied him. I found his drugs and put them in his beer."

"That is one hundred percent okay."

She shakes her head.

"Of course it is. He did the same thing to you."

"No. You don't understand. They didn't work right away."

I wait for her to continue, but she stalls. Her face collapses, her eyes go dead. There's more. She takes a breath and searches for the strength to tell me what happened, what she and Tarkin did in that trophy room while DeShawn Hill and Marcus Daubney ransacked Tarkin's bedroom. She doesn't cry when she tells me. She holds those tears in, keeps them right at the edge of her eyelids, like she'd rather die than let them go. I can see the effort it's taking, so I don't say a word. I don't want to break whatever spell she's cast to get through this. I just sit and listen until she's gotten everything out.

Tears come to my eyes, too, but I don't release them. If she can be strong, so can I. Tarkin Shaw doesn't deserve our tears. He deserves nothing.

"I didn't know what else to do," she says. "I didn't want—" She squeezes her eyes closed.

She didn't want what happened to me to happen to her.

I know what she's feeling right now, because I felt the same way once. Ashamed and wronged and responsible all at once. Dirty and guilty and like the world was out to get me. But the world isn't out to get you. That's the worst part. The world keeps on going like none of this ever happened. Monday comes around, the school week resumes. And somehow you have to make your way through it knowing what you know.

I don't have the words to make any of this okay for her. All I can do is hold her as tightly as she held me the day I told her my story on that rock behind her house. So that's what I do. I hold her and tell her that she is gold. She is everything.

And Tarkin Shaw is nothing.

ANI / **LYDIA**

> Wow, just wow.

I KNOW!!!

> I can't believe he was blackmailing her the whole time.

Like it's evil and super pathetic at the same time.

> The worst part is that we doubted Suze. We literally let a guy come between us. That's not cool.

I know. I feel like a traitor. To be fair tho, she sort of made us do it.

Because she was being BLACKMAILED!!

Yeah, but how were we supposed to know that?

I feel like we should have somehow. This was a friend fail. We have to own that. Especially me. I was such a bitch.

You were mad.

No, Ani. We should have been there for her.

Nikki says Suze wants to put it all behind her, so maybe we should just do that. For Suze's sake.

I feel like Tarkin's getting away with something tho.

I know. It's so unfair.

He should pay for what he did.

True. But let's just stay close to Suze. Make sure he doesn't try anything at school.

Oh, he better not try anything.

I will kill that motherfucker.

Breathe, Lydia. Don't forget to breathe.

TUESDAY

DESHAWN

At the bike rack the next morning at school, Marcus is super nervous. He keeps scanning the parking lot in search of Tarkin Shaw.

"Do you know what kind of car he drives?" he asks me.

I don't. I tell him to calm down. For one thing, Shaw doesn't even know we were in his house last night. For another, I'm pretty sure he won't try anything today. After the beatdown I gave him yesterday, I don't think his ego could take it. I'm not saying that to be cocky, I'm just saying how it is. Guys like Shaw are all about being on top, being invincible. Or at least looking that way. Inside they're soft as shit.

As we walk to homeroom, I can sense people staring at me, whispering, because of what happened yesterday.

"You're a celebrity," Marcus says under his breath.

I don't want to be a celebrity though. I like it better when people ignore me. I don't know how to hide it when I'm bored. And the kind of stuff most people talk about is boring as shit. If you say something boring to me, you'll know from my face exactly what I'm thinking.

Near homeroom, we spot Suze at Nikki Petronzio's locker with Lydia and Ani. I'm so glad she has her friends again. Those girls are tight, and when your world's been turned upside-down, that's who you need. The hood of Suze's gray sweatshirt is up and only a wisp of light brown hair sticks out. She's leaning against the locker next to Nikki's, sneaking looks around the hallway, probably scanning for Tarkin Shaw, too. When she catches my eye around the edge of her hoodie, she smiles, and it lights me up inside.

AFTER EACH CLASS, I cruise by Shaw's locker to see if he's shown up. I'm on high alert, ready to jump in and be Suze's bodyguard if need be. But by fifth period, it's clear that "the Tarks," as he likes to be known, is taking the day off. No surprise there. If Suze gave him the same drugs he gave her, which I'm pretty sure is either Rohypnol or GHB, he'll be feeling the same way she felt. I googled both drugs last night. Mr. All-State Wrestling champ can expect a day's worth of headaches, nausea, dizziness, and confusion. Feast on that, wrestler boy.

I like to imagine Shaw waking up with a crushing headache, tapping at his laptop and wondering why the screen is black. I picture him tearing his house apart in search of his phone, the remains of which are somewhere off the coast of Gloucester by now. Suze said the drugs stole her memory, so who knows how much he'll remember from the night before. Will he remember when it "got weird" with Suze? I wish I knew what that meant. I mean, I think I do. Mostly, I wish I could have prevented it, whatever it was. Marcus told me Shaw was naked on that couch, and it hurts my heart to think of what that means. Should I have barged into that room as soon we got there, rather than heading upstairs to find the pictures? Or would that have messed up the whole plan?

I wonder if Shaw will even remember what happened. Maybe he'll remember that he was supposed to have a "date" with Suze last night, which means he'll figure out at some point that it was Suze who turned the tables on him, using his own drugs against him. There's a certain symmetry to that. Symmetry is beautiful.

Now that I think of it, we should have taken pictures of Shaw's naked body while he was lying there on that couch. Then Suze could have threatened to upload them unless he did something *she* wanted, which would be even more symmetrical. I wonder what Suze would want, though. Maybe she'd make him volunteer at some excellent charity, or quit the wrestling team, or apologize to Amber Laynes and Nikki Petronzio and all the other girls he's hurt. Just imagine if you could hold something like that over a person's head and make sure they never hurt anyone again. That would be the best use of blackmail ever.

Marcus tells me that the rumor mill is in general agreement that Shaw is skipping school today because of yesterday's incident in the hallway. Not that he's physically injured, just humiliated. Guys like Shaw have super-sensitive egos, which is why they have to strut around acting like little kings. They're not kings, though. That's the point. They hate themselves for whatever reason, and they project all that hate outward, which is a sad and pointless way to live. Also, it seems like a lot of effort, and for what?

As for the rumors, I agree with Marcus that they're "icing on the cake." Justice is having a pretty good day today. What is justice, after all, but a kind of symmetry? You do something bad to someone, so something bad happens to you. Maybe, if enough people believe that I'm responsible for destroying Tarkin Shaw's ego, it will have a domino effect on other aspiring bullies. Maybe I've toppled their role model. That would be both symmetrical and awesome.

Of course, I'd prefer that none of this ever happened in the first place. But what the three of us did last night is a boost to the integrity of the universe. We made things better—not just for Suze, but for everyone. I like that. I like it a lot.

MARCUS

**"Area Youth Wakes Up Naked,
Confused, Missing Hard Drives"**

**"Varsity Wrestler Strikes Out
with Fake Girlfriend"**

**"Nerd Duo Help Coolest Girl in School
Turn Tables on Sex Monster"**

Those are just some of the headlines I come up with for the article I'm writing in my head. It beats listening to Mrs. Miller drone on about *Wuthering Heights*. How am I supposed to care about a stupid ghost story when a major news story has broken right in front of me? It has all the hallmarks of a great one too: drugs, sex, larceny, kids destroying each other with technology. It could be a real exposé. Even kind of a think piece. I could use the factual details—the who, what, when, where, and how—to riff on Big Issues.

But no, I can't print a single word of this pending masterpiece, because there's no way to do it without implicating myself in a crime. A grubby burglary, no less. Plus the evidence of Shaw's malfeasance is gone, smashed up and sent out to sea.

I guess I'll have to settle for feeling quietly smug. In lieu of paying attention to Mrs. Miller as she plods through *Wuthering Heights*, I indulge in imaginary ripostes with Tarkin Shaw. E.g., *Yes, Tarkin, you may have hands the size of feet, but you're not so tough once the drugs kick in, are you? Undone by two nerds and a girl. That's gotta hurt.* Not that I'd ever say any of these things to his face. I may have a mouth on me, but I also have a brain and a well-developed sense of self-preservation.

DeShawn isn't paying attention to Mrs. Miller either. His face has that peculiar DeShawnian glow of deep distraction. No one drifts off into imaginary worlds like DeShawn. I bet he's feeling like a hero today, and why shouldn't he? He was right about Suze. Those spooky instincts were spot-on once again. And as much as I doubted the feasibility of his plan, I'm glad I got to be a part of it. It's not every day you get to rescue the coolest girl in school from an alpha dillweed like Tarkin Shaw. We should get a reward for this shit. I'm sure if DeShawn could claim a reward it would be something noble and decent, like the knowledge that no one would ever hurt Suze Tilman again. Or world peace.

My desires are more modest. All I want is to write up this amazing story of teen degeneracy and comeuppance and shoot it over to Schnell at the *Bugle*, cc'ing Elena, just to make her jealous.

IT'S NEAR THE end of English class when we hear the first walkie-talkies. You don't usually hear walkie-talkies at school, so it gets everyone's attention. Mrs. Miller, picking up on the sudden flurry of fidgeting in the classroom, urges everyone to settle down because she still has some *Wuthering Heights* to cram into our supple, uncaring minds. When the bell finally cuts her off and we all empty out into the hallway, it's clear that something is awry. Nobody seems to know what exactly, only that the police are on the premises, talking with Principal Everett in his office. This encourages wild speculation, which goes rippling through the hallway. A bomb threat. A terrorist attack. A kid with a gun. Unlike some schools, Jonesville High has never done an active shooter drill. Principal Everett is a self-proclaimed pacifist who believes, adorably, that if you assume the best about people, they'll rise to the occasion. A nice thought, unless there actually is a shooter on campus, in which case we're all screwed.

When the late bell rings, DeShawn and I rush to Spanish class and sit in our usual seats in the back.

"Why are the cops here?" he asks, like I have a police scanner in my backpack.

It's only at that moment, seeing the fear in

DeShawn's eyes, that I realize the possible implications of the cops being at school. Technically, DeShawn and I are both guilty of a crime. What if Shaw's brother, Mason, saw us creeping around his house last night? What if he was on the other side of that bedroom door, peeping through the keyhole while we ransacked his brother's room? Maybe the noise from his video game wasn't masking *our* thieving, but *his* spying.

Holy shit! What if the cops are here to arrest us?

Quickly, I run through all the ramifications. The cops can't bust us for breaking and entering because Tarkin's door was unlocked. We walked right in. That has to count for something, right? Isn't an unlocked door an implicit invitation to enter? Plus, we're minors. Don't you get your first burglary for free? Maybe a fine, some community service? Surely we're not talking jail time.

"I can't go to juvie, man," DeShawn whispers, his face slick with fear. "Kids get knifed in their sleep at juvie."

Jesus, juvie. I haven't even considered that. What a terrifying prospect. It's fair to say that DeShawn and I are not the types who'd thrive in juvie. We'd be pawns, fodder, the hapless fuel consumed by vastly tougher kids looking to bootstrap themselves to full-blown sociopaths.

I actually know nothing about juvie. I never thought I'd need to. It doesn't come up when you live the way I live. Detention, maybe, but not juvie.

"Marcus, I'm kind of freaking out." DeShawn's gone gray again, with those undertones of green. He's broadcasting guilt before anyone even suspects us of a thing.

"Just relax," I tell him. "We don't even know why they're here. Could be totally unrelated. Could be a bomb."

Please let it be a bomb. Oh God, please let it be a bomb.

But if it isn't a bomb, if the police *are* here to arrest us, surely they'll understand *why* we stole those things. It's justifiable. Illegal, sure, but totally justifiable. A judge will have to see that. DeShawn and I aren't common thieves. We're heroes. Or maybe some combination of the two. Hero-thieves. Like Robin Hood, only we steal from predatory douchebags who totally have it coming. Surely there's a loophole in the criminal justice system for that.

Then again, even if we could explain the reason behind our one isolated instance of totally-out-of-character lawbreaking, the exculpatory evidence is gone. Damn it, I knew we should have made a copy of those pictures. My God, we suck at crime!

"My mom'll kill me," DeShawn says, breathlessly. "First the fight, then this?"

"Just don't say anything."

Stacey Gilinsky arrives at the door, wide-eyed and on the verge of an announcement. A bomb in the girls' room, a depressed kid with a gun, a teacher with a classroom full of hostages. Everyone freezes in anticipation as her hands fly up and tent over her nose.

That's when I notice that our Spanish teacher, Mr. Fiore, hasn't arrived yet.

Stacey Gilinsky starts crying, quietly but wetly, her face contorting into sickening shapes. I breathe deeply and share a look with DeShawn. Whatever it is, it's not about us, because no way would Stacey Gilinsky care that much if the police were there to arrest DeShawn and me.

Brianna Christakos slides out from behind her desk, walks up to Stacey, and asks her what's wrong. Receiving no reply, she hugs Stacey. Stacey sobs and shakes silently. Whatever it is, she can't bring herself to say it.

A kid goes to the window and reports that there are two patrol cars in the parking lot.

"Bomb," someone says. "It's gotta be a bomb."

But where is Mr. Fiore?

"I'm outta here," Marcel Sloane says.

A few kids get up and follow him out the door, shouldering right past Stacey Gilinsky who is still shaking—and still, despite Brianna's best efforts, unable to spit the bad news out.

"Should we go?" DeShawn asks. "Should we just—"

One of the kids who just walked out into the hallway returns, ashen. Steve Gomez is his name, a quiet kid, a math nerd.

"Holy shit," he says. "Tarkin Shaw is dead."

ANI / **LYDIA**

Can you believe it? I don't believe it. Do you think it's true? It can't be true right?

Why would Everett make that announcement if it wasn't true?

But dead as in like actually dead? What does this mean?

It means he's dead, Ani. As in not alive any more. As in never coming back to school. As in definitely not going to the homecoming dance.

I know, I know I'm not dealing with it at all tho. I said such horrible things about him last night.

We all did because he's a total scumbag. That doesn't change just because he's dead. Maybe he deserved to die.

You shouldn't say that.

After what he did to Suze? And Nikki? And god knows how many other girls?

Oh my God. Suze. What's going to happen to her now?

That's what I'm worried about too.

I want to help her.

Me too.

But how?

I've been thinking about that. What if we told the police she was with us last night?

What, like at your house?

Or at Nikki's. She did go there and we did all FaceTime.

So you mean like be her alibi?

That's the word I was looking for.

Wouldn't that be illegal for us to lie like that?

Yeah but they'd never know. Who's to say she wasn't at Nikki's house earlier than she actually got there. Where is Nikki anyway? Nikki, answer us. We need to brainstorm.

She's calling me now.

NIKKI

I'm alone in the library when the news arrives. Albert Dennison delivers it, standing stiffly at the librarian's desk next to the big dictionary on its stand. His voice is hoarse and too quiet. He has to repeat the phrase "um, guys, Tarkin Shaw is dead" three times before enough people hear it to make an impression. Then the whole library freaks out. Except for me. I go stiff. I can hear everyone else crying, gasping, exclaiming. *Oh my God. Is it true? Can it be? Tarkin Shaw? How is this possible?* In the background, I hear this persistent chirping, and it takes me awhile to figure out it's my phone. My group chat with Ani and Lydia is in overdrive. When I finally come to my senses and read it, I cannot *believe* what those two are texting. Don't they know anything about evidence? Why not just go to the police and straight up drop a dime on Suze? I call Ani right away because she's (usually, anyway) the sensible one.

"Get off your damn phones," I say, looking around to make sure no one's close enough to hear me. Nobody's paying any attention. They're too busy consoling each other over the "tragic" news.

Is it tragic? I feel like it might be, but not in the way everyone assumes.

"Oh, right," Ani says. "We should delete those messages."

"Yeah. You should."

"But what about the police? Do you think they'll arrest Suze?"

Will they? What do they know? Details of the night before sharpen and click into place.

"He died at home," I say. "Who's to say Suze was even there?"

"What about those guys?" Ani says. "Marcus and DeShawn."

Right. Those two. Karate Boy and Bigmouth. I wish I knew more about them. Especially that De-Shawn kid. He seems like a full-on weirdo to me. Math nerd with a violent streak. That can't be good. Plus, Suze said he was following her around school yesterday because he "intuited" that her relationship with Tarkin was a sham. Well, good for him. I guess he must be a mind reader too. And his friend, Marcus? He's even mouthier than Lydia. Dropping shade on Tarkin in public, telling him Suze was about to dump his ass.

"Do you think they'll say anything?" Ani asks.

"It wouldn't be smart," I say. "They were there, too."

"Right," she says. "That would make them accessories."

Accessories to *murder*.

That's when it hits me why this news is so tragic. It's not because he's dead. It's because he's even more dangerous dead than he was alive. Only Tarkin Shaw could figure out how to do that.

DESHAWN

After school, Marcus and I race to the bike racks like demons are chasing us. We make it to my house in record time then ride straight over my front lawn so we can dump our bikes and go directly into the hole, because that's where we go when we need to figure stuff out. But when we get to the basement door, Suze is crouched on the stoop, hugging her knees.

"Nobody knows I'm here," she says. "I parked down the street."

I dump my bike and crouch in front of her. She isn't crying, but she's so pale she looks like a ghost.

"Have you guys told anyone about last night?" she asks.

"No," I say. Who would we have told? Marcus and I don't talk to anyone but each other.

"What about your parents? Do they know where you were?"

"They think I was in the hole," I tell her.

"The hole?"

"My basement. I don't usually see them much after dinner. They didn't even know I was gone."

"My mom thinks I was here too," Marcus says.

"What about your dad?"

Marcus shakes his head. His dad left two years ago. He doesn't like to talk about it.

"What about your parents?" I ask.

"They don't know anything. They think I was at Nikki's."

Then she tells us that she actually *did* go to Nikki's after Chebacco Bridge and told her everything.

"Great," Marcus says. "And if Nikki knows, that means Lydia and Ani know too, right?"

"They won't say anything," Suze says.

"What if the police go to them?" he asks.

"Why would the police go to *them*?"

"Maybe they'll question everyone who knew Tarkin Shaw."

"They weren't even friends with him," she says. "They hated him."

"Enough to kill him?"

"What?" she says.

"Yeah, what are you talking about, Marcus?"

"I'm just saying, if it's a known fact that they hated him, maybe the police *will* question them. What will they say then?"

"Yeah, but Marcus," I say. "We don't even know if the police are treating this as suspicious."

"The police were at school," he says. "That tells me they're suspicious."

Suze drops her face in her hands. "I can't believe he's dead."

"Wait a minute," I say. "Are we even sure it was the roofies that killed him?"

"They'll do an autopsy," Marcus says. "They'll come up with a time of death, a window."

"And a cause of death," Suze adds. "Roofies, or whatever that was."

"Do roofies actually kill people?" I ask.

"Obviously," Marcus says.

But I don't think it *is* so obvious. We don't even know for sure what those drugs were. Maybe they were aspirin.

"They're going to find the Rohypnol," Marcus says. "Or whatever it was. Let's just assume that."

"It belonged to him though," I say. "You got it from his stash, right?"

Suze nods.

"Exactly," I say. "It was in his trophy room. In his house. So he overdosed on his own drugs."

"People don't roofie themselves," Marcus says.

Suze stands up and starts pacing between the stoop and the clothesline. I think Marcus is stressing her out.

"What if he wanted to die?" I say quietly.

"Tarkin Shaw?" Marcus says. "The cockiest, most inflated egomaniac alive? Why would *he* want to die?"

"You said yourself that everyone was talking about how embarrassed he was after I dropped him at school."

Suze whips around to face us. "Is that true? Were people really saying that?"

"Yeah," I say. "Tell her, Marcus. Everyone was saying that's why he skipped school. Because he was *humiliated*. Remember? That's what you said."

Marcus nods.

"And remember how mad he got when you told him Suze was about to dump him? He actually got violent."

"He got violent with *me*, DeShawn. Not with himself."

"All I'm saying is this is not someone who was happy. This is someone who was so obsessed with his image he had a fake girlfriend."

Suze nods, lingering by the clothesline.

"Then why were the police at school?" Marcus asks.

"Maybe they just went there to tell Principal Everett so he could make that announcement."

During sixth period, Principal Everett's voice came over the PA system to announce that his door was open in case anyone wanted to "talk things out." He also said grief counselors would be at school tomorrow. But that could mean anything. It doesn't necessarily mean the police are seeing this as a homicide. They could be treating it as a suicide. Maybe the police were there to warn Everett about the possibility of copycats.

Marcus's phone chirps, which makes us all jump. He takes it out of his pocket and looks at the screen. "Elena," he says. Then he goes to the swing set to take the call out of earshot.

When I explain to Suze that Elena's a reporter, she collapses on the basement stoop.

"No, no, no," I say. "She calls Marcus all the time. It doesn't mean the cops are on to us."

"Us? I think you mean *me*."

"No." I sit down next to her. "I mean us."

MARCUS

Elena makes no attempt to keep the excitement out of her voice when she asks me if I've heard about "this Tarkin Shaw thing."

"Yeah, of course," I tell her, trying to sound as casual as possible. "Everyone's heard about it. What are the police saying?"

"They're not ready to make an official statement yet. No evidence of heart trouble or any underlying medical conditions that would cause him to drop dead like that, though. Evidence of sex, semen."

"*Semen*?"

"Yes, Marcus. You *are* aware of what semen is, right? What have you heard about the kid's relationship with his parents?"

"Um . . . nothing. Why?"

"Any abuse, sexual or otherwise?"

"Do they think he was abused?"

"Kid's found dead, naked, semen stains on the couch? Fifty bucks says they find drugs, maybe Rohypnol, some kind of downer, muscle relaxer. There were beer bottles around. They'll be testing those."

Yes, they will be testing those beer bottles, and that's where they'll find the drugs Suze gave him, along with her fingerprints. She may as well have left them a note.

"What about suicide?" I ask.

"People usually compose themselves for suicide. This kid was a mess. How well did you know him?"

"Not at all."

"You were asking a lot of questions about him yesterday."

"Oh, right. Yeah, he's a jerk. That's what I know about him."

"Come on, help me out here. What are his class-mates saying? What about his girlfriend?"

"What girlfriend?"

"For Chrissake, you wrote about her in that arti-cle, the one about that party."

"That was a joke!"

"I know it was a joke, but was it true? Did she really throw herself at him? What was her name again? Hold on." I can hear those nail-bitten fin-gers banging away at her laptop as she retrieves the joke article I sent her.

"I made all that up," I say.

"You didn't make up the party. That really hap-pened. What about the rest of it? Was she really carried out of there drunk? Here it is. Suze Tilman. What do we know about her?"

"I don't know anything about her."

"You wrote that she doesn't normally drink. Is that true?"

DeShawn, as it turns out, was right about that part. It was one of the many tidbits I gleaned from the rumor mill about Tara Budzynski's party. The fact that Suze Tilman, who doesn't drink, who doesn't normally lower herself to attend parties at all, got full-on wasted like an Amish girl during Rumspringa. I remember the gleam in Becca De-Paul's eye as she told her rabbity little friend, Eliza Banks, about it. "She thinks she's above all that. Ha!" Kids seemed to take a lot of pleasure from the fact that the formerly too-cool-for-school Suze Tilman was now drunkenly slobbering over Tarkin Shaw.

"It wasn't an article," I remind Elena. "It was a joke."

"Yeah, but was that part true? Does she normally drink or not?"

"What difference does it make?"

"It makes a lot of difference, actually. Because if she doesn't drink, but she got drunk that night, we could be dealing with a good girl gone bad."

"Are you actually serious right now?"

"Whoa. You sound defensive. Are you involved with this girl?"

"No! I don't even—"

"Why did you pick her to feature in that article?"

"It wasn't an article!"

"There were a lot of kids at that party. You could have written about any of them. This beef you have with Tarkin Shaw—"

"I don't have a beef with Tarkin Shaw."

"Is it about this girl? Were you sneaking around with Tarkin Shaw's girlfriend?"

I realize at exactly this moment that I have to get off the phone. I've never been on the receiving end of Elena's interview style, but now I understand why it's so effective. She's sly and relentless. And she's not afraid to get personal. A few more questions and I'll be handing her the truth on a bun with pickles.

"Look, I'm really sorry," I tell her. "But I have to go. I've got a friend here. I can try talking to Suze Tilman at school if you want. See if she knows anything."

"That's okay. I'll get to her myself. But work with me on this one, Marcus. You could be a real asset. A source on the inside. I'll make sure you get some kind of credit, too. This could be big."

She hangs up, and a few seconds later, Suze's cell phone rings.

"Don't answer that!" I tell her as I run back to the stoop.

Suze looks at the phone number. "I don't recognize it."

"Just ignore it," I say. "Trust me."

"Is it that reporter?"

"Yes. If you don't recognize the number, don't answer the phone. She'll use different numbers."

"What does she want?"

What does any reporter want? To tell a great

story. I can already see the one that Elena's roughing into shape. Suze Tilman, good girl gone bad. Tarkin Shaw, star athlete taken before his time. Alcohol, drugs, sex. The perfect scandal. And that's before you know the true facts of the case.

"Just . . . don't talk to anyone," I tell Suze.

"Trust me. I won't."

FROM THE JONESVILLE *BUGLE*:

All-State Wrestler Found Dead
By Elena DePiero

A varsity high school wrestler was found dead in his Jonesville home early Tuesday morning.

Tarkin Shaw, 17, was discovered by his parents shortly after midnight in their home in Cedar Vale. The cause of death is not known at this time.

Shaw was a senior at Jonesville High.

Jonesville High principal, Francis Everett, has said that grief counselors will be available for students throughout the week.

"We're all heartbroken over this tragic loss," said Everett. "Tarkin Shaw was well-loved in this community, and I know I speak for the entire staff and student body when I say that he will be sorely missed. My thoughts and prayers are with his family now."

Shaw, 6'3" and 221 pounds, was captain of the Jonesville High varsity wrestling team.

He placed first at the Massachusetts All-State Wrestling Championship last year and was considered by many to have a bright future in the sport.

"He was the glue that kept the team together," said wrestling coach Dwayne Lassa. "Everybody looked up to 'the Tarks' and took their cues from him. This is a terrible loss."

Shaw's parents, Darren and Nicole Shaw, could not be reached for comment. The police are asking anyone who may have information about the young man's death to come forward.

WEDNESDAY

NIKKI

On Wednesday morning, Suze picks me up in her silver Prius so we can drive to school together.

"Do you want me to drive?" I ask.

"No," she says, backing out of the driveway. "It's good to have something concrete to focus on."

"You sure you don't want to skip today?"

"I can't be home."

"You haven't told your parents yet?"

She shakes her head. Suze's dad was hospitalized for anxiety last year and I know she feels protective of him.

"Why don't you at least tell your mom?"

I love Suze's mom. She's super smart and totally open-minded.

"She can't keep things from my dad. They're like . . . a hive mind. What good would it do, anyway?"

"Suze," I say. "You don't have to handle *everything* on your own."

Suze nods, but she doesn't say anything. Handling things on her own is sort of her thing. Once, when her parents were teaching at Trinity College in Dublin, she hitchhiked all the way around Ireland with a nineteen-year-old college student she met at a Kings of Leon concert. Her parents didn't even know. They thought she was staying with relatives at a farmhouse in Dingle. She was fifteen.

After driving in silence for a while she pulls into a Cumberland Farms parking lot then slumps over the steering wheel. "I fucked up," she says. "Didn't I?"

"You did what you had to do."

She looks up, desperate. "Do you really think that? I mean, I could have just—"

"No. You did the right thing."

"Would you have done it?"

I want to say yes, and it's not just to comfort her. I'd give anything to be as resourceful as Suze. But the truth is I don't know what I would have done in that room. I also don't know what I would have done if Tarkin had taken nude pictures of me. Would I have gone to the police and risked having them published? Would I have tried to delete them like she did, and risk being caught? It's so easy after the fact—when you have time to think and you already know the consequences—to figure out what the right course of action *would* have been. But in the moment when it's all unfolding in real time and you're too scared even to think straight, almost anything you do is going to be wrong.

"Fuck Tarkin Shaw," I tell her. "He brought this on himself. They were his drugs."

"Yeah, but he's dead, Nikki. He's dead because of me."

"Nobody knows that, though. Nobody even knows you were there."

I can tell that she *wants* to take comfort from this, but it's not easy. She can't undo what happened that night. The best-case scenario is getting away with murder. And that can't sit well. Suze is a kind person, a loving person, a bright, optimistic, adventurous person. I can almost see the cogs turning in her mind as she tries to fit this horrible incident into everything that came before it in her life. She wasn't meant to kill someone, not even accidentally. Not even in self-defense.

WHEN WE PULL into the high school parking lot, Lydia and Ani are waiting outside of Ani's car.

"Shields up," Ani says when we get out of Suze's car.

"Shield's fucking up," Lydia says.

Suze spots Marcus Daubney and DeShawn Hill locking their bikes up across the parking lot.

"I don't trust those guys," Lydia says.

"Yeah, Suze," I say. "I think you should steer clear of them for a while."

"Why?"

"Because they got in a fight with Tarkin the day before he died. Remember?"

"Yeah, and I'm his so-called girlfriend."

"So let's just play it like that. You're his girl-friend. You're in mourning. And they're just two strangers who have nothing to do with you."

When we get to the entrance, I let Lydia and Ani take Suze inside. "Meet at my locker," I tell them. I hold the door for a few sophomores who rush in, then wait while Marcus and DeShawn approach.

"Have the police questioned you?" I ask quietly.

"No," Marcus says. "Have they questioned *you*?"

"Why would they question me?"

Marcus shrugs suggestively, like maybe he knows something.

"Well?" I say, but he says nothing. He's bluffing. He doesn't know shit.

"You guys need to keep your distance from Suze," I tell them.

"Suze?" Marcus says. "Suze who?"

He's such a smart-ass.

"Is that what she wants?" DeShawn asks.

"Actually," Marcus says. "Nikki's right. We should lay low. No need to advertise our association."

"How is she, though?" DeShawn asks. "Is she okay?"

I step inside with them and we hang back while some more stragglers rush in.

"Don't worry about Suze," I tell him. "We've got this now."

INSIDE IT'S NOISY as hell. Yesterday, after the initial shock, everyone was quiet. It was like church. Maybe they were all genuinely traumatized, but I think a lot of them were afraid of saying the wrong thing. There's a right way to mourn, a right way to express shock. Too much and everyone will think you're faking it. Too little and they'll think you're a heartless monster. Now everyone's talking. Theorizing, consoling each other, crying, hugging. They must have all agreed on the right way to mourn.

On the way to my locker, I catch Kesha Belmont telling her dopey friend Tilly about the time she dropped her book in the hallway and Tarkin picked it up for her. "He was *so* sweet," she gushes.

Sweet, my ass. He was probably taking pictures up her skirt.

A few lockers down, Brent Samms is telling his friends about the time in study hall when Tarkin told this "sick joke" about a dead prostitute and nobody laughed. "But then I laughed," he says. "And Tarkin pointed to me like he was so happy that somebody got the joke." All of Brent's friends nod grimly, as if this anecdote represents a deep intellectual connection with Tarkin Shaw.

I guess that's the accepted grief protocol they've all agreed on: memorializing him like he was a saint. It's such bullshit. I want to barge into Principal Everett's office, get on the PA system and announce to the whole school: "Hey assholes, your hero died from his own rape drugs. Memorialize that."

But we're not doing that today. Today we're supporting Suze while she mourns her dead "boyfriend," whom she definitely did not accidentally kill with roofies.

AT MY LOCKER, Suze has her hoodie up and is pulling the ties so tightly her face is nearly swallowed up. Martina Landry, a senior football cheerleader who's actually friends with Tarkin, heads over to us, eyes red, her face the picture of tragedy.

"What does this bitch want?" Lydia says under her breath.

"Hi Suze," Martina says, dripping with compassion. "I just want to say how sorry I am." She reaches out to touch the sleeve of Suze's hoodie and Suze shrinks back, pulling her ties even tighter. I put my arm around Suze while Lydia shoves her way between Martina and us.

"Suze is in shock right now," Lydia says. "She can't talk to anyone."

"No, I get it," Martina says. "I *totally* get it. We're all in shock. Tarkin was . . . he was just so amazing." She starts sobbing over the last syllable, and her friends crowd around her and walk her away.

"He was just so *amazing*," Lydia mocks.

"Shock?" Ani says.

"I was improvising."

"No, shock is good," I say. "That'll keep people away. Suze, you're in shock."

"Got it," she says.

I think she actually still is.

As for me, I still can't believe he's dead. And I still don't know what to feel about it.

I WALK SUZE to most of her classes that day, keeping all of the would-be condolence-offering posers at bay with the force of my cold stare. I have perfected that. It's one of my core competencies. I am a one-woman Shield, an impenetrable fortress of ice-cold bitch, and it feels good. It's what Ani and Lydia did for me freshman year, when the wrestlers teased me relentlessly and I could barely face coming to school. They put themselves between me and the world. Now I get to do that for Suze.

Between third and fourth period, while I'm walking Suze to chem lab, Marcus Daubney walks toward us and flicks his head to the side like he wants me to join him.

"It's okay," Suze says. "Go talk to him. Find out what he wants."

She slips inside chem lab and Marcus catches up with me.

"Just keep walking," he says under his breath.

"Dude, it's okay if *we* talk."

"I know that."

"But keep a leash on your friend. Tell him to stop making googoo eyes at Suze. What's wrong with him, anyway?"

"Nothing's wrong with him. He's a caring person."

"If you say so. Did you need something?"

"Yes. I need you to get the word to Suze that the lab reports came back. The police know about the Rohypnol. He died of respiratory depression. She gave him too much."

"Where'd you hear this?"

"I have sources."

"What sources?"

We've arrived at my calculus classroom, so I stop and lower my voice. "Dude, what sources?"

"I'm not at liberty to divulge that."

"Are you talking about the police? Do you have a source at the police station?"

Marcus looks around to make sure no one's listening. "I'm a reporter, Nikki. I have sources everywhere."

The late bell rings, and he rushes off down the hallway, leaving me to wonder if he's completely full of shit, or only partially full of shit.

MARCUS

After fourth period, I'm heading to study hall in the cafeteria. I check my phone just as Elena calls to ask if I've turned up any leads at school.

"Lots of tears," I tell her. "But no hard intel. I guess he roofied himself to death, right?"

"Unlikely."

"Why? What have you heard?"

Elena's the one with the source at the police precinct. Not me. The last time I called the precinct in search of a quote about some vandalism at the community pool, the cop who answered the phone laughed out loud, then hung up on me. They don't do that to Elena. Luckily, she's been generously sharing what she learns, in the hope that I can enhance her intel with the intel I'm picking up at school. So far, it's a pretty one-way relationship, since no one at Jonesville High knows anything.

I head into the cafeteria and sit by myself at a table near the window, far away from anyone else.

"That kid's phone is missing," she tells me. "And

his computer's hard drive was removed. You hear anything about that?"

So, the police know about the stolen goods— some of them, anyway. They probably haven't bothered to check the printer. Still, this is a big chunk of bad news. Inevitable, probably—when you leave a dead body behind, people tend to go looking for clues—but I was hoping the base-level incompetence of the Jonesville police force would work to our advantage.

"Nope," I lie. "Haven't heard anything about that. What are they thinking? Robbery gone awry?"

Elena laughs. "Yeah, right. No way this was a robbery. Nothing else was missing."

"So what *are* the police thinking?"

"Thinking is not the Jonesville police force's strong suit, Marcus. I'm wondering if he dumped those things himself. Maybe he had something to hide. You hear anything about that? Any rumors of a secret life? You know these jock types. Super hetero. Maybe something along those lines?"

A pair of freshman girls eyeball me as they walk past toward an empty table, sucking green smoothies through a straw.

I lower my voice. "What? Like he was secretly gay and had gay porn on his computer that he wanted to hide? Sure. It's definitely possible." I like this angle. It ticks off several boxes, the most important being that it implicates no one in Shaw's death but Shaw himself. "I mean, if he *was* gay," I add, just to milk the angle. "He definitely wasn't open about it. And the suicide rate for gay teens is pretty high, right?"

"Suicides usually leave clues, though," she says. "His parents told the police this was totally out of the blue."

"Yeah, but kids don't tell their parents everything."

"Which is why I need you. Somebody knows something. His friends, his teammates, his girlfriend. Get me *something*."

"I'm trying."

"Well, stop trying. Get it."

She hangs up without saying goodbye.

The thing is, I *could* get it for her. I could get everything for her. That's the rank, unholy irony of the situation. My byline could sit atop a shocking (and gorgeously written, it goes without saying) tale of drugs, theft, and sexual violence, a searing portrait of a sexual predator that everyone would be talking about. It's already half-written in my head. Maybe it seems petty or vain to be focusing on my dashed journalistic ambitions right now, given the much larger catastrophe of my legal situation (not to mention the tragedy of a young man's death), but stories like this don't land in your lap every day. Also, just because I'm not writing it, that doesn't mean Elena won't figure it all out and write it herself.

LUNCH PERIOD.

DeShawn slides into the bench opposite me and says, "What now?"

"Huh?"

"You're upset."

I've been sulking ever since my phone call with Elena.

"The cops know about the stuff we took."

DeShawn panics, turns gray.

"Well, they know it's missing," I finesse. "They don't know who took it. Or why."

DeShawn takes a moment to process the information, scour it, sort it, figure out just how bad it is.

"So it could be a robber?" he says hopefully.

"Yeah, sure. A robber came in, roofied Shaw, then took his phone and hard drive, but nothing else? It's pretty niche, robbery-wise."

Now it's DeShawn's turn to sulk.

We should have known better. *I* should have known better. Maybe it's not our fault that Shaw is dead. After all, we had no idea Suze was going to dabble in pharmaceuticals. But we did go in there with a desperate girl, and desperate people do desperate things. Not to mention, we left her alone in a room with a known predator. What were we thinking? Of all our crackpot collaborations, this was the most reckless. Nothing else even comes close. Prior to this, the dumbest thing we ever did was an all-night stakeout of our eighth-grade shop teacher, Mr. Lawrence. I'd heard a rumor that he was dealing meth. We found no evidence of meth dealing, just a fondness for microwave nachos and *RuPaul's Drag Race*. So yeah, that was dumb. But at least nobody *died*.

"Okay forget about robbery," DeShawn says. "What if he destroyed the stuff himself?"

"Then committed suicide?"

DeShawn nods hungrily.

"Because he was gay?" I say. "And didn't want anyone to know?"

"Yeah. That."

"Elena says his parents are convinced he would never kill himself."

And this is the other area of concern. According to Elena, the Shaws wield a lot of influence over the local police, possibly through their friendship with Timothy Cochrane. I doubt they'll let the police drop this without a thorough investigation.

"All they need to do," I remind him, "is test that beer bottle for fingerprints."

"Yeah, but are Suze's fingerprints even in the system? She's never committed a crime."

"Before now."

"I don't consider what she did a crime."

"Right, DeShawn. Justifiable roofying. Because that's a thing."

"It should be."

"Okay, fine. But we have to deal with the world as it is, not as it should be."

"You know that I will never accept that philosophy. And look, even if they do find her fingerprints, all that means is that she touched his beer bottle. Maybe she had a sip. It doesn't mean she gave him the drugs."

"But she *did* give him the drugs."

"But they don't know that. They don't even know she was there."

"They texted each other. He invited her over. Remember?"

"But his phone is gone."

"Which also looks suspicious."

"What about motive? What's her motive?"

"Hmmm, let me think. The *pictures*."

"What pictures?" he says. "They're gone."

"So I guess it's all just fine and dandy. We're totally in the clear." I'm being sarcastic, of course, but DeShawn isn't even paying attention to me anymore. He's looking past me, his face clouding as he spies Lydia and Ani at their usual table.

"How come Suze and Nikki aren't there?" he asks.

"Maybe they're avoiding crowds," I say. "Suze looked pretty sheepish this morning. I don't think she's holding up so well."

"I wish I could talk to her."

"You can't. We're keeping our distance, remember?"

"I guess."

"We don't know Suze Tilman. She's not our

186

friend. You don't have a massive crush on her. And we've certainly never participated in a burglary, homicide, and cover-up with her."

"All right, I get it."

"Appearances matter, DeShawn. It's all we have going for us right now—the fact that nothing ties us to Suze or Tarkin."

Just then, Nikki shows up alone. She looks troubled, her sharp features contracted into a tight scowl. When she sits down, Lydia and Ani huddle close to hear what she has to say.

"Something's wrong," DeShawn says.

I tell him to relax, but it's no use. DeShawn's intuition is firing like a bug zapper on a hot July night. Just moments after he says, "Something's happening. I can feel it," the cafeteria begins to buzz. At first, I can't decipher the source. No one's fighting or shouting. No one's crying, and there have been isolated outbursts of crying ever since the news of Tarkin's death broke. But now, everyone's quietly talking and texting. This isn't unusual in and of itself, but the synchronized nature of it is. It's as if everyone has simultaneously received the same alert. When the volume of chatter rises so suddenly it catches the attention of the teachers on lunch duty, I know DeShawn is right. Some new mutation of Jonesville High bullshit is in the throes of birth. The words "Suze Tilman" drift across the cafeteria, followed a few seconds later by "sex.com."

That's when I know. Not in my brain. My brain

is still parsing the data, trying to arrange it into a sensible narrative. But in my gut, I know. Even before I touch my phone.

"What?" DeShawn asks, sensing I'm a few steps ahead of him.

"Oh my God," someone says. "It's under her *name*."

I whip out my phone and head straight to sex. com. I type "Suze Tilman" in the search bar.

And there she is.

"What?" DeShawn pleads. "It's not—please tell me it's not—"

I don't answer. My eyes are glued to my phone.

"Stop looking," he says.

But I can't stop looking, and it's not for any prurient reasons. There's no thrill in seeing Suze naked like this. Not when you know how these pictures came to be. They're an abomination, a sick violation. It's the reporter in me. I need to see, to witness, to *know*.

"I said stop looking!" DeShawn shouts as he knocks the phone out of my hand. It clatters to the floor and slides under the next table to a chorus of "ooohs" and "aaaahs."

"DeShawn," I whisper. With a simple shake of the head, I try to broadcast: *We have no dog in this fight, remember? We don't know Suze Tilman.*

It's a lot to ask of a headshake, and it doesn't seem to register with DeShawn. While I slip under the table to retrieve my phone, he stands up and scans the cafeteria, staring in open-mouthed horror at all the kids scrolling through these images. "The fuck you all looking at?" he shouts.

A bunch of kids look up at him, then return immediately to their phones. Between the spectacle of DeShawn shouting and the pageant of nude pics scrolling down their phones, there's no contest. The naked girl wins.

I walk back to him and put my hand on his shoulder. "Buddy," I whisper. "You really need to calm down."

His breath comes in short, rough bursts through his nose. His hands clench into fists. He may be trying to calm himself down, but it's not working. If anything, he's amping himself up. He moves away from our table and I assume he's planning to walk this off, but two tables over, his arm shoots out and slaps the phone out of a freshman girl's hand. The girl squeals in fright, then clambers after her phone. I speedwalk after him, trying not to look panicked, but he outpaces me easily, grabbing at another phone. "Are you proud of yourselves?" he barks. "You think she wants to be seen like this?"

"Um, yeah!" some guy yells back. I can't see who it is, but he gets a round of applause.

With every passing second, more people look up from their phones, spot DeShawn patrolling the cafeteria like a vulture, then look at their phones again and connect the two. Russ Minichek, one of the varsity wrestlers, gives me a dirty look as I rush after DeShawn. I shrug helplessly. *Yep, that's my pal DeShawn. What a goofy guy. No idea what this is all about.*

Then DeShawn spots Minichek. "Were you there?" he says, pointing directly at him.

Minichek stares back, icily. I put myself between the two of them in attempt to be a buffer, a skinny, ineffectual buffer.

"Were you?" DeShawn asks around me. "Could you have stopped it?"

"The fuck's it got to do with you?" Minichek says.

"Okay, okay, guys," I say, putting my hands out like a referee in a boxing match.

"Sit down," one of the other wrestlers says to me while the others laugh glibly.

Meanwhile DeShawn stalks past me so quickly I can't grab him. While I trail after him like an impotent puppy, Minichek pulls his great bulk out of the bench and readies himself. The other wrestlers follow suit, forming a tight scrum behind Minichek, who I guess is their new leader.

"DeShawn, come on," I say through clenched teeth. "It's two against nine here. What are you planning to do? Take on the entire wrestling team?"

"Try it," the other wrestler says. I think his name is Aaron Paulson.

"Were any of you there?" DeShawn demands. "Did you know what was happening?"

"Buddy, this is pointless," I whisper. "It's too late. There's nothing we can do."

"But you could have," DeShawn says, pointing to Minichek. "Couldn't you?"

Just then there's a commotion over by the windows and some girl's voice rings out, "Oh my God, the police are here!"

Over everyone's heads I can just make out a police cruiser parked outside. As I'll find out later, they're only here to speak with Principal Everett, probably to find out if Shaw was exhibiting any suicidal tendencies at school. But since they're on the premises anyway, Everett decides to press them into service for this other situation. They come in with Everett in a tight huddle at the other end of the cafeteria. Two of the teachers on lunch duty head over to fill them in on what's happening while I try to nudge DeShawn away from the wrestlers and back to our nice, anonymous table where people can go back to ignoring us.

"The cops are here," I whisper.

"Good," he says, standing firm. "Tell them to ask these douchebags what they did."

Minichek takes a step forward. "You better watch your mouth."

"Or what?" DeShawn says, taking an equal step forward.

A crowd has formed around us and through them I spot Everett pointing in our direction while speaking to Officer Scaletti, a jowly Italian-American man I remember from a stranger danger assembly in middle school. His partner, a scarecrowish woman with a long blond ponytail under her police hat, confers with Mr. Barber, a history teacher.

"Buddy," I whisper. But I don't even get the next part out because the next thing I know, DeShawn's in handcuffs. He's so laser-focused on Russ Minichek, trying to burn a confession out of him with the power of his stare, Officer Scaletti walks straight up to him and cuffs him. No jiu jitsu magic this time. DeShawn is stunned. But only for a second. Then he realizes what's happening and, with an eerie calm, says to me: "Call my mom."

"Why are you arresting *him*?" I say. But Scaletti and his partner don't answer. They just take DeShawn out of there.

He doesn't resist. He knows better than that. His parents had The Talk with him a long time ago.

I look to Principal Everett for an explanation but he shakes his head like this is all *my* fault, then heads toward the exit himself.

"Excuse me," I say running up to him.

He stops and faces me. "I think that's enough out of you today, Marcus."

"What the hell did *I* do?"

"The two of you need to change your attitude and get your anger in check. I will *not* have violence in this school."

As he heads to the exit, I watch helplessly through the cafeteria windows as DeShawn is deposited in the back of the police car. My mind reels back to a school safety assembly we had in June of last year.

"Hey Everett!" I shout.

He turns back with a warning look.

"I thought we weren't supposed to be bystanders," I say. "I thought you wanted us all to be upstanders. Remember that? Look out for each other? Have the courage to stand up?"

This gets a predictable round of guffaws and titters from my fellow classmates, who remember that assembly with the same lack of reverence as me. Everett looks flummoxed for a second then he raises a single finger and says, "That was your last warning."

As he walks out of there, I shout after him: "When was DeShawn's last warning?"

But he doesn't answer and he doesn't turn around.

NIKKI

I don't know what DeShawn Hill was thinking, freaking out like that in the cafeteria. It's bad enough Suze has these pictures to contend with. Now she's got some karate-chopping supernerd smacking people's phones out of their hands? Seriously? These boys need to step off and let the Shield take over. Which is exactly what we have planned. After school, Ani and Lydia come to my place so that Ani can use her mad hacker skills to try to figure out who posted those pictures. We know it wasn't Tarkin, because he's dead.

Suze has gone home to break the news to her parents. She's kept them in the dark so far, but now that the pictures are online—and searchable under her own name!—she has no choice but to tell them. Her plan is to tell them that Tarkin drugged and photographed her, but nothing else. She's not going to tell them about going to Tarkin's house and roofying him to death. *That* is a secret we all plan to take to the grave. The pictures are bad enough. I can't imagine my parents seeing something like that. It would be the end of them. But at least her parents won't blame her for it the way my parents probably would. I remember my dad getting on my case in fifth grade when I complained about a boy in school who grabbed my ass. He was all, *Why are you wearing such tight jeans if you don't want your ass grabbed? That's on you, Nikki.* And I was like, *Actually, my jeans are so tight because in case you didn't notice, I gained ten pounds this year because . . . um, puberty?* My dad and I didn't speak for about a month after that. I felt like trash, and he felt like his cute little girl was growing up too fast.

The thing is, I *wasn't* growing up too fast. I was still a little girl in my head. I didn't want boys grabbing at me. That was the farthest thing from my mind. All I wanted was to play softball and hang out with my friends. It's just that my *body* was growing up. I had hips and breasts and boys thought that made me fair game. Like all of this extra meat on my bones was created for their personal entertainment. *Ooh, a butt, let's grab it. A bra strap, let's snap it.* But they were fifth graders. You can't expect much from them. I did expect more from my dad. I wanted him to have my back on this, to tell me that it wasn't my fault. I wanted him to acknowledge that it was the boys being horrible, not me. But he's old-school. In his mind, the boys weren't being horrible, they were just being boys. And my mom agreed with him, which kind of broke my heart. She told me it was my responsibility to watch myself and make sure the boys had nothing to grab. How do you even do that?

Suze's parents are completely different. I remember this long conversation I had with Suze's mom one day in their kitchen over graham crackers and lemonade. Suze's mom was raised Catholic like me, but now she's an atheist. She said the most important thing a girl has to do—especially a Catholic girl—is to "erase the shame." She said our society is patriarchal and that what it wants more than anything is to make women and girls hate themselves. And one another. So we shouldn't do it, because then we're just playing their game. She also said that biology makes us sexually mature in our early teens, so why pretend that it doesn't? That's what they use the shame for, "to put us at war with our bodies." Needless to say, I didn't relay this conversation to my own parents. They already think Suze is "a bit of a strange one." If they knew that her mom was basically endorsing premarital sex, they'd probably forbid me from seeing her.

Ani sits cross-legged on my bed with her laptop on my pillow and headphones on. She's been coding since she was seven. She has all these crazy smart ideas about math and data and stuff. I always do my best to pay attention when she goes on about it, but honestly, I don't know what she's saying half the time. While Ani dives into a trance to do her thing, Lydia stands at my window, huffing and fuming about how medieval she wants to get on whoever posted these pictures.

"Ani's going to worm straight up into this punk's business and dox him, right?"

"No," I remind her. "The last thing Suze needs is more attention right now. We're just going to find the little d-bag and get him to take the pictures down."

"What if it's a girl?"

"Oh, you know what, Lydia? If it's a girl, then gloves off. You do your thing."

Lydia smiles deviously and punches her fist against her palm. "There's a special place in hell for women who don't support women."

"Taylor Swift?"

"Katie Couric."

"Actually, it's Madeleine Albright," Ani says, without looking up from her laptop. "And it's for women who don't *help* other women."

Live and learn.

A minute later, Ani whips off her earbuds and smiles at her laptop like it just handed her a free Cinnabon. Lydia and I join her on the bed. On the screen is one of those swirl drawings people use for avatars when they're too lazy to upload a photo.

"Asshammer15?" Lydia says. "Who's that supposed to be?"

"He's the one who posted the pictures."

"Did you get a real name?" I ask.

"Of course. But don't you want to know how I found out first? It's totally genius. He goes by asshammer, dickmonster, and dinoweenie. Same guy. Thinks he's so clever, hiding behind all these handles. Real nasty too, big on fat-shaming, loves to tell girls they're ugly. But I nailed him. Traced the little troll through a dozen sites all the way back to his Facebook page. Idiot."

Ani gets colorful when she talks about hacking. She thinks the Internet is practically alive, has some weird theories about how everything in the universe is made up of data—but supposedly in a beautiful way that isn't as depressing as that sounds.

"So . . . do we have a name?"

"Oh, I have it all. Name, address, phone number, current whereabouts. He's on sex.com right now, commenting on the pictures. I can dox that little fuck lickety-split. Want to see?"

"No," I tell her. "No doxing. We don't want to start a war. Trolls always win those things."

Ani sulks. She's in Lydia's camp. She's probably thinking, *What's the point of having all these mad hacker skills if you can't use them to fight evil?* But, unlike Lydia, Ani can be reasonable.

"Meet asshammer15," she says. "Aka dickmonster, aka dinoweenie." A few taps and she brings up the dude's Facebook page.

It's Sean Princely, a sophomore, a short, red-haired, squirrelly-looking kid, who also happens to be a junior varsity wrestler.

"Oh, I am going to dropkick that little Ewok," Lydia says.

"You're not doing anything," I tell her.

"There's more," Ani says. "The pictures aren't only up on sex.com. They've actually been on Porn-Hole since Monday."

"PornHole?" I say. "Wait a minute. Tarkin was still alive on Monday."

"I know," Ani said. "I don't think it was Tarkin who posted them though. It was this guy." On the screen now is a picture of Pepe the Frog with the name Cocktosen.

"Who's John Cocktosen?"

"It's an '80s movie reference," she says. "I'm pretty sure it's Mason Shaw."

"Tarkin's little *brother*?"

"I swear to God, Nikki!" Lydia says, blaming *me* for the fact that she can't just straight-up murder somebody over this.

"Wait," I say. "So Tarkin shared the photos with him?"

"Gross," Lydia says.

"Either that or Mason found them," Ani says. "You know how little brothers are. Mine is always trying to hack my passwords. Either way, Mason put them on PornHole and that's probably where Princely saw them. Princely's a regular there. Comments all the time. Really gross stuff, too."

"But if they're already on PornHole," I say, the words themselves tasting like poison in my mouth, "why did he go to the trouble of posting them on sex.com?"

"They weren't tagged on PornHole," Ani says. "And sex.com has a better search function. You can type Suze's name and the pictures come right up."

"Yeah," I say, stammering a bit. "But *why*?"

Ani shrugs and looks at me like *I'm a hacker, not a shrink.*

Lydia gnaws on her thumbnail, trying to resist the urge to hit something. "Ten bucks says they did it for the lols."

Maybe she's right. There's no need to search for fancy motivations here. To some guys, there's nothing funnier than a humiliated girl. Especially a humiliated naked girl. And Suze is an amazing trophy for these little monsters, given that she's hands-down the coolest girl in school. It must make them feel like big men to be able to take her down like this.

"I haven't even gotten to Reddit yet," Ani says. She puts her headphones on and goes back under.

Lydia and I stand back and watch as her fingers fly across the keyboard. Neither of us can tell what she's doing as she jumps from site to site. A few minutes into it, she whips off her earbuds and stares in horror.

"What the hell?" Lydia says.

On the screen are over a dozen photos of naked girls, all from Jonesville High. There's Julie Baslitz, making duck lips and squeezing her tits together. Alicia Ramirez looking over her shoulder while sticking her butt out.

"These are from PornHole," Ani says. "I searched everything uploaded by John Cocktosen, aka Mason Shaw."

"But those are clearly selfies," I say. "Are you telling me Alica Ramirez is sending nude selfies to Mason Shaw? She's a senior. He's a freshman. And that one's Izzy Rigoletto. She graduated last year. Mason was in middle school."

"I'm just showing you what I found," she says.

She scrolls down to some more pictures of Jonesville High girls. Danielle Jameson, Belinda Christaldi, Morgan Tremaine. Only these ones look different. In fact, they look more like the pictures of Suze. Their eyes are closed or half-open. They look sleepy or shy.

Or drugged.

"Jesus," Lydia says.

I feel the skin on my arm prickling.

Then Ani brings up six more photos and we all gasp.

"What the hell?" Lydia says.

The photos are of Amber Laynes. She's lying naked on a green blanket with her eyes half-closed.

"Where is that?" Lydia asks.

"I don't know," Ani says.

The pictures are close on her body. The only other thing you can see is that green blanket and the bottom of a black plastic water bottle near her head.

Both of her hands are in frame in some of them, so she definitely didn't take the pictures herself.

It's hard to tell whether she posed for them or not, though. They're a lot like the photos of Suze. When you know what really happened, it's easy to see that she was drugged. But if you don't know the story, you could just as easily assume she was posing. A little drunk, maybe—that would explain the droopy eyes—but aware, and consenting. They tell a certain story about Amber Laynes, and it's the same story the pictures of Suze tell.

Here I am. Look all you want.

SUZE

When I was fourteen, I took a train from Madrid to Barcelona by myself. My parents didn't know. They were teaching at the University of Madrid and they thought I was at my friend's house in Segovia. That's what I told them. It was my first time sneaking out on my own. To be honest, I was a little bit scared. I remember hiding under the brim of this big sunhat I'd borrowed from my mother. I put these huge cheap sunglasses on and just watched people and listened to them speaking to each other on the train. I practiced understanding Spanish at full speed. I didn't speak to anyone though. The sunglasses made me feel invisible and I liked that. When I got to Barcelona I wore them everywhere. They felt like armor, like a shield. Nobody could tell how nervous I was, or that I was basically a kid who should have been home with her parents. Even the other travelers at the youth hostel treated me like I was one of them, a university student. A few of them invited me to a party on the beach with some local students and I went along. I was pretty nervous about it, especially since they kept speaking to each other in Catalan, which I didn't speak. The party was at this seaside paella restaurant and everyone there was older than me. They drank wine and smoked cigarettes. They spoke Catalan and occasionally translated something into Spanish for my benefit. My Spanish wasn't very good at that point so I mostly smiled and nodded. I'm pretty sure they thought I was stupid or boring. After a while, I wandered over to a table under a big umbrella and just watched and listened from a slight distance. Nobody bothered me. I'm not sure they even knew I was there any more. I liked that feeling. It made me feel free. Like the world was this great big show I could either experience up close like they were all doing, or watch from a slight distance like I was doing. Either way, it was up to me. And that weekend I liked being invisible.

I've lived in six different countries. I've enrolled in ten different schools. And one thing I can tell you is that when you're the new girl, you're never invisible. People notice the new girl and they always have the same questions. *Who are you? Where do you come from? Why do you talk like that? Why do you dress like that?* I've never fit in anywhere, but ever since that weekend in Barcelona, I haven't cared about it, either. You don't have to fit in to feel okay. If you want, you can just opt out of the whole game. Which is what I choose to do no matter where I am. I don't go chasing popularity. I don't even need to be liked. If you think I'm weird or stuck up or that I'm faking my English accent (though, seriously, the arrogance of believing a person would fake an accent just to impress you), go ahead. It doesn't matter. As long as I have a few close friends, like Nikki, Ani, and Lydia, that's all I need.

But there is something different about Jonesville. And I don't just mean Tarkin Shaw. He's a monster. A peculiarly American sort of monster—sorry, USA, but it's true. I've hung out with guys all over the world and I'm not saying they're all princes, but I've never met anyone as toxic as the average Jonesville "dude." But it's not just Tarkin and his posse of douchebags that makes Jonesville so unique. It's everybody else. Kids who don't even know me, kids who've never even spoken to me feel like they own a piece of me now. It started even before the pictures came out. When I showed up on Monday as Tarkin's "girlfriend," that's when it started. When they could sink their teeth into the story about how I "threw myself" at him at Tara Budzynski's party, their whole concept of who I was changed. I made sense now. I wasn't the weirdo foreigner who hung out with the mean girls. I was Tarkin's latest conquest, his property. And I could have lived with that. It was just an act and I didn't think it would go on for that long. But this new version of me, the nude exhibitionist with her head thrown back, is something I can't live with. Because I could never be that girl. And because of the pictures, I always will be.

My parents are doing their best to be supportive. But they don't even know the whole story. They don't know about what I did to Tarkin in that trophy room, or what I let him do to me. I think my father would freak out. He's only just keeping a lid on his anxiety as it is. My parents only know about the pictures. My mother keeps telling me that they shouldn't matter at all. "It's the human body," she says breezily. "Everybody has one."

And I get what she's saying. I honestly do. But there's a reason we don't all walk around naked. There's a reason we put curtains on our windows and take showers in private. It's the same reason I let Tarkin parade me around school as his fake "girlfriend" in the first place. Because I don't want everybody to see me naked. That's a privilege I've only conferred on three boys: Hans, Piotr, and Andy from London. *I* let them. *I* wanted it. It was *my* choice.

And no, Mom, it isn't just "the human body." It's *my* human body. Tarkin took that from me, and I want it back. I want to own myself again. I want to be the one to decide who gets to see me. I want my armor, my shield. I want to be free.

But most of all, I want to be invisible.

DESHAWN

"Do you know what it's like to get a phone call like that?"

My mother has already asked me this ten times. We're at the dining table, where we've been sitting for sixteen minutes. Five Chinese food containers sit in front of us, but my little sister, Kiara, is the only one eating. She slurps up lo mein noodles while my mom fumes and my dad tries to calm her down.

"Desi," he says, in his calmest voice.

"No, Barry, I want to know if our son knows what it feels like to get that phone call."

Of course I don't know what it's like to get that call. I'm not my own mother. But yes, I'm sure it must have been eight different kinds of shitty to get a phone call at work from the Jonesville police saying *Your son's been arrested.* I'm not stupid. But she's been asking me this question ever since she picked me up at the police station. She asked me on the way home. She asked me at Kowloon's, where we stopped to pick up dinner. And she's asked me three times since we sat down to *not* eat. I don't know how to answer her, other than saying *I'm sorry*, which I've already done ten times.

"Principal Everett says this is strike two," she says. "What is going on with you?"

"We just want to know why you did it," my dad says.

"I told you already."

My dad crinkles up his face in confusion. "Because they had no right?"

"Yeah. They had no right to look at those pictures."

"But what's it got to do with you?" My mother now. She's angry and afraid, and angry that I've made her afraid. My mom likes to be in control. She's the calm, grounded one, the one who makes sure I have my gym uniform on gym days, the one who counts the number of broccoli spears my sister and I eat so we get enough folates. Whatever it is, my mom is on it.

"And this is the girl who came to visit you the other night?" she says.

"Yeah."

"So she's a friend of yours."

"Not really."

"Then I'll ask the question again, DeShawn. What's. It. Got. To. Do. With. You?"

There's no way to answer this question honestly. I can't tell her it's got to do with me because I'm the one who broke into Shaw's house to steal those pictures. All for nothing, as it turns out. I can't tell my mom anything. And I know how it looks. Believe me. I know it wasn't the smartest thing to go swiping at all those cell phones in the cafeteria like that. I know I made a fool of myself, trying to stink-eye a confession out of Russ Minichek and his friends. I didn't do it because it was smart. I did it because instinct took over. I never said I was perfect.

"Look," my dad says. "Who is this girl? I've never heard you mention her before. Now all of a sudden you're picking fights over her?"

My little sister takes a break from her pork lo mein to gawp at me. Kiara's ten and just this side of boy-crazy. She has a new crush every week and a notebook where she keeps track of them. She's never heard me talk about a girl before, so she's as curious as my parents about this new development.

"I told you, I don't really know her that well. I just didn't think anyone had the right to look at those pictures."

My mom brings her palms down hard on the table. "This isn't making any sense, DeShawn. The girl puts a bunch of naked pictures up on the Internet and—"

My dad puts his hand out to stop her. They both look at Kiara. My sister doesn't know the full story yet, but she's picked up on some of it. She's well aware that this conversation is quickly becoming "inappropriate" for her.

"Kiara, honey," my mom says. "Why don't you take your plate into the kitchen?"

"Do I have to?"

"Move it."

With a big, ten-year-old huff, she picks up her plate and heads out of the dining room, closing the door behind her. It won't make any difference. She'll still be able to hear everything we say. I guess it allows my parents to tick off some kind of box, though.

"And no screens!" my mother shouts to her. Then, more quietly to my dad, "I don't want her seeing any of this stuff online."

"Agreed."

"She didn't put those pictures online herself," I tell them. "Someone else did."

"How do you know that?" my mom asks.

"I just do. Okay?" I push my chair back.

"Where do you think you're going? We're not through here."

I was hoping to go downstairs to the hole, because this conversation is going nowhere. But I know better than to defy my mother right now. She's got a lot of anger built up over this and she has to spend every last cent of it before I'm free to go.

"Now," she says. "How do you know she didn't put those pictures up there herself?"

"Have you seen them?" I ask.

She and my dad share an awkward look, which means they've definitely seen the pictures.

"Does it look like she took those herself?" I ask.

"Well, I am not an expert in that type of photography, DeShawn."

"She was drugged. I have it on good authority."

"What authority?"

"Does it matter?"

"Are we talking about Marcus?" my mother asks. "Mr. Woodward and Bernstein himself? Is he your authority?" I guess my expression gives it away, because she says, "Of course it's Marcus. I might have known he'd be involved with this."

"Nobody's *involved* with anything. I was just standing up for a girl, all right?"

"A white girl."

"What difference does it make that she's white?"

"The difference it makes is that a white girl can fight her own battles. You are a Black boy, DeShawn. You are a Black boy who now has a disciplinary record. First that fight with Tarkin Shaw"—she whispers—"who's *dead* now. And now this. What's going on with you?"

"I told you that wasn't a fight. I was defending Marcus."

"Marcus again."

"Yeah. I was standing up for him."

"Well, aren't you just a hero."

"I never said that."

"Good, because I don't think MIT is going to see it that way either. Do you think they're going to reward you for this type of behavior? Do you think the dean of admissions is scratching his head right now, going *Hmmm, let's see now, I think what MIT really needs is to get some violent Black kids up in here.* Is that what you think, DeShawn?"

Of course I don't think that. I don't even disagree with her. I know the world is unfair. I know I have to walk the line twice as straight as any white kid just to be treated equally. I can't defend my actions to *her*. I know how she thinks. She's *my* mother, not Suze's. Her only concern is making sure Kiara and I get what we deserve in life. Other people's kids are other people's concerns.

But my dad is different. He's soft where she's hard. He's generous where she's ruthless. So I look at him when I say, "I didn't think it was right that they were all looking at her like that. Without her permission."

In my peripheral vision, I can see my mom shaking her head, like this is the dumbest thing she's heard in a day full of dumb shit. But I know my dad understands. He's the one who told me, "Sometimes you've got to stand up for the little guy when he can't stand up for himself." Well, that's what Suze is right now. She's the little guy.

"Do you realize what could have happened?" my mother says. "Do you realize the phone call I *could* have gotten instead of the one I did get?"

Yeah, I know. I saw those guns in their holsters. I know how the whole thing could have gone down. I know and I'm sorry and no matter how many times I say it, it's not going to make any difference. But

I say it anyway. I promise her that I'll never knock anyone's phone out of their hand again. I'll never defend Marcus when someone attacks him. I'll never stand up to protect a girl who's been violated. I've learned my lesson. I'm going to take care of myself from now on and let other people take care of their own stuff. I don't think my mom believes me, but after a while she runs out of steam. When my dad starts serving himself some chicken chow mein, I know this part of the disciplinary action is over.

When we've finished eating, I clear the dishes and put stuff away with my sister. Then I head to the basement door.

"DeShawn," my mom says.

I brace for another lecture. I have no doubt she'll find something else I did wrong today.

But she doesn't say anything. She just looks at me like she's about to cry. Then she mouths the words *I love you.*

I know she does. And I *am* sorry for the pain I caused her. I know how lucky I am to have a mom like her. She's the mom you'd ask for if you had that power. A little bit pushy, but not too much. She's the one who sent me to science camp when I was nine. I didn't want to go because I was too shy and terrified about meeting new kids. But she made me, and I wound up loving it. She's the one who got me a tutor in math when I came home with a B instead of an A. She's the reason I want to go to MIT and the reason I believe I can. The last thing I want to do is cause her pain. I make a heart with my hands at my chest then point to her. She pretends to catch it in her fist and presses it to her own chest. It's a thing we used to do when I was little, back when she'd drop me off at school.

WHEN I GET downstairs, my head's still spinning. My heart is full of so many emotions I don't know what to do with them. Was it reckless to expose myself like that? Should I have stood by and done nothing while people ridiculed Suze and leered at those pictures? Doing nothing seemed wrong. But doing something didn't exactly make things better. I can't figure it out. And the only thing that feels right is sitting in my favorite chair and working on one of my projects. Things are understandable in the hole. There are problems to solve, gears that stick, and all I have to do is pick up my tools and get to it.

I pick up the pewter fire truck for my Etsy client in San Diego. It's based on a photograph she sent me, and I can't get it exactly right. Every time I shape the ladder, it comes out wrong. In the photograph, the fire truck is on a 3/4 angle, and I have to imagine what it would look like in 3-D, which is always the challenge with projects like this.

I know I can figure this out, but I'm having trouble focusing. I put on Earl Sweatshirt, but I can't get into the zone. The zone is where I do my best work.

It's where I feel most like a machine, like I'm one with the motion of my tools. But I can't get there now, because my mind keeps drifting away—to my mother and the fight we just had, to the scene in the cafeteria, which still feels unreal, to the cops stuffing me into the back of their patrol car. To Suze. Where is she right now? What is she feeling? I put the fire truck down and start working on Terence and his damaged arm. This I know I can fix.

After a while, the drone of Earl Sweatshirt's voice captures me and I get into the zone. I start feeling at one with the soldering iron and the motion of Terence's gears. I don't know how long I'm in the zone, because time basically disappears when I'm there. I only know I've been in it because something pulls me out. In this case, it's a knock on the basement window. But there's no text from Marcus, which means someone else is out there. Worst case: Tarkin Shaw's wrestler buddies. Those guys definitely have it in for me. One-on-one, I could take them, no problem. But all at once? No way.

The curtains are open a crack. I can see something white and fluttery on the other side. I press myself against the wall and peek between the edge of the curtain and the window frame, but I can't see who it is, just that fluttery thing, like a giant moth. Then I see the feet. Black Chuck Taylors. When I whip the curtains open, she crouches down to see me. "Can I come in?" she mouths. I shake my head and motion for her to meet me around the back.

She gives me the thumbs-up then takes off across the front lawn, her gauzy top ruffling out from the bottom of her hoodie.

It's 10:17 at night. My parents and sister will be asleep by now, so I don't have to worry about them. I slip through the basement door and find Suze waiting for me, as out of place as she was the first time she came to see me.

"I heard about what happened at school," she says. "Are you okay?"

I nod.

"They're not charging you?"

"No. I think Everett's just trying to make an example out of me."

She points to the low stone retaining wall at the edge of my back yard. "What's on the other side?" she asks.

"Woods, a path, a pond. Do you want to go for a walk?"

She nods, so I lead her over the wall and into the woods. There's only a sliver of moon, so it's not easy to find the path that leads to the pond. Everything is overgrown. Branches and vines cling to us.

"So what happened at the police station?" she asks while I hold back a vine for her.

"They just asked me a bunch of questions."

"Like what?"

"Why did I do it? Do I have mental health issues?"

"Did they ask if you knew me?"

"Yup."

"What did you tell them?"

"Nothing. I didn't say a word."

"You just blanked them?"

"Uh-huh."

"Wow."

That was part of The Talk my parents had with me when I was nine. Don't ever talk to the police, no matter what they want and no matter how innocent you are. If you're arrested, keep your mouth shut and insist on a lawyer. Or, in my case, wait for your mom to show up and drag your ass out of there.

When we finally make it through the woods, I'm surprised by how small the pond is. My sister and I used to skate here, but now you'd barely have any room to move. It looks like the reeds and swamp grass are overgrown, but also, sometimes things just look smaller when you revisit them. I lead Suze to the big, flat rock we used to sit on to change into our skates. There are some beer cans and cigarette packs around the base of it, which means other kids from the neighborhood have been coming back here. Probably Daryl Parkness and Joey Delouche, smoking pot and lighting insects on fire.

Suze sits next to me and squints at the black water through the reeds. "Did they ask you anything about Tarkin?"

"No. Marcus says the police are pretty clueless."

"Well, that's some good news."

The sound of a frog draws her attention to the pond, but there's nothing to see. Just the marsh reeds waving slightly.

"I didn't look at them, you know," I say.

She turns back to me.

"The pictures."

"Oh."

"I would never look at them."

She looks down. "Like my mom says, it's just the human body. Everybody has one."

"True."

"Thanks, though. For not looking at them. It means a lot, actually." She sighs then tilts her head back and looks up at the sky. "Do you know stars?"

"Constellations? Not really."

"Ooh," she says, pointing. "There's Cassiopeia."

I look up, but I can't see it.

"Over there," she says. "Just on the edge of that tree. It's like a funny shaped *W*. Right there."

I bring my head closer to hers and look up.

"See?" she says, drawing a *W* in the air.

"Oh yeah," I say. "W." I'm so close I can smell her shampoo. Flowers and spice. Meadows and Christmas.

"Nikki calls that Wonder Woman," she says. "It's like she's watching over us."

"She's cool."

"Nikki?"

"I meant Wonder Woman. But yeah, Nikki's cool too. I'm not sure she likes me, though."

"No. She's just a bit possessive. I think she resents that I came to you for help. Instead of her."

"Oh."

"Can I ask you a question, DeShawn?"

I nod. The sound of my name in her voice still gets to me.

"Remember when you saw me with Tarkin on Monday, when I bumped into you in the hall?"

"Yeah."

"How did you know something was wrong? Even Nikki didn't pick up on that."

I think back. It was only two days ago, but it feels like forever, like the whole world turned on the axis of that day. "Something was missing," I say. "It was like you turned off the light inside. You weren't you anymore."

"You saw that?"

"That light was . . ."

"What?"

"Your light is very special." She looks at me quizzically. "To me," I say. I know I'm not nailing this, but I don't want to scare her with my actual thought, which is: *I love everything about you.*

"I noticed you, too," she says. "Before all of this, I mean. I noticed you noticing me."

"Yeah?"

"I like how you sort of keep yourself apart."

"Really? I think most kids just think I'm awkward. Or shy."

"They're not really seeing you."

"I guess not."

"You know what I wish?" she says. "I wish we could see through each other's eyes." She looks right at me. "You know what I see?"

"What?" I ask nervously.

"I see strength. I see courage. I see kindness."

"Like Wonder Woman?"

She laughs. "Just like Wonder Woman."

"You know what I see when I look at you?"

"What?"

"I see the light again."

"Really?"

"Yeah. It's faint. But it's still there."

"God, I wish I could see that," she says.

"You'd be amazed."

The next thing I know, her lips are on mine and it's the softest thing I've ever felt, softer than the cashmere baby blanket I keep at the bottom of my T-shirt drawer and only take out when I'm feeling sad. I've only kissed one girl before. Her name was Sonja and we met at science camp. Her lips were soft, too. But she kissed in short bursts and, since I'd never done it before, I thought that was how you did it. I was wrong. *This* is how you kiss. Deep and slow and gentle. It feels like it could go on forever, and that's exactly what I want.

"Help me forget?" she says.

"Forget what?"

"Everything."

She puts a hand on either side of my face, kisses me again, then pulls me down to the rock with her. When her soft hair falls onto my neck and face my bones feel like they're melting, like they're molten, like I'm made of liquid fire. Time stops, but it's nothing like being in the zone. Instead, I'm hyper-aware of everything that's happening—the spicy, floral smell of her, the soft wetness of her tongue, the weight of her thighs on either side of my hips.

She pulls away suddenly and sits back, then slides out of her hoodie. She pulls her gauzy white top over her head. She's not wearing a bra.

"Is this okay?" she says.

I want to say yes, but yes feels inadequate, like there should be a different, much bigger word for this. I'm pretty sure I nod. At least I can feel the cold, rough rock rubbing against the back of my head. She grabs the hem of my hoodie and T-shirt, and when she leans forward to lift them off of me, her warm breast grazes my cheek. It's like being kissed by angels. We slide out of the rest of our clothes until we're lying naked side by side, the deep groove of her waist and the long silhouette of her hip and legs backlit by the neighbors' porch light in the distance.

"I've never done this," I whisper.

"I have."

"Okay."

"You don't have to, DeShawn."

"I want to."

"Are you sure? Because I don't want you to feel like—"

"I'm sure," I say. I've never been more sure of anything.

She reaches over to her hoodie on the ground and pulls out a metallic blue square. It takes me a second to realize what it is.

A condom.

She lays it down on the rock above our heads. "Whenever you're ready," she says. "*If* you're ready."

This is it, I think. Something huge is about to happen. Something momentous and life-changing. But before I can drown in these thoughts, my body takes over. Our arms and legs interlock and find each other in in new and thrilling ways and, even though I've never done this before, I know exactly how to do it. So does she. Everything about her body meshes with mine and together we become the most beautiful machine. All the grace and symmetry that's usually missing from the world is there with us.

And nothing else is.

Not Tarkin Shaw, or the pictures, or the horrible kids leering at her. No one can see us but that W in the sky. It's just me and Suze, the cold rock, the whispering marsh reeds, and that shiny blue square above my head, waiting, for whenever I'm ready.

MARCUS

I'm at my desk in my room, obsessively reading and refreshing articles about Tarkin Shaw, when Nikki calls. I guess we're not hiding *our* association from the police. If Jonesville's finest are interested, they'll know that the formerly frosty Nikki Petronzio has included me in her circle of tolerable humans.

"It was Sean Princely," she says.

"What?"

"He posted the pictures," she explains.

I try to summon up a face to go with the name.

"Sophomore?" she says. "Wrestler? Red hair?"

"Oh yeah, that guy." Smarmy is how I'd describe him. Hangs on the varsity wrestlers' every word, reliably laughs at their so-called jokes.

"He got the pictures from PornHole," she says, "which is where Mason Shaw posted them."

"*Mason* Shaw?"

"Yup. Tarkin's little brother."

"Why would *he* post them?"

She sighs. "Don't ask me to grasp the minds of

assholes, Marcus. Anyway, the pictures are already on four different sites. That we know of. I don't think Suze is going to be able to delete them all."

"That sucks."

"Tell me about it."

"How's she doing?"

"She's gone analog."

"What does that mean?"

"Not answering her phone. Not going online. Cleansing. She does that sometimes."

That sounds like a very good idea. I think if I were Suze Tilman, I'd stay offline for as long as possible. Maybe forever.

"There were other pictures too," she says.

"Of Suze?"

"Other girls. Like lots of other girls. From Jonesville."

"Who?"

"Danielle Jameson, Izzy Rigoletto, Alica Ramirez, Amber Laynes, Taryn—"

"Whoa. Did you say Amber Laynes?"

"Mm-hmm. A lot of them look like they were all taken in the same place."

"Where?"

"A bed with a green blanket."

"That doesn't exactly narrow it down."

"Some of them are selfies too."

"Wait. Did you say a *green* blanket?"

"Yeah."

"Could it have been a comforter or a bedspread?"

"I guess so."

"Could it have been a bedspread with Pepe the Frog on it?"

Over the phone I hear her typing something. "Yeah, it was that bright green color. And there was a black spot that could have been an eye."

"Well, guess who has a Pepe the Frog bedspread."

"Tarkin?"

"Yup."

"Of course he does. Of course he's into that alt-right shit. Does he have a black water bottle too?"

"Yes," I say. "With the Jonesville Eagle mascot on it."

"I bet it's him, then," she says. "I bet a lot of those pictures were taken in his room."

"Plus we found a stash of nudes there. Printouts."

"Of who?"

"I only saw a few—Marcela Desjardins, Lena Schmidt."

"My God," she says. "How many girls was he doing this to?"

I can barely fathom it. It seems like virtually the entire student body has passed through the Tarkin Shaw porn machine, whether they wanted to or not. I knew the guy was bad news. But the scale of this is taking my breath away.

"What did you do with them?" Nikki asks.

"What?"

"The printouts. Where are they?"

"DeShawn took them. To destroy, of course."

"Are you sure?"

"Yes, I'm sure."

I have no doubt that DeShawn burned the pictures just like he said he would. I don't tell Nikki how much I opposed the decision. I'm more convinced than ever that we should have saved them.

"Anyway," she says. "That's all I know."

"Hey, Nikki?"

"Yeah?"

I want to ask about her past with Tarkin Shaw. I know something happened between them her freshman year and I can only assume that it snaps right into what we're learning about him now. The reporter in me wants to dive in and pry out all of the details. But something about the sorrow in her voice stops me.

"Thanks for calling," I say.

"Sure," she says. Then she hangs up.

I spend the next half hour wondering who's to blame for Tarkin Shaw's rampage across the female population of Jonesville High. Other than Tarkin himself, of course. Could someone have stopped him? Did his coach know? His parents? Principal Everett had to have known *something*. I find myself staring at the green Post-it stuck on my wall wondering to myself: If journalism's *first* obligation is to the truth, what's its second obligation?

Then my cell phone rings. Elena.

"So the photos," she says.

"Huh?"

"The photos, Marcus. The nudie pics of the dead kid's girlfriend, Suze Tilman?"

Her matter-of-fact tone annoys me. They're not "nudie pics." I hate when people minimize with language. I hate when they say "We have a little problem" when they mean "We have a *big* problem."

"Marcus!" she barks at me.

"What?"

"Did you know about them?"

"Yeah, sure, everyone knows about them."

"Everyone at Jonesville High?"

"Well I don't know about literally everyone."

"Any reason you didn't call me immediately when you heard about them?"

Oh no, here we go again. I have to explain myself to Elena, bullshit detector extraordinaire. "I don't know," I say. "I guess I didn't think they were . . ." I have to wince my way through the next word because it's such an obvious lie. "*Relevant*?"

"Oh, come on," she scoffs. Predictably, I have to admit. "A jock dies under mysterious circumstances then two days later a bunch of nudie pics of his girlfriend surface. And you think that's not *relevant*? You're supposed to be my eyes and ears at the high school, Marcus. *Everything* having to do with Tarkin Shaw is relevant. Jesus."

I slump over my laptop. "Sorry."

"Don't be sorry. Be sharp."

"Okay," she says. "What do we know about the pictures? What's the buzz at school?"

I snap upright. This I *can* answer because "the buzz at school" is pretty wide of the mark. "There are a few theories," I tell her.

"Such as?"

"Suze is an aspiring porn star and the photos are her calling card?"

"Unlikely."

"Another theory is that the whole photographic opus is an homage to her dead boyfriend."

"Next."

"She was a slut all along, only we never knew?"

"Any meat on those bones?"

"Are you asking me if she's a slut? Because I generally don't think of girls in those terms."

"Well, you win the woke Olympics. Congratulations. I'm asking what we know about her, Marcus."

"I don't think anyone really does know her. She only moved here six months ago, and she pretty much keeps tight with her friends."

"Well, that's some shit intel."

"Sorry. What are the police saying?"

"They're saying she's one hot piece of ass. What do you think they're saying? Fucking yokels."

I force out a laugh, which is what I assume a person not actually implicated in the death of Tarkin Shaw would do. In any event, the police not knowing things is my favorite bit of intel from Elena.

"You've seen them, right?" she asks.

"The photos? Yeah." I say it casually, like they're no big deal, just another example of a kid being stupid. But when I catch my faux shrug in the mirror to my right, it does not convince. I'm a bad actor. Thank God this conversation is over the phone and not in person.

"So what do you think of them?" she asks.

"It is what it is, I guess."

"See, I'm not so sure. Something about those pictures doesn't look right to me. Did you notice anything unusual about them?"

"Um—"

"Of course not. You were too busy looking at her tits. To me, she looks drugged. The way her eyes sort of droop. Did you catch that?"

"Um . . . ?" Don't answer. Keep it vague. Don't get trapped by easy-to-discredit details.

"And we know the Shaw kid was drugged. So I'm wondering if there's a connection."

"What kind of connection?"

"That's what I'd like to find out. Did they hang out with any sketchy people?"

"I really don't know who they hung out with."

"Could be a sextortion thing. That's what I was thinking."

I've never heard the word before and immediately start Googling. From Wikipedia:

Sextortion is a form of sexual exploitation that employs non-physical forms of coercion to extort sexual favors from the victim. . . Sextortion also refers to a form of blackmail in which

sexual information or images are used to extort
sexual favors from the victim.

"It's all the rage," Elena says. "You get a nude
photo of someone, then you use it to get more photos, or sex, even cash. I read about a guy pulling
down twenty thousand a month from girls paying
him to take their nudes down. It's a real growth
area, crime-wise. And the law's patchy, can't keep
up with it."

"Is that how the cops are leaning, then?" I ask,
my throat drying up. "Sextortion?"

"Nah, the cops are still trying to figure out how
to pull their heads out of each other's asses. I doubt
they even know what the word means. I'm just
throwing stuff at the wall here, trying to see what
sticks. Something about this whole thing isn't add-
ing up. Do you think little miss good girl gone bad
published those pictures herself?"

"You should probably stop making Rihanna ref-
erences, Elena."

"You have a problem with Rihanna?"

"I have no problem with Rihanna at all. I just
think—"

"Answer the question, then."

"What question?"

"Do you think she published those pictures
herself?"

"I have no idea."

"What are they saying at school? What are her
friends saying?"

230

"I don't know any of her friends."

"Well, what do *you* think?"

"How should I know? I don't know her."

"Really?" Elena purrs. "You see, that's interesting, Marcus."

Oh God. She's setting me up. I can feel it. "Why is that interesting?" I almost squeak.

"It's interesting because my sources at the precinct tell me that you got into a fight with Tarkin Shaw the day before he died. And apparently the fight was about this girl."

Shit!

"The police told you that?"

"They tell me a lot."

I freeze and go silent, which is the stupidest course of action. Nothing gives a person away more obviously than flabbergasted silence. It's as good as a written confession. Of course the police know about my fight with Tarkin Shaw. Principal Everett probably told them all about it. That's basic police work. Even the Jonesville police are capable of that.

"It wasn't a *fight*," I say, way too late.

"So you're saying my sources are wrong?"

"Shaw attacked me. There was no fight."

"Look, let's just get this out of the way up front. It wasn't you who killed Tarkin Shaw, was it?"

"Are you crazy?"

"You pick a fight with him, then the next day he turns up dead?"

I stand up and start pacing while trying to keep

my voice calm. "I didn't pick a fight with him. I told you, he attacked me."

"Why?"

"Because he's a dick. Sorry, *was* a dick."

"So it *wasn't* about Suze Tilman? Because they told me it was. What happened? Did Tarkin see the two of you together or something?"

"How should I know?"

"Well, either he did or he didn't. Let me ask you this. Were you seeing Suze Tilman behind Tarkin's back?"

"No."

"Are you sure?"

"How could I not be sure if I was seeing someone?"

"Did you take those pictures?"

"Oh come on."

"Is that why the Shaw kid attacked you? Was he jealous? Were you getting too close to her?"

"I don't even know her."

"You wrote that article about her."

"I told you, that was a joke!"

"Pretty elaborate joke. Pretty well-researched, too."

"Well, maybe if Schnell gave me a decent assignment once in a while, I wouldn't have to kill time writing joke articles."

"Don't change the subject."

"Elena, you don't honestly believe I murdered Tarkin Shaw."

After a purposefully agonizing pause meant

either to extract a full confession or just inflict maximum pain, she says, "No. You're not the type."

I slouch back into my chair, relieved. "Well thanks, Elena. It's good to know you don't think I'm a *murderer*."

"Don't be so touchy."

"Well, it's pretty disconcerting to be accused of killing someone."

"Anyone can be a killer."

"Even you?"

"Are you kidding? I have murderous thoughts twelve times a day."

"I'll keep that in mind."

"Why didn't you tell me, though?"

"Tell you what?"

"About that fight with Shaw? Or those photographs? You're hiding something."

"I'm not hiding anything."

Which, I realize far too late, is *exactly* what people say when they're hiding something big.

"Oh, Marcus, Marcus. Please tell me this girl isn't working you over."

"What do you mean?"

"Well, look. Here's how I'm leaning. And please correct me if I'm wrong, because I really want to get this right. Either Tilman and the Shaw kid were both being sextorted by whoever posted those pictures. Or—and I have to admit, I like this angle even better—Shaw was sextorting Tilman and she killed him over it."

Holy shit! Elena just broke open the story.

"Ha!" I yelp. "That's insane!" I hope she isn't clocking my shallow breathing. "I mean, that seems really far-fetched, unless you have proof. Do you have proof?"

"No," she says, cold as ice. "Not yet. But I've got an insider at Jonesville High with a connection to the girl, don't I? The cops are way behind. Let's you and me bust this thing open ourselves. Get an exclusive."

"Elena." I struggle to keep the panic out of my voice. I have to assure her that I am nothing but a fellow journalist here. Not a witness, and certainly not an accomplice. "I honestly don't have any connection to Suze Tilman."

"Sure you don't."

It's only after Elena hangs up to take another call that I realize the only people who ever say the word "honestly" are the ones who are lying their asses off.

Like me.

ANI / **LYDIA**

Did u see what Sean Princely wrote on Facebook tonight?

Why would I ever be on Facebook?

Just look. He's saying Tarkin killed himself because he was ashamed of Suze.

Hold on.

...

OMG, that little shit!

Yup. And all the varsity wrestlers are backing him up, saying Suze is this great big slut for posting those pictures.

Princely's JV. I bet he's trying to impress the varsity guys by pretending to be concerned about Tarkin and his "reputation."

If those guys knew it was Princely who posted the pictures, I bet they'd straight up kill that little Ewok.

Too bad we can't tell them.

Maybe we can.

Nikki says no way. We're not supposed to say anything.

Nikki says. Nikki says. She's not the boss of this. Suze is.

Yeah, but Suze has gone analog.

Exactly. So how do we know what she wants? We can't just sit here and do nothing while people say evil shit about her.

But what can we do?

I have an idea. Come to my house.

Lydia, you're scaring me.

No, you'll love it. Trust me. We're gonna be legends.

NIKKI

Sean Princely is having a field day on Facebook. I guess posting the photos wasn't enough of a thrill—he has to trash-talk Suze on multiple platforms. I know for a fact that Suze has never said a word to him, so I don't know why he has such a vendetta against her. But he's not alone. All the wrestlers are piling up on her now. Here's Taran Boid, from the JV squad:

> *I'm just glad Tarkin's not around to see her like this. What a disgrace.*

You know what's a disgrace? Worshipping rapey blackmailers like Tarkin Shaw. *That's* a disgrace.

And what's with all the hostility toward Suze? If you honestly believe she was Tarkin's for-real girlfriend, shouldn't you be defending her? It's like no matter the circumstances, they always choose humiliation. And other people hop right on the bandwagon.

She comes off as so snobby and sophisticated but look at her. Can you say desperate?

That's not even a wrestler. That's Becca DePaul, some random freshman girl. Way to look out for a sister, *Becks.* Hope you like your special place in hell.

And here's Martina Landry, the cheerleader who had the nerve to try to console Suze at school today:

I bet he was about to dump her and she took these pictures to win him back. Sad.

What gives, Martina? Where's all that compassion you were dripping with? They're obviously taking their cues from the wrestlers, because hey, why not sell out another girl to win the approval of a bunch of jocks? I want to scream, *Look at the photos, people. She. Was. Drugged. Is that not obvious to you? Suze's eyes don't usually droop like that.* But I guess if the wrestlers say Suze is this giant slut, it must be true, because whatever they say goes. And everyone falls in line. The wrestlers are like gods at our school, all because they won the championship once. The *division* championship. Not even state.

It's spooky how quickly everyone's turned on her. Suze never did anything but mind her own business, keep to herself, and be nice to people. Maybe she wasn't chatty or outgoing, but she was always nice. She's way nicer than me, that's for sure. Now everyone thinks they're better than her just because they've seen her naked. Like that makes sense.

At least Suze and her parents managed to get the photos off of sex.com and PornHole. But it hardly matters. There'll be screenshots. They'll never really disappear. Stupid Internet. Ani keeps telling me that the Internet is "morally neutral" and only reflects "the values of the end user." But screw that. If you ask me, the Internet was invented to humiliate girls.

Around 10:15, I'm sitting on my bed with my laptop and I get a call from Marcus. He's freaking out because this reporter he knows figured out that Tarkin was blackmailing Suze with those pictures.

"Good," I tell him, "because everyone else thinks she took those pictures herself. You should see Sean Princely's Facebook feed right now."

"What? Why?"

I can hear his fingers tapping through the phone.

"They're saying Suze is this big slut," I tell him. "And that Tarkin killed himself because he was so ashamed of her. It's disgusting."

"No. That's perfect."

"How is that perfect? They're saying she's an exhibitionist. No, wait—an exhibitionist whore."

"Yes. An exhibitionist. That's great. We need to encourage that theory."

"Excuse me? Suze is *not* an exhibitionist."

"I know, but listen. Have you ever heard of sextortion?"

"No."

He tells me about people who use naked photos of girls to get money and sex from them. He even emails me links to some examples, because apparently this is a thing now. Surprise, surprise, Tarkin Shaw wasn't even original. All over the world, girls are getting Shawed by scumholes just like him, sad losers who can't get a girl on their own so they have to commit blackmail, or *sextortion*. I'm not naïve. I've been clued in to the dark side of the male sex ever since freshman year, but this is more than I can process right now. I've had about enough of people being horrible. I don't need fancy new names for it.

"The problem, Nikki, is that my colleague has figured out that Suze was being sextorted by Tarkin."

"So?"

"So that's motive."

"For what?"

"For killing Tarkin Shaw."

Of course it's motive for killing Tarkin Shaw. And a damn fine one at that. But then I realize what he's actually telling me and it's like stepping into a bath of icy water. "So she knows."

"She suspects," he says. "She can't prove it yet."

"How did she figure it out?"

"The pictures. She thought Suze looked drugged."

"Because she *was* drugged."

"And that's what we need to fix," he says. "We need to make it clear that Suze took those pictures herself. That she sent them to Shaw and she doesn't even mind that people are looking at them."

"Hah! You're not serious."

"I am, Nikki. I mean, why would she mind? She's a beautiful girl. She has a beautiful body."

"That's a weird thing to say."

"I didn't mean it like that. Her body's—I mean, your body is also very—"

"Oh my God. I wasn't fishing for a compliment."

"I know, I know, I was just saying—that you both have equally—"

"Stop talking."

"Sorry."

He shuts up, but I can hear him breathing heavily on the other end. I'm practically hyperventilating myself. If I'm not mistaken, what Marcus is telling me is that Suze should come forward and confirm exactly what Tarkin tried to convey with those pictures in the first place: namely, that they're selfies. So in addition to pretending that she's the willing girlfriend of a serial sex predator, she also has to pretend that she was so enamored of him that she sent him nudes. Because, hey, why not? She's a beautiful girl with a beautiful body.

"Can I talk now?" Marcus says.

"If you say the wrong thing, I might kill you."

"Look, I realize how awful this is."

"Do you?"

"Yes."

"He drugged, stripped, and photographed my best friend."

"I know," he says. "And it's horrible. I get that. I really do."

"Do you?"

"Yes. The problem is, Elena knows too. And if she figured it out, it's only a matter of time before the cops do."

"So what are you telling me? That it's already too late?"

"No. Right now it's just a theory. And the theory Elena's working with is that Suze Tilman is an innocent, teetotaling virgin who got blackmailed."

"She's not a virgin."

"That's great. That's perfect. Those are exactly the kinds of details we need."

"Why?"

"It works against the good-girl-gone-bad angle."

"The—what?"

"That's the story Elena wants to tell. Suze was innocent and pure, she got blackmailed, so she fought back and killed her blackmailer. We need to destroy that theory."

By exposing Suze's sexual history. And by pretending Suze is totally fine with people looking at naked pictures of her. Which she took herself. For Tarkin Shaw! It just keeps going. Deeper and deeper down the rabbit hole of *revolting*. What's next? Uploading her gynecology records?

"Look, Elena's itching to scoop this story," he says. "I wouldn't put it past her to publish before the cops even put two and two together. She's dying to be first on this, so we need to act fast. We need to get in there with a new story before Elena gets in there with hers. And hers is the truth. The truth has a way of leaving clues."

"Like the pictures," I say, utterly defeated.

"And like Tarkin Shaw's dead body."

I'm going to be sick. I'm going to choke on my own rage and die.

"This is weapons-grade sneaky shit," he says. "Will you call her? Will you get her on board with this? We need you. She won't listen to me."

Is there any limit to the debasement to which we have to subject ourselves because of the shit they do to us? Is there any escape at all?

"Nikki?"

"Yeah, I'll call her," I say. Then I hang up, throw my phone across the room, and scream.

MARCUS

As soon as I hang up with Nikki, I call Elena and tell her what my "source" revealed about Suze Tilman.

"She's a free spirit. Definitely not a virgin, and no hang-ups about nudity. Totally sex-positive. Bit of an exhibitionist, actually."

"Really," she murmurs, voice dripping with suspicion.

"Yup."

"And this comes from . . . ?"

"Nikki Petronzio. Suze's best friend. Knows her like the back of her hand. She says Suze doesn't even care that people are looking at those pictures."

"So why'd she ditch school early today?"

Man, how does Elena know that? The woman has eyes everywhere.

"Mourning," I say. "Nikki says she's really broken up about Shaw. True love, I guess."

"True love plus nudie pics, huh?"

"Yup," I say, "kids these days." I throw in a fake laugh. I need to work on that.

While I'm lying my ass off, I frantically Google fresh verbiage on the prevalence of teen sexting. "Everybody's doing it. 'Send pics.' It's basically how you ask someone out."

"Hmmm," is Elena's reply. *Hmmm*, with an extra scoop of skepticism. Then she jumps off to take another call.

It's a seed. That's all. I've planted a seed of doubt in Elena's sextortion theory. We'll need more than that. Nikki's a solid source, but it's not enough. What we need is for Suze to step up and claim the photos openly. To say, *Yeah, I took them. Big deal. Everybody calm down. Let me get back to mourning my boyfriend, Tarkin Shaw, whom I love uncomplicatedly.* Until some approximation of those words comes out of Suze Tilman's mouth or gets posted online, Elena's sextortion theory will remain a live wire. Because the truth is, even though everyone *is* apparently sending nude pics around, they're also committing suicide over it. And right there you have a serviceable definition of my idiot peers: reckless, unthinking attention-seekers, desperate for approval and totally incapable of self-preservation.

Unfortunately, Suze Tilman is not, as we say in the press, available for comment. According to Nikki, whom I've been calling every ten minutes for the last hour, Suze is still "analog." I find this outrageous. If you're going to roofie someone to death, at the very least you owe your unwilling co-conspirators the courtesy of remaining reachable for emergency planning. Nikki doesn't necessarily disagree with me. She finds Suze exasperating too.

"So why are you friends with her?" I ask her over the phone.

"Why are you friends with DeShawn?" she shoots back.

Despite her hostility, I find myself warming to the sound of Nikki's voice. It's soothing, in a degrading sort of way. I think I have a thing for mean girls. I'm not sure what this says about me.

"No way can you compare those two. DeShawn is the smartest person I know."

"Ditto for Suze."

"And the kindest."

"Double ditto."

Clearly Nikki and I are seeing something different in our respective best friends. But I guess that's the nature of best friends. You see something in the person that no one else sees.

"Can you call her again?"

"Suze is down for the count," she says. "As soon as she turns her phone back on, she'll call me. It'll probably be tomorrow, though. Go to sleep."

"Are *you* going to sleep?"

"No."

"Me neither."

We hang up and I go back to scouring the press coverage of Shaw's death. Most of the items refer to the investigation as "ongoing," but none of them mention homicide. Maybe I'm working myself into a tizzy over nothing. If all goes well, the story will fade into oblivion. Never mind Elena's thirst for a juicy sextortion angle, or her lust to paint Suze Tilman as a "good girl gone bad." That's just her ambition talking. She wants this story to be big, because she wants out of local news. But if the police have any inkling that DeShawn, Suze, and I are involved in Shaw's death, surely they would have questioned us by now. They already know about the fight with Shaw. Obviously, they don't consider it relevant. And why would they? Shaw's a known bully. He throws his weight around all the time. If anything, the fight bolsters the suicide angle. Varsity wrestling captain humiliated in public by a quiet nerd two-thirds his size? Instant ego death. The suicide angle practically announces itself.

Things are looking good. Tomorrow, Nikki will talk to Suze, Suze will swallow her pride and publicly claim the photographs—I don't envy her having to make *that* performance—and the live wire of Elena's sextortion theory will blink out and die. Tarkin Shaw's death will be ruled a suicide, and Elena and the rest of the press bothering to cover the story will go back to covering road deaths and local politics. All I have to do is make it through this one sleepless night.

AROUND ELEVEN O'CLOCK, this happens:

> *Wanted: Sean Princely, aka asshammer15,*
> *for the crime of posting pornographic images*

without the subject's consent. Also, for being a snarky little troll who negs random girls online because he's too much of a wussbag to say anything in person.

Reward for capture: the pure joy of seeing justice done for once in this sick, ugly world.

Above the post is a blurry photo of Sean Princely, mouth wide open, eyes half-closed, freckled face blotchy and overheated. It's a close-up, possibly taken from a wrestling match where, it's safe to say, he isn't winning. And which genius posted this on her Facebook page for all the world to see? Why, none other than Lydia Moreau.

I pick up the phone and call Nikki. I'm shaking—terror and irritation simultaneously. Obviously, there's been some horrible miscommunication on strategy. When I get her voicemail, I leave a message for her to call me ASAP. Meanwhile, the comments section below the post explodes.

PRINCELY: *shut up, you whore. i didn't post shit.*

LYDIA: *liar. we caught you. cops are gonna love seeing your browser history. met any nice prostitutes on any of those escort service sites you like so much?*

PRINCELY: *YOU'RE a prostitute.*

LYDIA: *and you broke the law. enjoy prison. bring lube.*

EMMA CHAMPLAIN: *wait, Lydia, how do you know he posted those pictures of Suze?*

LYDIA: *hacked straight into his business.*

EMMA CHAMPLAIN: *woah. how did you do that?*

ANI: *she didn't. i did. it's all documented too. so Sean, if you're still reading, you can stop deleting your accounts. It's too late for that.*

PRINCELY: *you're fucking dead.*

LYDIA: *really? you want to elaborate on that? cuz i think the cops really like death threats. how are you planning to kill her?*

BRENDAN STICIC: *dude, srsly, shut up. you're gonna get in even more trouble.*

PRINCELY: *i didn't do anything. these bitches are totally lying. Suze Tilman posted those pictures. why don't you go arrest her?*

It's not *quite* the Algonquin Round Table.

ABOUT TEN MINUTES into the debate, Nikki finally calls back. "Ani and Lydia have gone rogue."

"Really? You think?"

"I tried calling to tell them the new plan, but they wouldn't even pick up. I think they're avoiding me."

"Why?"

"It's Lydia. She wants to punish someone. And she knows I would not approve of this stupid Wanted post."

"This is the exact opposite of what we need right now."

"You think I don't know that?"

"We have to shut it down."

"What do you think I've been trying to do? They're not answering their phones."

"Where are they?"

"MIA. They're avoiding me, obviously."

"So track them down. Please tell me you're all on FriendFinder."

"Shoot. I didn't think of that."

"I'm sending you my address. Pick me up."

EIGHT-AND-A-HALF minutes later, Nikki pulls into my driveway, barely stopping long enough for me to jump into the passenger seat of her little blue hatchback. She throws me her phone so I can monitor Lydia and Ani's dots, then screeches out of there and heads for Main Street. Lydia and Ani are at the Dunkin's in Beverly, but by the time we cross the town line, Ani's dot disappears from the screen. A few seconds later, Lydia's dot disappears, too.

"They're on to me," Nikki says. "They must be tracking my dot."

Dunkin's is between a Stop & Shop and a craft store called Sandee's This 'n That, at the far end of an ocean-sized parking lot that is mostly empty because of the time. Nikki speeds through it and parks right near the entrance of Dunkin's. We rush inside and scan the place, but it's empty. Nikki checks the bathrooms, while I approach the twenty-something beardster who is manning the counter on his own.

"A short, pixie-ish blond and a curvy Indian girl. Have you seen them?"

He has. But he says they just left in a big hurry.

Nikki emerges from the women's bathroom, shaking her head.

"Think," I say. "Where could they be?"

"Obviously they're not going to show up any place *I'd* look. They're probably just driving around."

Dunkin's is dead, has that stale feeling of a party that's over except for the last few, clueless stragglers. I drop into a booth and check the status on Lydia's Wanted post. Fifty-three comments so far, ranging from incredulous to vicious, and full of dire spelling. Though no definitive consensus has been reached on Sean Princely's guilt vis-à-vis the posting of the photos, or on the precise whoreishness of Suze Tilman, the dialectic has expanded. Not only is Suze Tilman's character under discussion, so are Lydia's, Ani's, and, of course, by association, Nikki's. Nikki slides into the booth across from me and taps at her phone.

"Don't look," I tell her. "It's ugly."

"You think no one's ever talked trash about me before? Please. You weren't there my freshman year."

True. I was still in middle school. Slightly more innocent times.

As she scrolls and refreshes, I can't tell if she's actively avoiding conversation with me or legitimately getting sucked into the hullabaloo online. Nothing makes it easier to ignore someone right in front of you than your own phone.

Lydia's post seems to have hardened the battle lines. It's the wrestlers versus the mean girls and nearly everybody's taking the wrestlers' side. I have never understood the wrestlers' social cachet. I mean, sure, they're jocks, they're strong, a few of them are all-right looking, I guess. But not one of them has an ounce of charisma. At least Lydia and Ani are funny. They have spirit. When they insult you, they put some finesse into it.

But now that Sean Princely's been accused of something, everyone seems to be rallying around him. It was the same way with Amber Laynes. She was one of the most popular girls at school, the life of the party. (Not that I'd ever been to any of those parties, but you hear things.) As soon as she accused Shaw of rape, everyone turned on her. No, more than that—they tore her down. Her fun-loving, party-going ways were recast as evidence of her depravity. Now she was a slut and a liar and someone who threw herself at Tarkin, so he couldn't have raped her. *You can't rape a slut* seemed to be the theory, and *Tarkin Shaw doesn't need to use force to get a girl.* Everything people loved about Amber, they now hated. And the rank hypocrisy of that didn't even register for them. It was like they'd convinced themselves that they'd never liked her in the first place. *Oceania was at war with Eurasia; therefore Oceania had always been at war with Eurasia.* That's Orwell, and yes, I sometimes pay attention in class.

Nikki deposits two Dunkaccinos and a cinnamon raisin bagel onto the table. I didn't even realize she'd gotten up, that's how deeply I've disappeared into the online miasma. I reach into my pocket to give her some money, then realize I haven't brought my wallet.

"Don't worry about it," she says, and goes back to her phone.

I text DeShawn to see if he's read any of this. People being cruel to Suze is enough to send him over the edge. But DeShawn doesn't answer his phone. Best-case scenario really. Sleep through the whole mess.

"One thing," Nikki says. "They're all arguing about whether Sean or Suze posted the pictures right?"

"Yeah."

"But no one's questioning whether Suze actually *took* the pictures. That's the important thing, right? That people think she took them herself?"

"Yeah. That's the important bit."

"Well, it looks like everyone's in agreement on that point."

She's right. The Jonesville High hive mind has more or less settled on the thesis that Suze Tilman, who once seemed so aloof and sophisticated, so foreign and stylish, is actually a vain exhibitionist who would do anything to hold onto Tarkin Shaw.

I wonder what Elena thinks. It's 11:29. I haven't heard from her in a while, which means either she hasn't seen any of this Facebook stuff yet, or she doesn't find it relevant. If she does find out about it—and I have to assume she will, because she knows *everything*—then I'm going to have to make sure I tell her about it first. She already thinks I'm hiding things from her. I need to reassure her that I'm not. I take a screenshot of a particularly juicy bit of slut-shaming and text it to her. She gets back to me right away, with:

What does Suze Tilman have to say about all of this?

I show Nikki and she shrugs, so I text back:

According to her best friend, Suze wouldn't even care. She's too broken up about Shaw to care about anything else.

Elena texts back:

Maybe.

I don't like it. Elena has it bad for Suze Tilman. I wonder why. You'd think she'd feel some sense of camaraderie with a fellow female. It can't be good for women to promote this kind of misogynist trash-talking. Then again, Elena can be pretty single-minded. I guess, in the end, the story matters more.

"Hey, Nikki," I say. "Can I ask you something?"

I'm thinking about a particular detail from the scene of the crime, something Elena revealed to me the day we found out Shaw was dead. It was the detail that I think excited Elena the most. "Did Suze tell you what happened in Shaw's trophy room that night?"

"The night he died?"

I nod. "Because she wouldn't tell us. All she'd say was that something, quote, unquote, *weird* happened."

I wait for Nikki to fill in the blank there, but she just looks at me, dead-eyed, a rough-edged chunk of bagel in her hand.

I lower my voice so the beardster behind the counter, who's been artlessly eavesdropping on us ever since we came in, can't hear. "The police found semen on the couch. They haven't revealed that to the public yet."

"So how do you know about it?"

"Sources."

Nikki stares back blankly, but not in a way that means she doesn't know what I'm talking about. She knows. But she doesn't want to tell me.

"What happened?"

When she doesn't answer, I lower my voice to a whisper. "Did he rape her?"

"Why are you whispering?"

I flick my eyes to the beardster restocking napkins while openly staring at us.

"Well, did he?" I ask.

"Does it matter?"

"Of course it matters."

"Why?"

"Well, either she was raped, or—"

"Or what?"

"Or"—I lower my voice even more—"or she had sex with him."

"And?"

"Well, which is it?"

"Does it matter?"

"You're asking if it matters whether she was raped or not?"

"Yeah. Why does it matter?"

"It matters because there's a big difference between those two things."

"No, to *you*, Marcus. Why does it matter to *you*?"

"I'm just trying to understand."

"Sure you are." She drops her chunk of bagel onto the table as if she's lost her appetite, then sinks back against the booth and disappears into her phone.

"Why are you mad at me?" I ask.

She keeps her eyes on her phone while shrugging. "I thought you were different."

"What's that supposed to mean?"

"Judging her."

"I'm not *judging her*."

"Yes, you are."

"Nikki—"

She puts her phone down and looks at me. "What if I told you she was raped by Tarkin that night?"

"Was she?"

"If she was, would that make you feel differently about her?"

"Different from what?"

"Different from how you'd feel if she had sex with him? Would that make her a good girl? Instead of a bad girl?"

"I never said that. Those are Elena's words, not mine."

"But you're the one who needs to know so badly, so answer the question. What if she *did* have sex with him?"

"Why are you grilling *me*?"

"It changes the way you think about her," she says, "doesn't it?"

"No."

"Liar."

"Why are you attacking me?"

"You think *you're* being attacked? Ha! You have no idea."

"Nikki," I say very softly. But she won't look at me now. She's back into her phone. "Nikki, please, I'm just trying to understand."

She looks up suddenly, her eyes flashing. "What if she had sex with him because if she didn't he would have raped her anyway?"

"Is . . . that what happened?"

"What if it is?"

"But we were right there. All she had to do was scream."

She looks down and shakes her head like this is a ridiculous idea. "Screaming is the last thing on your mind. Screaming will only enrage him."

I'm about to say something, but I stop and let that settle, because I don't think Nikki's talking about Suze right now.

"Plus you're in this . . . vulnerable position. You don't want to be seen like that."

"But there were two of us," I say. "And one of us was DeShawn."

"Right. A real pair of heroes."

"I never said I was a hero."

"Good, because based on what Suze told me about the plan that night, you running in there to save her would have meant Tarkin posting those pictures."

"Yeah, but they're just pictures."

"*Just* pictures?"

She taps at her phone, then turns it around for me to see.

i hope that bitch kills herself. and her skank friends too.

such a fake two-faced cow. i always knew their was something up with her.

She scrolls down and shows me this eloquent exchange between Lydia and one of the varsity wrestlers:

AARON PAULSON: *sluts like Suze Tilman are the reason hate-fucking was invented.*

LYDIA MOREAU: *misogynist turd, go back under your rock. nobody cares about your brain-dead theories*

AARON PAULSON: *shut up slut*

LYDIA MOREAU: *make me, shit for brains.*

AARON PAULSON: *next time I see you, slut. right after I'm done hatefucking your friends.*

"Just words, right?" She scrolls for more, but I wave her off. Undeterred, she holds the phone up for me to see.

Aaron Paulson has started a new hashtag:

#RapeLydiaMoreau

I open my mouth to say something, but I come up empty.

"This is what happens when you cross a wrestler," she says. "They don't just defend themselves. They destroy you. And don't tell me you could have prevented it. And don't tell me she could have gone to the police. Nobody cares. They always win. You know what being a hero is? It's being able to have sex with someone you hate. *Now* do you understand?"

I don't answer, because she already knows I don't understand. Her question wasn't really a question. It was an accusation, a demonstration of the difference between us, the unbridgeable gulf. I couldn't possibly understand because I've never been in that position.

"You want to know what I think?" she says. "I think Suze knew this shit would happen if the pictures got out. She knew what Tarkin was. I told her. I told her all about him. So yeah, she had sex with that monster to try to prevent this. And you know what, good for her. Because no way would I be able to do something like that. I'd try to fight him off, which would mean instead of screwing some guy to get what I wanted, I'd be getting raped instead. So if that's what Suze did, that was just Suze being smart. That's what I say."

She goes back to her phone, scrolls, refreshes, pretends I'm not even there. I wish I weren't. I wish I were home and all of this was unreal. I feel like I'm drowning, like this can't possibly be true, even though I know that it is. When did rape become something you have to manage? Not avoid. Manage. Has it always been this way?

"Nikki."

She lowers her head, keeps her eyes on her phone.

"Nikki?"

She sniffles, then tries to cover it up by wiping at her nose and coughing, pretending she has a cold.

"Nikki?" I whisper.

"What!" Her eyes glisten.

The guy behind the counter openly gawks at us now.

"Do you mind?" I say to him. Then I turn to Nikki and lower my voice. "Did something like that happen to you? Because—"

"Stop," she says. She puts her phone down and stares at me full-on. "I'm not here to tell you my story. So don't ask me about it. Okay? I'm here for Suze. That's all."

After a long, suffocating silence that stretches over us like a sheet of rubber, I mutter, "I'm sorry," because it's the only thing I can think of. I'm sorry. I'm heartbroken. And I've never been more ashamed of being male. What I was going to say, before she put up her hand to stop me, was, "Whatever he did, it says nothing about you."

After a while, she looks up sadly and says, "Don't be sorry. Be one of the good guys."

And all this time I thought I was.

AFTER THAT, we take refuge in our phones. The pageant of misspelled insults and violent threats is easier to take than the tense, pregnant air between us. Around midnight, the music shuts off, the guy behind the counter tells us he's closing, and we head to the door. Out in the parking lot, Nikki tells me she wants to go check on Suze to make sure she's okay.

"I can't risk being seen there," I tell her.

"I'll drop you off first."

"Actually, no. I'll stay in the car and duck down. I want to know she's safe, too."

Nikki narrows her eyes at me.

"I do care about her, you know. I *was* just trying to understand. I swear, Nikki."

She stares through me, like she's trying to catch me in a lie. But then she softens and lets out a little laugh. "Good luck with that. She's my best friend and sometimes I don't understand her."

It's late and there are only a few cars on the roads. When we get back to Jonesville, most of the houses are dark. On Elm Street, we pass Jason Sipwicz's house, a kid who used to go to day camp with me. It's a neat little Cape Cod–style house with a perfectly manicured lawn I can remember Jason's father trimming with actual scissors. Inside that neat little home, Jason is angrily thumbing out rape and death threats against Suze, Nikki, Lydia, and Ani. He's not even a wrestler. Just another kid joining in the fun. In houses all over Jonesville, kids are doing the same thing. Not the delinquent, mouth-breathing creeps you'd expect it from, either, but the quiet ones, like Jason.

"Uh oh," Nikki says.

We've just turned onto Roberts Road, a neighborhood of small, cookie-cutter, colonial-style houses. A police car sits in front of a white one with a small front lawn and a cement walkway.

"Is that—"

"Suze's house," she says.

I pull up my hoodie and duck below the window. "Drive past."

She drives all the way to the end of the cul-de-sac. When she rolls past Suze's house again, I chance a peek over the car door and see straight into the Tilmans' living room, where two adults I've never seen before (Suze's parents, presumably) speak with the two police officers who arrested De-Shawn in the cafeteria.

"They know," I say. "It's over. We're screwed."

Nikki says nothing. But she doesn't stick around. She drives away so no one will see me there.

THURSDAY

DESHAWN

I feel like a changed man. I feel like a *man*. Yesterday I was a boy and I didn't even realize it. I don't know how to describe what happened last night. I guess that's what poets are for. It hardly feels real, like if I think about it too much, I might realize it was all a dream. But I can't stop thinking about it. As I ride my bike to school, it's all I can think about. And I know it wasn't a dream, because there's a sore spot on the back of my head from scraping against that rock. I keep pressing on it, and the ache brings me back to the pond, to Suze sitting on top of me with her hair in her face. So soft. So impossibly soft. I have to pull over every few blocks just to catch my breath.

She came to *me* last night. Not Nikki or her other friends. Me. When she wanted to forget, she came to *me*. She brought a condom with her because she wanted to have sex with me. It didn't just happen. She planned it. She planned it with me.

About halfway to the junction of Cherry and Main, where I usually meet Marcus, I hear a strange *bip-bip-bip*. I reach for the phone in my front pocket, but it's not that. It's farther away, behind me. I ignore it and pick up my pace. I can't wait to see Suze at school, even if I can't actually talk to her, because we're supposed to be hiding our association, I can look at her. I can feel those big, dark eyes on mine as she remembers last night too. I can luxuriate in the secret that only we share.

I push my legs as hard as they'll go. The ragged sound of my breath is like an animal's, an animal that's pushing its limits. I love that feeling. My body is a good machine. I've always known that, always been able to master and control it. When I tell myself I want to kick higher, I keep working until I get there. If I want to ride faster, I do. Now, I have even more juice because thinking about Suze makes me powerful. I am mighty and nimble and I make love like an angel.

The sound returns. *Bip-bip.* A car horn? No, something electronic. I ride faster, put it behind me. Whatever it is, it has nothing to do with me. I'm on a mission to get to school so I can see Suze's face. Her dark pink lips, the wrinkle above her nose when she smiles, her long beautiful neck, her—

"Pull over!"

I peer over my shoulder and spot a police cruiser.

"Pull. Over."

A black minivan drives past. They must be after whoever's driving it. But when the siren squeals behind me, I realize they didn't speed up and chase it down. In fact, they're driving behind *me*.

268

When I get to the corner of Cherry and Main, I look for Marcus, but he's not there yet. I'm probably early because I've been riding so hard.

"Pull! Over!"

That's when I realize they're talking to me. They want *me* to pull over.

I turn left onto Main Street then again onto Elm. I don't even know where I'm going. I just know I have to get away. Are they here to arrest me? To question me? Do they know about Suze?

Suze. I have to warn her. I have to lose this police car and get to school by some other route. Elm Street slips beneath my wheels like water, like air, like pure speed. At the end of Elm Street there's an entrance to the woods. I know I'm sleek enough—even on my bike—to slip around the chain link fence and keep going down the rocky path. I can ride straight through, dump my bike and sneak into school to warn Suze.

But then my mother's words come to me:

Never run from the police.

In my mind's eye, I see my father nodding his head, like this is the Number One Thing I have to know. If I stop knowing everything else in life, I have to know this.

Never run from the police.

Now I understand why they had The Talk with me so many times, why they drilled it into me, or tried to anyway. They wanted it to be an instinct. Not a rule, but an automatic reflex. Because in the heat of the moment, you forget everything. When the police show up, all you want to do is run.

Do you realize the phone call I could have gotten instead of the one I did get?

I'm closing in on the chain link fence. The woods beyond it are thick and dark, the perfect cover. Once I'm on the other side, they can chase all they want and they'll never catch me.

But I promised my parents.

And I don't want to die.

I stop and let my bike drop to the dirt in front of the fence, then I turn around to face the patrol car as it screeches to a halt. I throw my hands in the air. I remember that part. *Let them see your hands, make sure they can see that you don't have a weapon. Don't make any sudden moves. Don't reach for anything in your pockets.* It's all coming back because they made me recite this again and again. I understand why, too. It's so you don't have to summon the memory or the reasons from your head. It's just stuck in there, like the seven times table.

I stand spread-legged in front of the chain link fence with my bike at my feet. My hands are over my head and my fingers are wide open, so they can see that there's nothing in there. Officer Scaletti gets out of the patrol car first and waddles over, jowls shaking. His partner, Officer Dagmoor, comes out afterward. These are the officers who arrested me in the cafeteria. Officer Dagmoor stands in front of the car and points her gun right at my chest.

"Why did you run?" Officer Scaletti asks me.

Don't speak. Don't say a word. You have the right to remain silent. There is nothing to be gained from speaking to the police.

I stare into the barrel of Officer Dagmoor's gun. She has a wide stance and a straight back. She's fit, strong, knows how to carry herself. The brim of her blue hat dips low, but I can make out her eyes. They're cold and focused. She's ready to put a bullet in my heart.

"We just wanted to talk to you," Officer Scaletti says while grabbing my right wrist. "Now we gotta do this." He cuffs me then walks me back to the patrol car.

Probable cause. I remember that now from The Talk. It's why you should never run from the police. If you run, it gives them a reason to arrest you.

Officer Scaletti opens the back door and puts his hand on my head right where it's bruised from that rock by the pond. But I don't say anything. I let him put me in the car. It's the same one as last time, the same smell of Burger King onion rings and ketchup. Officer Dagmoor gets into the passenger seat and puts her hat on the dashboard. Her fingernails are shiny red. She never looks at me. The car sags when Scaletti gets in behind the wheel.

"You find that game for your nephew?" Scaletti asks Dagmoor, like I'm not even there.

"Got him a gift card instead."

"Probably better."

Scaletti backs up and drives off, leaving my bike in front of the chain link fence, which means someone will probably steal it later. But I don't mention that. I keep my mouth shut for the whole ride. And they don't ask me a thing.

NIKKI

When I pull into the school parking lot the next morning, I put the car in park and just sit behind the wheel. I've been calling Suze nonstop since last night, but she's still not picking up. I don't know what's happened to her, if she's been arrested, or if she's just lying low. When the first bell rings, I watch people rush to the entrance, but I don't move. Ani's Volvo sits two spaces down, which means she and Lydia are already inside. I know I have to talk to them about what happened last night, but I want to wait until the last possible second. I keep looking at the parking lot entrance, hoping to see Suze's silver Prius rounding the corner. But it doesn't, and when the late bell rings, I drag myself out to face the inevitable.

Inside the school, I keep my head down. After last night's multi-platform slut-shaming festival, I can feel people's eyes on me, roaming, judging, sizing me up, comparing what they see to what they've heard, what they've read. I've kept as low a profile as I possibly could here, which has earned me a reputation as a mean girl. That's fine. I'd rather be mean and ignored than nice and noticed. Now I'm back in the limelight. It's like freshman year all over again.

"There's the bitch," I hear some guy mutter. He's with a group of sophomores, so I don't even know which one said it. I detour into the girls' room and lock myself in a stall.

Those guys don't matter. They mean nothing. I just have to remember that. Other people's opinions are just that: *other* people's opinions. This philosophy was the bonus of surviving freshman year and it served me well. It was like a hard shell that stood between them and me. I just have to regrow that shell.

When I step out of the stall, Missy Devry is just coming into the bathroom, pulling stray bobby pins out of her French twist. She clocks me, does a quick internal assessment, then averts her eyes and heads to the mirror to fix her hair. But I can read everything in that glance. She knows. She's read what people have written. She won't bother being cruel about it. She's a quiet girl, she's endured her share of bullying, largely because of her ample breasts (honestly, that's all it takes). But she also doesn't want to be associated with me in any way.

I have this powerful urge to explain myself to her, to set the record straight. Not just about Suze and Tarkin, but about *me* and Tarkin. To tell her that what he said about me freshman year was wrong.

Why do I still want that? Why do I still care? Where is that goddamn shell?

When I head back into the hallway, I keep my eyes on the green linoleum floor. My inner monologue is going: *I am Wonder Woman's shield. I am impenetrable. You don't matter. And you don't matter. You especially don't matter.* I still don't feel protected, but by the time I get to the East Wing I've started to feel numb, which is something. It's like slipping under an old blanket, one of the heavy ones you only use in winter. When I arrive at my locker, someone has taped a picture to it. Radley Sebert and his mousy pal, Elliott something-or-other, have obviously seen it too, because they're cowering two lockers down.

"What the hell, Sebert?" I say.

Sebert's a sophomore, scrawny and meek. "It was Tony Petrof," he says. "I saw him tape it there."

Tony Petrof, as in Tony "Mad Dog" Petrof, a varsity wrestler. Paint me shocked. And what did this budding artistic genius create? Only a shitty inkjet print of my face photoshopped onto some naked girl's body. She's fake-tan orange with even faker tits, like giant water balloons. My God do these bozos find big tits funny.

"I was going to take it down for you," Radley Sebert says, "but—"

But Tony "Mad Dog" Petrof would have kicked his ass into the next century over something like that.

"Don't worry about it," I tell him, like it doesn't even bother me. That's another thing I learned freshman year. If you're not okay with what's happening to you, the trick is to act like someone who is. Fake it. Picture the hardest, coldest, meanest bad-ass you can think of—personally, I like Cersei Lannister for this—then just pretend you're her. Don't ever let them think they've gotten to you. It won't inspire sympathy. It just makes them come after you harder. They smell weakness like a jackal smells an injured gazelle.

I rip the picture down and stuff it into my backpack, then grab my books for the first two periods and make my way to Ani and Lydia's lockers around the corner.

"Hey, slut. How are your slut friends?" Brendan Manaforte drops that one as a drive-by, then high-fives his buddy, Pete.

I have about a million comebacks, but I don't want to engage him. That was another lesson from freshman year. Don't ever defend yourself. They'll just come back at you harder. And meaner. Trolls always win because they play by different rules. They have no conscience, no decency, and no empathy. And it doesn't matter how irrational their claims are, or how soundly you discredit them, they'll just change tacks and come at you another way. Their arsenal is infinite, because all they care about is inflicting pain. It doesn't matter if it's online or IRL.

When Ani sees me coming, she cringes, like she knows I'm mad about what she did last night. Lydia is digging around the bottom of her locker. I know I have to get these two in line. They can't be out there freestyling on Facebook to satisfy Lydia's hunger for vengeance. But at that moment, all I feel for them is love. I'm not even mad at them. They're my girls. And sometimes you just need your girls around you. I go straight up to Ani and hug her.

"Did we mess up?" she says into my shoulder. "With that post? Is Suze mad at us?"

Lydia stands up, defiant. "No, we didn't mess up, Ani. That shitstain Princely had it coming." She slams her locker door shut.

Someone has Sharpied WHORE on it in huge black letters. Surprisingly, they've spelled it right. Probably the one word they actually know how to spell. Lydia opens up a black lipstick she found on her locker floor and writes "Sean Princely is a . . ." above it.

"Have you seen Suze yet?" Ani asks me.

"No. I don't think we'll be seeing Suze today."

"Good," Lydia says. "She doesn't need to be here for this. People are disgusting. Not that she should care what anyone thinks. Let them say what they want."

"Yeah, you know what, though." Ani's voice is shaking. "I'm not really into being threatened with gang rape."

"Then start carrying this." Lydia pulls a set of keys out of her pocket.

"What am I supposed to do with keys?"

"Actually, there's a lot you can do with keys. But this"—she shakes the black plastic medallion they're dangling from—"is a panic alarm."

Ani looks around nervously, then shoves Lydia's hand back down. "Oh my God, Lydia, are you even allowed to have that here?"

Lydia shrugs then stuffs it into the front pocket of her jeans.

"Where'd you even get that?" I ask her.

"My dad. He thinks I should carry a gun. And actually? I'm starting to think he's right."

"But you're against guns," Ani says.

"My opinion is evolving."

"Lydia!"

"I believe in the Second Amendment. But only for girls." Lydia looks from Ani to me, her face hardening. "Are *you* going to lecture me now?"

"About guns?"

"No, about that post. You think we were wrong to do it, right?"

Lydia wants to fight, which is typical. Fighting is her go-to strategy. She and I have been down this road plenty of times before. We'll get into a big messy argument and she'll go off and sulk for a while. Then she'll come back like it never happened. No apology, no admission of guilt. She's like a little kid that way. Never holds a grudge. Buy her a Froyo and everything is forgotten. Put some sprinkles on it, she's your friend for life. I sort of love that about her. I carry grudges forever.

"I don't even see why you're mad at us," she says.

"Do I look mad?"

"Chasing us to Dunkin's."

"You wouldn't answer your phone."

"'Cause we knew you'd tell us to take it down."

"Yes, I would."

"Well, what does Suze think? Because I know you think she wants us to keep everything hushed up, but does she actually want people thinking she put those pictures out there herself? Because that's what everybody's saying."

"I don't know, I haven't talked to her. But the police have." That knocks the defiant look off of Lydia's face.

Ani grabs my arm. "Are you serious?"

"They were at her house last night."

"To question her?"

"Maybe."

"Oh my God," Ani says. "Did they arrest her?"

"I don't know. I had Marcus with me, so I couldn't stick around. All I saw was two cops talking to Suze's parents in the living room."

"Maybe they were just there to question her," Lydia says. She whips out her phone and tries to call Suze, but it's no use. Suze isn't answering.

"There's more," I say. I tell them about the reporter who figured out that Tarkin was sextorting

Suze. I tell them the cops probably figured it out, too, because of the pictures, and how they could call that a motive for killing Tarkin.

Lydia keeps calling Suze, texting her, searching for her dot on FriendFinder. "Damn it, where is she?"

"Oh my God," Ani says. "Do you think she's in jail?"

"I don't know, Ani," I say.

But I can't rule it out.

BETWEEN THIRD AND fourth period, Marcus spots the three of us walking to the gym and heads after us.

"Not this guy," Lydia says.

"No, he's all right," I tell her.

"Since when?"

Marcus looks nervous as he catches up and walks with us. "Any word from Suze?" he asks.

I shake my head.

"Did you tell them about—"

"Yeah, we know," Lydia says.

"About the police?"

"Yeah. And about your friend the reporter."

"She's not a friend. She's a colleague."

"Whatever. We're up to speed on the new *spin*."

"Our friend, the exhibitionist," Ani adds, cringing.

"I know it sucks," he says. "But—"

"Yeah, okay, whatever," Lydia says. I may have

softened a bit on the Marcus Daubney question, but Lydia still sees him as an interloper. The fact that he was there when Tarkin died makes it a bit too easy for her to blame this whole mess on him. Which doesn't actually make sense. But that's Lydia for you.

Just then a handful of varsity wrestlers head our way, doing that stupid walk where their thighs get in the way because they're so bulked up. They move like boulders stacked on top of other boulders. They don't say anything, they just slow down and look at us real cold. I don't want Lydia getting any ideas about lashing out, so I grab her arm and dig my fingers into it, which is something my mom used to do in church when I acted up. It always brought me right in line.

"Yo, Daubney," Russ Minichek says, "careful you don't catch anything."

"Yeah. Those bitches are crawling with crotch critters." Aaron Paulson has to laugh at his own "joke" because no one else does.

"I'm good," Marcus says. "Thanks for your concern, though."

"What did you just say?" Minichek gets right up in Marcus's face. He's about four inches taller than Marcus and twice as wide.

But Marcus doesn't flinch. "Is that how you big yourself up?" he says. "Picking on girls? Trolling them online? Oh, learn to spell, by the way."

"You're fucking dead," Minichek says.

Marcus's eyes wander up to the ceiling. "Now, where have I heard that before?"

Minichek grabs him by the T-shirt and slams him into a locker. "Where's your boyfriend now?"

"Ow," Marcus says. "Is that all you guys can do? Push people up against lockers? No wonder your team had such a shitty record last year."

My God, the mouth on this kid. It's like he's drawn to trouble. On the other hand, I'm sick of the wrestlers throwing their weight around this place. And I'm sick of being afraid of them. I shove my arm between Minichek and Marcus and try to pry them apart. Minichek is much stronger than me, but just like Tarkin, he'd never be seen hitting a girl. He twists my arm away, which frees up Marcus to kick him in the shins.

"Motherfucker!" Minichek yells.

Marcus grabs my hand and pulls me away.

Then Lydia jumps in with a punch to the back of Minichek's neck. It's her dad's signature move, something he calls the "dirty win." Minichek howls in protest.

Ani, meanwhile, has shrunk back and pressed herself against someone's locker. She's just shaking, waiting for this to end. Paulson and the other wrestlers go after Lydia now, grabbing her by the arms and dragging her away. But she's so full of muscle and rage, she doesn't go easy. She kicks and squirms like a pissed-off weasel.

Then there's a noise so loud, so piercing, that everyone ducks and cringes in pain.

It's Lydia's panic alarm, reverberating off the walls. It sounds like a car alarm, but inside your head.

"HOW CAN I convince you kids that fighting is not the answer?"

Principal Everett leans over his desk, aiming his bald patch at me, Ani, Lydia, Marcus, Minichek and four other wrestlers. Lydia's black panic alarm sits on the desk between his hands.

"Marcus," he says, "I'm disappointed to see you in here. Again."

"Well, maybe you can convince the wrestling team that I am not interested in a physical relationship. Because they won't take my word for it."

That mouth of his. It's like he's physically incapable of not stirring the pot. But I feel like I should defend him, since he defended us. Or tried to, at least.

"Yeah, this was all them," I say. "We were just minding our own business trying to get to class on time when these guys came over and accused us of having STIs. Which is not true."

"We're *grieving*," Aaron Paulson says. "We're in mourning because of the Tarks, and they've been talking shi—I mean, trash about us."

"Excuse me," Lydia says. "I never said anything about *you*. All I did was write the truth, which is that Sean Princely hacked those pictures out of Tarkin Shaw's computer, which, by the way, Suze only meant for his eyes."

Extra points for shoehorning the new spin into the situation.

"Then," she goes on, "he posted them *illegally*, and without her knowledge or consent, on a porn site. How is that supposed to be okay, Principal Everett? Why isn't Sean Princely in here?"

"Um, excuse me," Tony "Mad Dog" Petrof says, "but is it legal to break someone's eardrums with that alarm thing?"

"Is it legal to threaten someone with gang rape?" Lydia shoots back.

Principal Everett's mouth drops open, like he's about to say something. Then he runs his hand over his bald patch and sits down like someone's just knocked the wind out of him. When he finally speaks, he sounds queasy and disgusted. "What are you kids *doing* to each other?"

Ha! Old man doesn't know the half of it. If he heard even a fraction of the vile shit that floats around in this place, he wouldn't sit here so smugly with his inspirational posters and naïve pep talks about "the power of communication." If you ask me, we need less communication at this school, not more. Kids should walk from class to class in total silence, stewing on whatever happens to be the bullshit of the week. If I were principal, that would be my first rule. No talking. Ever.

"So are you going to expel me?" Lydia asks him, eyeballing the panic alarm. "Because I only used that for my own self-defense and I can prove it."

"I'm not expelling anyone."

"Really?" Marcus says. "Not even them?" He sticks his thumb out at the wrestlers. "How many fights do they get to start before one of them gets kicked out? Are you waiting for them to actually kill someone? Because I wouldn't put it past them. This loser may have bruised my ribs. And Tarkin Shaw almost broke my face."

"Don't you say his name!" Aaron Paulson shouts. "Don't you *ever* say his name."

"I'll say what I want," Marcus says, "and at least I have the balls to say it out in the open. Not like you guys, making rape and death threats online."

"What's this now?" Principal Everett asks. He looks nervous. Like maybe he doesn't want the answer to his own question.

"It's all online," I say. "If you're so concerned, why don't you look?"

"Yeah," Lydia adds. "There's nothing subtle about it. They literally threatened to rape and murder us on Facebook."

"That was a joke," Paulson says.

"A joke?" I say. "Really?" If anyone knows what these sports douches are capable of, it's me. And joking is definitely not on their list of talents. I can feel myself getting angry and I do my best to rein it in, because I know that it will backfire somehow.

"Last night you threatened to *rape and murder* us. Then today you and your posse surround us in the hallway. And we're supposed to assume you're *joking*?"

"I think they call that a pattern of abuse," Marcus says.

"Yeah," Lydia agrees, pointing to Marcus. "I read about that. Oh, oh, show him the picture, Nikki. You know, the one on your locker."

Everett's face darkens. "What picture?"

I pull it out of my backpack, uncrinkle it, and slap it down on Principal Everett's desk. "That's not my body, by the way."

Everett glances at it, winces, then turns it upside down. "Wh . . . what is that?" He looks embarrassed, like right about now he's questioning his decision to pursue a career in education.

I point at Tony Petrof. "He taped it to my locker."

"I did not."

"You were seen, you idiot. There were witnesses."

"Yeah," Lydia says, "and I bet Ani can hack into your computer and find the porn website you took the picture from. Right, Ani?"

Ani doesn't want to answer. She's too freaked out by this whole thing. But her pride as a hacker is too powerful to override, so she nods her head very quickly.

"I bet it's super violent, too," Lydia says. "That's what they're into. Violent hate porn. You know what you should do, Principal Everett? You should expel all the wrestlers and cancel the wrestling program. To send a message."

The wrestlers harrumph, fidget, and smirk, like no way would this ever happen because wrestling is so important. Oh my God, they won their division once. *Once*, like a million years ago.

Everett shakes his head. "Look, we have got to get a handle on things here, okay? This is a good school, and—"

"No, it's not," Marcus says. "Wakefield is a good school. Fenwick is a good school. Jonesville High is a substandard piece of crap. Everyone knows that. The only thing Jonesville High ever did to distinguish itself was win one lousy division championship in wrestling. And that was, like, five years ago. Talk about clinging to past glory. Is that why you let the wrestlers act like such dicks? Or is it their parents and all the money they have? Is that how you got Amber Laynes to drop out of school? Did Shaw's parents get to you?"

Marcus may have overplayed his hand here, because now Everett is pissed. "Are you quite finished?"

"Not really. I have a lot of questions, Principal Everett. Like why did you call the cops on my friend, DeShawn, but not on the wrestlers? Is it because he's Black?"

Everett points at him like his finger is an actual gun, as if that's enough to stop this whole line of questioning.

287

"Should I take that as a yes?" Marcus says.

"I think you've made your point, Marcus. Maybe you ought to watch your mouth for a day or two. It might keep you out of trouble."

"Right. Silence the reporter," he says, "but not the violent thugs who keep attacking him. Got it."

"That's not what I said."

"It sort of is."

"Yeah," I say. "You definitely implied that, Principal Everett. Because I don't hear you criticizing the wrestlers for anything."

"All right, everyone out of here," Everett says. "Get back to class." He puts the panic alarm into a desk drawer and makes meaningful eye contact with Lydia. "If I catch any of you with one of these again, I'm calling the police. This ends *now*. Do you understand?"

"Sure," Lydia says. "But if one of these guys attacks me, that's on you, Principal Everett. You all right with that? Because I wouldn't be."

"Me neither," I say.

"Me neither," Marcus adds.

Principal Everett looks at us, then at the wrestlers, then back at us. But he doesn't say anything.

He just looks very, very tired.

DESHAWN

This is what I get for "resisting arrest." Officer Dagmoor takes my fingerprints with one of those electronic scanners, then she puts me in a tiny room with a yellow Formica table and four blue plastic chairs and tells me she'll be back "in a bit." She's not mean about it, but she's not nice, either. She seems distracted, like I don't actually matter that much. She has other things to attend to and she'll get around to me eventually.

"A bit" stretches out past an hour, then past two. Normally I'm okay with solitude. But this is different from being alone in the hole. This is being alone in a scary, threatening place. To keep myself from going crazy, I start picking at the table, trying to flake off bits of chipped Formica in interesting patterns. Up close, I realize it's yellowed, not yellow. It was once white. Not that this matters. Sometimes details soothe me.

After two and half hours have passed, Officer Dagmoor comes in with a can of soda and puts it on the table. I don't touch it because I don't drink soda. Officer Scaletti comes in behind her. They sit on the other side of the yellowed Formica table and stare at me—again, not angrily, just neutral, like they're waiting for something.

Eventually, Scaletti asks, "So why'd you run?"

I look down at the section of Formica I've chipped off. It sort of looks like a dog, or half of a dog.

"Maybe there's an innocent reason for it," Dagmoor says. "DeShawn, did you panic? Is that why you ran?" She's using a surprisingly gentle voice. Based on our previous encounters, I was expecting it to be sharper.

When I don't answer, they look at each other in frustration. I don't know why. I didn't answer their questions the last time I was here either. They ought to be used to it by now.

"Okay, look, here's the thing," Scaletti says. "Maybe you can help us out with this one. Tarkin Shaw. Tragic story, am I right? Seventeen years old, bright future, wrestling captain."

"It's a shame," Dagmoor says. "Real, real sad."

"Would you agree with that, DeShawn? Would you agree that it's sad?

Actually, I *don't* agree that it's sad. I agree that it's tragic, but not sad. There's a difference. Tragedy is a rational assessment of an event. Any time a young person dies it's tragic, because young people aren't supposed to die. Old people are. But it's only sad if the person's death diminishes the world in some way. From what I know about Tarkin Shaw, the world is better off without him. So no, I don't agree that his death is sad.

I say none of this.

"Okay, how about this," Scaletti says. "How about we knock off the bullshit and get down to business?"

"I think he wants to help us, Paul. Don't you, De-Shawn? You want to help us, right?"

Scaletti shifts his bulk uncomfortably and glares at Dagmoor like he's had enough of the silent treatment. Dagmoor looks like she feels bad for me. Or maybe she just wants me to think that. Possibly, they're setting up to play good cop/bad cop. But I can't be sure because I only have movies and TV to go by.

"Here's the thing, kid," Scaletti says. "We've been talking to Tarkin's parents, his brother, his coach, some of his friends—a lot of people, actually—and none of them said anything about the two of you being friends. You weren't friends, right? You and the Shaw kid? Did you hang out?"

"Did you text each other?" Dagmoor asks.

"Throw back a few beers?" Scaletti now. "No? Okay, that's what I thought. So, unless you tell us differently, we're going to assume you and Tarkin Shaw were not friends."

"Seems reasonable," Dagmoor says.

"Feel free to correct us, though."

"I don't think they were friends, Paul. I think we can move forward with that assumption. For now.

We can always revisit that later." She taps the table twice.

"So, here's what I can't figure out," Scaletti says. "If you and the Shaw kid weren't friends, why were your fingerprints all over his bedroom?"

He stares at me while his jowls settle, like he's just delivered the death blow. And all I can see is my stupid hands all over Shaw's stuff. His printer, his laptop, his bookshelves, his shoes, his bedside table. I touched almost every single thing in that room. And now, because I ran from the police, they have my fingerprints on file.

"*Fresh* prints," Scaletti adds. "Did you guys have a sleepover? Because there's a lot of people in the world I'm not friends with and none of them have ever left fingerprints in my bedroom. You let people who aren't friends into your bedroom, Ellen?"

"I'm not sure I want to talk about what goes on in my bedroom, Paul." She laughs good-naturedly and Scaletti joins in.

Do they know I'm panicking? I haven't spoken or moved, but what if there's some micro adjustment in my posture that they're trained to spot? Are they filming this? I don't see a camera anywhere.

"Did Tarkin invite you over?" Dagmoor asks. "Let's start with that."

"'Cause we're talking about a *lot* of prints, De-Shawn. Not just a few. You must have got real comfortable in there, touched a lot of things. Were you looking for something?"

"The place was a mess."

"Ha!" Scaletti says. "You should see my place."

"No thanks."

Now they both laugh, but it's not very convincing. I feel like they're putting on a show for me. And even though they're not very good at it, it's actually working. I'm scared as shit right now.

"Come on, DeShawn, help us out here," Dagmoor says. "If there's an innocent explanation, just tell us. Help us understand."

"You seem like a smart kid," Scaletti says. "You a smart kid?

"Straight As. That's what I hear. Plans for college. MIT, right? Isn't that what Principal Everett told us?"

Scaletti whistles. "MIT. Wow. Not a lot of Jonesville kids end up there. Sure would be a shame to jeopardize that."

"A real shame."

They both stare at me expectantly. I guess they're trying out the silent treatment, waiting for me to buckle. But that'll never work on me. I can be silent for hours, days. I could give up talking for good if I had to.

Scaletti's the first to break. "Listen kid, I know you think you're being smart here, keeping your mouth shut."

"Which is your right," Dagmoor says. "Let's not forget that."

"Yeah, yeah, he knows his rights. But let me paint a picture for you. Are you paying attention?"

"Ease up, Paul."

"No. I want this *genius* to understand what he's putting at risk here."

"Excuse my partner, DeShawn. He gets a little hot sometimes."

Good cop/bad cop, just like I thought. Only I would have gone the other way. Dagmoor is way more intimidating. She looks strong and icy, with the kind of focus you get from serious training. I wonder what she does. Maybe judo. Scaletti looks like his only exercise is shuffling over to the trash can with those Burger King wrappers. Plus his jowls shake every time he moves his head, which undermines his authority.

Still, I'm panicking. The fingerprints are a disaster. I never should have run. I never should have caused that scene in the cafeteria either. I've screwed everything up. I let instinct overrule reason. Why did I do that? I don't think Marcus would have made these mistakes. He has a big mouth, but he'd never run from the cops.

"This is a nice town," Scaletti says. "A nice, small, quiet town. I know we're not Wenham or Marblehead. But it's good people here. Good, hardworking people. They don't expect much, but they do expect their kids to wake up every day alive."

"My partner gets emotional sometimes."

"Damn right I get emotional. We've got a dead

kid on our hands. And people are looking to us to explain how that happened. You know what it's like to look a dead kid's parents in the eye?"

Dagmoor shakes her head. "It's the hardest part of the job."

"They want answers, DeShawn. They want to know why their son isn't going to college like you are. They want to know why their son will never get married, never have children. And these are influential people, the Shaws. When they want answers, they get them. Now, what am I supposed to tell them? Am I supposed to look these people in the eye and say, *Sorry your son's dead, but we can't help you. We've got nothing.*"

"They have a right to know, DeShawn. Don't you think?"

They wait me out. I guess they're playing on my sympathy. Or trying to. And I do feel bad for Tarkin Shaw's parents. I can't even imagine what it must feel like to lose a child. But this isn't about how I feel. It's about me being smart. And right now, being smart means being quiet. I have parents, too. And they don't want me winding up in jail because I couldn't keep my mouth shut.

Scaletti starts stroking his chin like he just thought of something. It's so fake. He should take acting classes. Or maybe just be honest. "But actually, we don't have *nothing*. We've got you in the dead kid's room, putting your hands all over his stuff."

"It does sort of jump out at you."

"We also have you beating the kid up the day before he died. How do you think that looks, De-Shawn? Do you think that paints a pretty picture?"

"Plus there's that ruckus in the cafeteria," Dagmoor adds.

"Holy shit, I forgot about that." No he didn't. "Wrap this puppy up, Ellen. I don't know why we're wasting our time here. We got this. We don't even need his statement."

"Hold on, hold on, Paul. Let's slow down. De-Shawn, at least help us understand *why* you did it." She cocks her head to the side, which I think is meant to convey sympathy. "Did he hurt you? Did he threaten you?" She waits. "You had to have a reason, DeShawn. Nobody does something like this for no reason. Come on, help us out. Are there extenuating circumstances? Did you have a thing with his girlfriend? Is that what this is about?"

Dagmoor has pretty eyes. Pretty, cold, blue eyes.

"If you don't help us," she says, "we can't help you. You know that, right? Keep us on your side here."

"Ah, forget him," Scaletti says. "He ain't talking. Thinks he's smarter than us."

Dagmoor narrows her icy blue eyes at me like she can see into my soul. But I know she can't. She's too busy seeing what she wants to see.

A killer.

MARCUS

I'm in the back of trig class alone, because De-Shawn has decided to take the day off from school. No call, no text, nothing. I waited longer than usual at the Cherry Street junction for him, too. It's not like DeShawn to be incommunicado. But then again, DeShawn has not been himself lately. Or, more accurately, he's been a peculiar version of himself. I keep looking for his dot on my phone, but he seems to have turned his off. We're not supposed to be on our phones in class, but I have devised clever ways around everything this school tries to stop me from doing. My phone is set to vibrate, and unlike other kids who openly gawp into their crotches and laugh idiotically at whatever moronic blurt someone has sent them, I know to take surreptitious glances downward and read my phone in small sips so as to give my teachers the illusion that I'm paying very close attention to whatever bullroar they're feeding me. As an added flourish, I can mask my downward glances with determined fake note-taking. I have whole pages

filled with random Spanish conjugations and pretend math.

About halfway through trig, my thigh vibrates.
It's a text from Elena.

We need to talk about DeShawn.

A short intake of breath. Stacey Galinsky, sitting
in the desk right in front of me, turns around annoyed. Beneath my desk, I slyly type out.

Why? What's going on?

Up at the whiteboard, Mr. Daniels turns around
suddenly and waits for one of us to fill in the blank
he's left in the equation. When no one volunteers,
he casts his disappointed eye among the rows in
search of a worthy victim, settling finally on Dawn
Jameson, who never answers anything.

"Um—" Dawn says.

Behind her, Prince Bouchard, class nerd, whispers the answer.

"Thank you, *Prince*," Mr. Daniels says, returning to the whiteboard.

My thigh vibrates again. Elena.

My place. Now. Cut school.

Two rows in front of me, Colin Marsalis drops
his cell phone to the floor with a hugely disruptive
clatter. Mr. Daniels springs for it like a panther and
deposits it into his desk drawer. After a single cas-
tigating glare around the class, he returns to the
whiteboard.

Although I've successfully masked my texting
so far, I'm practically hyperventilating on the back

of poor Stacey Galinsky's neck. Feeling my hot breath, she turns around and says, "What the hell, Daubney?"

Mr. Daniels whips around, irritated.

"He's breathing down my neck," Stacey says.

I freeze for a second, then realize that panic and nausea are probably very similar in appearance. "I think I'm about to puke," I say.

"Well, don't do it here." Mr. Daniels gestures at the door.

"Thanks," I say, holding my stomach as I exit the classroom.

Once in the hallway, I do not go to the bathroom, as Mr. Daniels undoubtedly expects. I head straight for the exit by the music room, which opens into the parking lot. I jog to the bike rack by the soccer field, calling DeShawn all the while. He doesn't pick up. What could Elena mean? Is he dead? Was he hit by a car on the way to school?

When I get to the bike rack, a handful of freshmen eyeball me curiously from the lacrosse game they're limply playing for gym class. I crouch down and unlock my bike as inconspicuously as possible. A lacrosse ball meanders over the lip of the field onto the parking lot in front of me and I crouch behind my bike to hide, which makes about as much sense as hiding behind an open window. Helen Pickering jogs lazily over to retrieve the ball, regards me with minor curiosity, then returns to the game.

WHEN ELENA DESCRIBED her neighborhood to me once, I assumed she was exaggerating. Turns out she was right. It *is* a slum. I didn't realize we had slums on the North Shore. Rough parts, sure, but this forlorn strip of degradation looks like it would be more at home in the more derelict parts of Boston. I lock my bike to a broken parking meter in front of a shoe repair place that's almost certainly a front for meth dealers. It says Sadie's Shoe Repair, but there are no shoes inside, just a reedy white guy sitting on a metal stool, eating an Italian ice with a butter knife. Elena lives above the dry cleaners next door, which looks like it's been abandoned for decades. I mount the rusty steps bolted to the outside of the building and bang on her door.

Eventually, she opens it wearing cutoff jean shorts and a shredded Nirvana T-shirt that reveals a crescent of suntanned stomach. "That was fast."

"Is he dead?"

"No."

I'm so relieved I practically melt onto her threshold.

She opens the door wider. "You coming in or what?"

I follow her inside the one-room apartment. She goes straight to the mini fridge and produces two cans of PBR. I crack mine open and the first swig goes straight to my head.

"So what's going on?" I ask.

Elena opens hers and has a sip. "Police arrested him this morning."

"What?!"

She picks up a yellow legal pad from the top of a pile of newspapers and scans her notes. "How well do you know him?"

"Wait. Back up. What did they arrest him for?"

"What do you *think* they arrested him for?"

"Um . . ." I trail off. I'm guessing they've arrested him for stealing Tarkin Shaw's hard drive, but something tells me it could be worse than that.

"Where was he on Monday night?" she asks.

"Monday?" I stall. Where *could* he have been? Where *would* he have been if we hadn't gone to Shaw's house that night? "He was in his basement."

Elena shifts weight, stares at me, incredulous.

"With me. It's where we hang. He has a whole robotics lab down there. Yeah." I pretend to think about that night. "We were definitely there Monday night."

"What were you doing?"

"Talking."

"About what?"

"Plastic and resin modeling, Marlon Brando movies, girls."

Lies of course. But they could be true. These are all topics we've covered in the past. I could spin off any number of facts about plastic and resin modeling. I could also name DeShawn's three favorite Marlon Brando movies: *On the Waterfront, Mutiny on the Bounty,* and *Apocalypse Now.*

"So why were his fingerprints found all over Tarkin Shaw's bedroom?"

A wave of nausea ripples through me.

"The police fingerprinted him after he fled on his bike," she says. "Came up with a match. Puts him at Shaw's house."

I sink into a vintage red chair, which releases a breathy sigh through the cracked leather. Fingerprints. Of course. DeShawn and I must have touched every single object in that room, every trophy, every stained coffee cup, every pungent, sweaty T-shirt.

"They like him for the murder," she says. "Schnell's waiting for the inches."

"He didn't do it."

"How do you know? And don't give me that bullshit about being in his basement. I know he was there."

She can't know that. She's bluffing. She has to be. The fingerprints are bad, but they don't prove that he was there Monday night. What if he was there over the weekend? Yeah, what if he broke into Shaw's house on Sunday night to steal his hard drive. That could work. That would explain the fingerprints. Sure, he'd still be guilty of theft, but at least it keeps him away from Shaw's death.

"Fine," she says. "I'll write it up as is." She reaches for her laptop underneath some magazines and opens the lid. "I thought you might have some information that could help your friend, but if you don't—"

"You can't write that. It's not true."

"It *is* true. They *did* arrest him."

"But he didn't do it."

She slams the laptop shut. "Then who did?"

When I don't answer right away, she seethes for a second then pulls out a dirty white Ikea folding chair and drags it right up to the red leather chair I'm sitting in. She turns it backward and sits down, a long bare leg on either side, her bare feet touching the tips of my sneakers. "Let's put a pin in DeShawn Hill for a minute," she says, quietly, calmly, like we're starting over and she's prepared to cut me some slack for being dishonest. "Talk to me about Suze Tilman."

"What about her?"

"Where is she? Have you heard from her? Has— what's that girl's name?" She leans back and grabs that yellow legal pad off the table, flips back a few pages. "Nikki Petronzio. Nice Italian name. Has Nikki heard from Suze?"

"I don't know. Why?"

"Suze wasn't at school today, right?"

"I—didn't see her, but—"

"Was Nikki?"

I nod vaguely, trying to give the impression that I hardly noticed Nikki.

"Did you talk to her?"

"No." As soon as I say it, I picture the two of us standing side by side in Principal Everett's office earlier in the day. Elena will no doubt find that out, too, if she hasn't already.

"What aren't you telling me?" she asks.

"Nothing. I swear."

303

"Marcus, please. You're a terrible liar."

"I'm not lying."

"Yes, you are. Every time you lie, you swallow first and your eyes flick to the right."

So help me God, I swallow nervously. And it takes all of my willpower to keep my eyes steady.

"It's a classic tell," she says. "It's kind of adorable."

At any other time, being found adorable by Elena DePiero would be the highlight of my day, especially with her sitting so close I can smell her fruity shampoo. But today she's not dangerously sexy. Today she's just dangerous.

"Is Suze—"

"Missing," she says. "Yes. The police went to her house last night to question her."

"To *question* her?" I thought they'd gone there to arrest her.

"Yeah. About her dead boyfriend. Remember him? Her parents said she was out walking in the woods or something. So the cops tell her parents to bring her in to the station the next morning, which is today. Her parents say fine, sure, no problem. They're certain little Suze wants to help in any way she can. Yadda yadda. Only they never show up. You really don't know about this?"

I shake my head.

"Well, that was this morning," she says. "So the cops go back to Tilman's house around noontime to ask what's up. And no answer. Nobody home."

"Wait, so her parents are gone too?"

Elena shrugs. "You tell me." She leans back, and as she sizes me up I feel like a goat dropped into a tiger's cage.

"Elena, I'm sorry but I have no idea where she or her parents are."

She stares me down, willing me to tell her everything I know.

"Fine," she says. "Then I'll just write about DeShawn."

"But he didn't do it."

"If it turns out the police arrested the wrong guy, I'll report that later."

"No! Elena, you know how that works. A correction never makes as big of a splash as the original story. Just having this article out there could destroy him."

"Then give me the real killer." She leans forward hungrily and I half-expect a second jaw to spring from her mouth and clamp around my neck. "I'm publishing something," she says. "And I want it out before the police make a statement."

"When's that going to happen?"

"Tomorrow morning. They want to meet with Shaw's family first."

So that's it. She wants her scoop. She wants to be in there with the story before the police make it public knowledge and the rest of the press dive in.

"So what's it gonna be?" She cocks her head and waits, then waits some more, her right leg bouncing gently against the seat of the chair. She's got me and she knows it. The biggest story of her career is dangling in front of her.

Deep in the base of my loins, I can feel something twisting. It's the unholy combination of Elena straddling that chair, plus the creeping dread of what's to come. She doesn't want DeShawn. He's small potatoes. A quiet male nerd with violent tendencies. That's old hat. Nowadays, there's one of those per week. Sure, it would do in a pinch, but in the end, most people would just see a Black kid accused of murder and shrug their shoulders. Suze Tilman, on the other hand? The beautiful outsider with a mysterious past? Now we're in Amanda Knox territory. If Elena breaks a story about a female killer ahead of the police, it will be the making of her. Those kinds of stories twist and morph and sprout wings and go on forever. Elena could ride that story way out of Jonesville. She could go national. She could go all the way to *CNN*. But only if she has the inside line.

That's why she needs me. The cops don't know yet that I was there that night, too, that my fingerprints are right next to DeShawn's, splattered all over Shaw's bedroom. As Elena so eloquently put it, the police "like" DeShawn for this crime. Maybe it's simple racism. Or the fact that he kicked Shaw's ass the day before he died. I don't know. But Elena knows that I'm the one with the real story and she's dangling DeShawn to get me to spill it.

Man, she's good.

"What's it gonna be, Marcus?" she says licking her lips.

"Give me one day," I tell her.

"You have until 9 a.m. tomorrow."

I peel myself out of the red leather chair with another noisy sigh and head to the door.

NIKKI

When I pull into my driveway after school, I'm surprised to find Marcus Daubney sitting on my front steps, scribbling in that reporter's notebook he always seems to have with him. His bike lies across our flagstone path, like he dumped it there in a hurry. I'm glad my parents are both at work, because I wouldn't want to explain what he's doing here. Truth be told, I can't explain Marcus Daubney. The boy confuses me. He's an annoying troublemaker. But he's smart. And useful. He doesn't even look up from his notebook until I get to the bottom step.

"Did you cut school early?" I ask.

"Yes," he says, snapping his notebook closed. "We need to find Suze."

I head up the steps slowly. "What do you mean?"

"She's missing."

"Missing? So she wasn't arrested?"

"Nope," he says, putting his notebook into his backpack. "They arrested DeShawn instead."

"What?" I drop my backpack on the top step and lean against the cement flowerbed.

"They took his fingerprints this morning," he says. "They matched them to the prints in Shaw's bedroom."

Fingerprints. That's bad news. You can't lie about something like that.

Marcus stands up and grabs his backpack. "We need to find her," he says.

I take out my phone and try calling her again. When her voicemail picks up, I try texting her like I've been doing all day. It doesn't deliver, which means her phone is turned off.

"Track her phone," he says.

I open the app, but Suze's dot isn't there. When she goes offline, she goes all the way.

"Come on." I head down the stairs. "Let's go to her house."

"I just came from there."

"And?"

"Nobody's home."

"Not even her dad?"

He shakes his head.

That's strange. Suze's father is always there. He works from home writing some book he's been revising for three years now. Suze says he doesn't even get dressed most days.

"The house seemed empty to me," Marcus says, walking down the steps slowly. "No cars in the driveway, either."

I sit on the steps and call Suze's mother. She answers on the second ring. When I tell her it's me, there's a long pause while she muffles the phone to talk to someone—Suze's father, presumably. I can hear traffic in the background so she must be in her car. When she comes back to the phone, she's crying.

"Suze never came home last night," she says. "She left the house around ten o'clock."

"Where did she go?"

"She told us she was going for a walk. We assumed she meant in the neighborhood, or the woods behind the house. We didn't even realize she'd taken her car until later on, after the police came. We've been calling and calling her."

"Have you checked the beach?"

"Wingaersheek, Crane, Singing Beach. All of them. We checked the nature preserve on Grapevine Road. All the places she likes to go. She hasn't called you?"

"No."

"I don't understand what's happening, Nikki. First, those awful photographs. Then the police came by to ask her about the boy who took them— you know, the one who died? Did you know him, Nikki?"

"No," I lie. "Not really." My stomach flips over because I hate lying to her. She's always been so kind and supportive.

"Do you think something's happened to her? Do you think whoever killed that boy—oh God, I can't even say it—"

"No, Mrs. Tilman. I'm sure it's nothing like that.

I'm sure she's just—you know how she likes to—" I almost say "disappear," then realize that's probably the last word she wants to hear.

Marcus's phone rings. He looks at the screen, then grabs his notebook and pen and rushes down the steps to take the call in our front yard. He paces back and forth in front of the birch trees, then jams his phone between his ear and shoulder so he can write something down.

"Nikki?" Mrs. Tilman says. "Are you still there?"

"Yeah, Mrs. Tilman. I'm here."

"You don't think she had anything to do with that boy's death, do you? She didn't—I mean, there's no way she—"

"No, Mrs. Tilman. I'm sure she had nothing to do with it."

Mrs. Tilman's heavy sigh fills me with guilt. She's always been straight with me. More like a mentor than a friend's mom.

"We've always let her make her own mistakes," she says. "We let her roam. We thought it would build her confidence to have that freedom. God, have we given her too much freedom?"

I know what my parents would say. They'd say, *Yes, you bohemian hippie weirdo, your daughter's a freak and you should rein her in. And send her to church while you're at it so she can learn to be ashamed like the rest of us.* My parents and Suze's parents are from opposite ends of the parenting spectrum. But *I* don't think they gave Suze too much freedom. I think the way they raised Suze is the reason she is who she is. I wouldn't change any of that.

Down on the front lawn, Marcus hangs up and shoves his phone in the front pocket of his jeans. I hang up with Mrs. Tilman, then head down the steps.

"Who was that?"

"Elena," he says. "They found Suze's car."

FIFTEEN MINUTES LATER, we reconvene in Ani's bedroom, which is a converted attic with sloped ceilings and a collection of beanbag chairs in rainbow colors. Ani's parents are much less nosy than mine. Plus, it's pizza night there. Ani's mother brings us a large pepperoni pizza and a two-liter bottle of diet cherry soda, then leaves us in peace. I settle into my favorite red beanbag chair with a slice and some soda. According to that reporter, Suze's car was found in Boston. The police traced it to a used car dealership using one of those LoJack systems. The car was sold for $800 cash, which, according to Kelley Blue Book, is half of its actual value.

"Sounds to me like she was in a hurry," Marcus says. He's trying to sit up straight in a lime-green beanbag chair, which makes his knees buckle outward like a cricket.

"We don't even know it was Suze who sold it," Lydia says. She's been pacing in the center of the room, where you can actually stand up straight. "Maybe it was stolen."

"Then where is she?" Marcus asks. "Walking around Jonesville?"

"She could be camping," Ani says, looking up from her laptop on the bed.

"Yeah," Lydia adds, "camping."

Marcus looks at me, incredulous. But in all honesty, I can't rule out that Suze is camping. It wouldn't be unlike her at all to pitch a tent in the woods somewhere just to get away for a few days. She's done it before.

"Okay," I say, "let's focus on what we know for sure."

"Fine," Lydia says petulantly.

The four of us are not exactly private detectives, but when you put Ani's computer skills together with Marcus's reporter skills, then add my flare for lists and spreadsheets, we're able to make some headway. I think Lydia is just angry because she doesn't have much to offer, other than pacing, stress-eating gummy bears, and being annoyed that Marcus is there.

I spend a lot of time on the phone with Suze's parents, who are basically in free fall, wondering if they screwed up by raising Suze the way they did. In terms of actually locating Suze, they're useless. Her phone's turned off. She's not with her car anymore. She left no note. None of her clothes are missing. Her suitcase is still there. Her laptop is still in her bedroom. Wherever she's gone, she left in a hurry, and—as we all know—when she unplugs, she goes all the way. I ask them to check whether any of their camping gear is missing, and while her father goes to the garage to check, I ask her mother if she can track Suze's bank and credit cards. But Suze's parents are comically low-tech. Suze does all their banking for them. I tell Suze's mother to look for a red heart-shaped Post-it inside a small cedar jewelry box in Suze's bedroom. That's where Suze keeps her logins and passwords. Luckily her mother trusts me enough to give me the information.

Five minutes after we hang up, her father calls back to report that all of the camping gear is still in the garage. But by now, Ani has gotten some hits with that bank information and we're able to piece together a timeline.

She left home some time after 10 p.m. That was the last time her parents saw her. At 11:53 p.m., she used her debit card at an ATM outside a Stop & Shop in Lynn, which is two towns south of Jonesville. She withdrew $1000, the daily maximum. At that same ATM, she also withdrew $2000 from a Visa card her parents gave her for "emergencies only." Then she waited until just after midnight so she could do the whole thing again at an ATM in Revere.

"So she's driving south," Ani says.

"Heading to Boston," Marcus adds, "where she sold her car."

"She's also loading up on cash," I say.

"Before someone turns off the cards," Marcus says.

I grab my phone. "I'll tell her parents not to turn off the cards. They're our best way of tracking her."

"And if she doesn't want to be tracked," he says, "she'll stop using them."

Lydia shoots him a dirty look.

"What?" he says. "You think she's draining her bank cards for no reason? Please. She's running."

"You don't know that," Lydia says.

"Then where is she?"

In place of a reply, Lydia shoves a green gummy bear in her mouth.

"We don't know for *sure* that she's running," Ani says.

"Yeah," Lydia mumbles around a sticky, green mouthful. "She's probably camping."

"In Boston?" Marcus scoffs.

"She could be on the Cape somewhere," Lydia says. "There's that spot in Eastham? That state park? You know, with the pond? Where we went that time?"

"Lydia," I say, "she doesn't have her camping gear with her."

"So. Maybe she bought new gear with all the cash she took out."

"You don't seriously believe she's camping," Marcus says.

"Why is he even here?" Lydia asks me.

"Um, guys?" Ani stares her laptop. "Suze used

315

that Visa card again, the emergency one. The charge just showed up." We all crowd around Ani's laptop on the bed. She has the "recent transactions" of that emergency Visa card open on her screen. Two of the transactions are the cash withdrawals we already knew about. The new one is for Avekian Brothers in the amount of $10,967.

"Whoa," Marcus says. "That's a lot of money. What did she buy?"

Ani clicks open another tab. Avekian Brothers is a jewelry shop in Boston.

Jewelry? I think to myself. Other than that yin-yang necklace she got from a friend in London, she doesn't wear jewelry. In her own words, "People aren't Christmas trees." There's a phone number on the Avekian Brothers website, so I call it. I ask for the manager, then tell him I need to know exactly what Suze purchased. He won't tell me because of "customer privacy."

"Excuse me," I tell him. "This is someone who might be in trouble."

"I can't help you," he says, then hangs up.

"Maybe someone stole her credit card?" Ani suggests.

Lydia takes out her phone and calls Avekian Brothers herself. But she doesn't ask for the manager. She pretends she's Suze and asks to speak to the salesperson who waited on her. She even manages to mimic Suze's trace of an English accent. She tells the saleswoman she has to fill out an expense report and needs to know the precise names of the items she just bought, otherwise her boss won't reimburse her for it. The saleswoman puts her on hold for a minute, then comes back and gives her the breakdown. Suze purchased six "gold bobble chain chokers," three "midweight gold chain necklaces," five "wide belcher chain bracelets," three "emerald-and-diamond princess rings," and four pairs of "ruby and diamond stud earrings."

When Lydia hangs up, we all sit in silence, trying to figure out why Suze would buy these things.

"Somebody must have stolen her credit card," Lydia says. "Maybe she left it in the car by accident."

"You *just* impersonated her on the phone," Marcus points out. "Obviously it was her buying the jewelry."

"Oh shut up!" Lydia flings herself off the bed and starts pacing with the bag of gummy bears in her fist.

"What's she doing in Boston, anyway?" Ani asks. "Who does she even know there?"

"No one," I say. "She's not in Boston."

Lydia whips around. "Her car's there."

"She's not in Boston."

"How do you know?" Lydia demands.

I know because I know how Suze thinks. "She had to know her car was traceable because of that LoJack thing," I say.

"So?" Lydia says.

"So that's why she sold it. Plus, she needs the cash. That's why she bought the jewelry, too."

"Why would she buy jewelry if she needed cash?" Ani asks. "Why wouldn't she just get cash?"

As soon as I put myself in Suze's frame of mind, it's so easy to see it.

"Because she already withdrew the daily maximum in cash," I say, "at that ATM in Revere."

"Right," Marcus says, "but there's a different limit for purchases."

"Exactly," I say. "Check the terms of the credit card, Ani. I bet it's maxed out."

Ani switches back to the credit card tab and finds the information. I'm right. Between the cash withdrawals and the visit to the jewelry store, the credit card is maxed. She won't be able to use it again until someone pays it off.

"But why jewelry?" Ani says.

It's so obvious now. I can't believe Ani doesn't see it.

"Oh God," Marcus says. "Of course."

"What?" Ani says. "Of course what?"

"Jewelry is portable," I say.

"And untraceable," Marcus adds.

Lydia scowls at him, then looks to me for confirmation.

"It'll hold its value," I say. "She can sell it anywhere. Add it all up. The cash, what she got for the car, the value of the jewelry—how much is that?"

Ani does a quick calculation on her phone.

"Fourteen thousand, seven hundred and sixty-seven dollars."

"Plus whatever cash she had on her," Marcus pipes up, know-it-all style.

Nobody says anything for a while as we ponder what Suze is doing right now, and where exactly she is. Lydia chomps on gummy bears while Ani refreshes the feed on the other bank card.

After a while, Marcus comes out with, "So I guess we can cross off the camping hypothesis?"

Lydia throws a handful of gummy bears at his head.

"She still has about seventeen hundred in her bank account," Ani says. "She'll probably try to withdraw that at some point. We can see where she is then."

"Maybe," I say.

But I'm doubtful. Suze has to know we're all looking for her. If she wanted to be found, she would have reached out to us. She would have called or texted. Marcus is right. She's not camping.

She's running. And Suze is a girl who can take care of herself on the road. She'll travel by train or bus, which require no ID. She'll hitchhike if it comes to it. She'll "sleep rough," like she did in Île de Ré, France, with some people she met on the beach. Suze isn't like us. She won't be calling home in a panic because her emergency credit card stopped working. She can sell that jewelry little by little as she needs it. Or sell it all at once and buy herself a new identity, get a fake passport, and head to Mexico or Canada. When the money runs out, she'll find a way to replace it. She'll ingratiate herself to some rich family and get a job tutoring their kids in English, like she did in Poland.

Suze told me she could make more money than both of her parents combined, if she put her mind to it. And I believe her. She's resourceful. Her parents were right to raise her the way they did. She'll be fine on her own. She's the perfect fugitive.

DESHAWN

As soon as you arrive at Haverland Juvenile Detention Center, they take everything: your shoes, your clothes, even your underwear, which seems like overkill. What dangerous thing am I going to do with my own underwear? In exchange for all of this stuff, they give you their stuff: a stiff red jumpsuit with HJD written on the back, a pair of boxy white sneakers with Velcro instead of laces so you don't hang yourself, and three pairs of white briefs. You have to wear someone *else's* underwear.

My "room" (they don't call it a cell) is six feet by ten feet, with a skinny window way up at the top that I can't even see out of. I share my "room" with this white kid from Swampscott named Richie Something Italian. He said his last name quickly, and I didn't want to ask him to repeat it because I didn't know how he'd take that. Everyone in here is scary as shit. And by everyone, I don't just mean the inmates. I mean the guards, too.

I suppose some of these kids are just waiting for a court hearing, like me, maybe for nonviolent crimes. They're still scary as shit. I am not prepared to rule out being knifed in my sleep. Richie Something Italian is in here because he stabbed his algebra teacher, which is an anecdote he took some pride in sharing with me. I didn't ask what his algebra teacher did to deserve being knifed because I didn't want to start up a conversation I might end up regretting. He looked disappointed at my lack of interest, then he went back to his comic books. He has a stack of them in the corner, but I don't dare touch them. That's not how I want to go down. He's asleep now on the top bunk, snoring.

While I lie in my own bed, not snoring, or sleeping, I keep thinking about my mom. When I saw her in that little meeting room here, she looked wrecked. Her mouth was drooped on one side like she'd had a stroke. But that was just her heart breaking. Because of me. Because I screwed everything up.

My mom and dad kept asking me, *Why? Why did you run from the police? Why would they arrest you in the first place? Why do they think you're responsible for the death of "that boy"? Does it have something to do with "that girl"?* I was afraid to say anything because I assumed someone was listening. I don't think any conversations in here are private. And I haven't figured out what to say yet. Keeping my mouth shut is the only thing I've done right so far, and I think I'll go on doing it. Maybe forever.

While I stare at the springs of Richie's bunk,

thoughts of Suze wash through me. It's like when you wade out into an icy lake going *Oh shit oh shit it's cold it's cold cold cold*, then a warm current wraps itself around your thigh and you think *Yes, that, more of that.* The weight of her, the warm, velvety skin of her neck, the glow of her dark eyes reflecting the porch light. *Yes, it really happened. I lost my virginity last night.*

And when the reality of that starts to fade and twist into something that feels like it might be a dream or fantasy, I press the back of my head against the thin mattress so I can feel that tender spot where the rock scraped it. *It's real. It actually happened. I had sex with Suze and it was the most beautiful gift the universe ever gave me.*

Then she disappears, and I remember I'm in juvie.

MARCUS

Suze Tilman is gone. I'm sure of it. She must have realized it was only a matter of time before the police arrested her for Shaw's death and so she got out of Jonesville while she could. She's seventeen, which means she could be charged as an adult. If I were facing murder charges, I'd consider the fugitive lifestyle, too, though based on what Nikki's told me, Suze will do a lot better than I ever would.

For now, they have DeShawn, locked up in juvie awaiting arraignment. And tomorrow morning, unless I do something, Elena's going to publish that ruinous article. Who cares if it's not true? It makes great copy. What Jonesville wants is an answer to why their jock god is dead. If that answer turns out to be DeShawn Hill, who's going to question it?

So here I sit, alone in my room, staring at my little green Post-it with its exhortation about "journalism's first obligation." My hands hover above my laptop as I try to come up with the perfect exculpatory article to replace Elena's incorrect one. I know I can do it. I could hand Elena Suze Tilman's head on a platter, with a heaping portion of evidence to go with it. There's Tarkin's text "inviting" Suze over that night—I'm sure the police would be able to subpoena that. The blackmail photos provide an obvious motive. There's even a photo of Suze being carried out of Tara Budzynski's house, where Tarkin took the blackmail photos. And if that's not a sumptuous-enough feast, there's me. I'm a witness. I was there when Tarkin Shaw died. I know exactly who did it, how, and why. It would be so easy to exonerate DeShawn and lay Shaw's murder at Suze Tilman's feet—which, after all, is where it belongs.

But as much as I want to put an end to all of this and rescue DeShawn from this mess, my fingers won't move. They won't even touch the keyboard. I've been staring at a blank screen for over an hour. In my head, the article is already written, but I can't seem to transfer it to my fingertips and onto that screen. Because I don't want Suze Tilman's head on a platter. I want her to get away with this. I want us all to get away with it. And the more I think about it, the more I realize that the cops might not even care what I know about Suze Tilman. The perfect exculpatory piece of journalism notwithstanding, they might just stick with DeShawn and his goddamn fingerprints. It wouldn't be the first time the police pinned a crime on a Black kid.

It's amazing how quickly the presumption of guilt gathered around DeShawn. According to

Elena, the police didn't set out to arrest him. They were planning to question him. They only arrested him when he ran. *Jesus, DeShawn, why did you run?* But, more to the point, why didn't the police try to question *me*? I got in a fight with Shaw the day before he died too. Hell, I'm the one who started that fight. DeShawn was only protecting me. So why did the police focus their attention on De-Shawn? Why is he in juvie awaiting "arraignment" while I'm safe at home, unquestioned and unarrested? I've never been a romantic about the criminal justice system, but I always figured it got things mostly right, give or take a mistake here and there, the inevitable dollop of corruption. But now I see it differently. It's too easy to get things wrong. It was too easy for Shaw and his influential family to get Amber Laynes to change her story. Hell, it was too easy for Mason Shaw and Sean Princely to post those pictures of Suze and get away with it. Why haven't *they* been arrested? Why aren't the cops chasing them down for questioning? And what about all those kids making rape and death threats against Nikki, Lydia, and Ani? Where's the law when it comes to that? Why is it that all of DeShawn's actions over the past week add up to the presumption of guilt, while all those other guys—including me—roam free? Why is Suze Tilman a fugitive when all she did was fight back? It's enough to make you question the entire system.

The little green Post-it looms, but my hands don't

move. I know I have to do something. I can't let De-Shawn go down for this. But the longer I stare at this blank screen with its blinking cursor, the more I realize journalism isn't going to save anyone. Not this time.

On my phone is a picture of DeShawn that I took when he got his black belt in karate. He looks so proud, standing against the white cement-block wall with his teacher shaking his hand. I love that picture. And I remember that moment. He'd worked so hard and he really wanted me to be there for him. When I look at it now, I realize exactly what I have to do.

NIKKI

I always half-suspected Suze would leave us. There's something about her that never belonged in Jonesville. But I didn't mind that, because I figured when she left, I'd catch up with her somewhere. After graduation, she was planning to go backpacking around South America while I went off to UMass. We were going to meet up in Paraguay during spring break. After that, I'd visit her in whatever yurt or kibbutz or backpackers' hostel she was staying at. It was such a beautiful dream. But it was tangible, too. It wasn't the kind of fantasy you know will never come true. I could feel it really happening. Now, as I drive home from Ani's on my own, I wonder if I'll ever see her again.

I'm rolling to a stop at the intersection of Grapevine Road and Topsfield Avenue when I get a call from an unfamiliar number. It's an area code I've never seen, definitely not from Massachusetts. I accept the call.

"Is it safe to talk, Nikki?"

It's Suze.

The car behind me beeps and flashes its beams at me, so I drive through the intersection, then pull into the first driveway I can find.

"Where are you?" I ask.

"It's probably best if I don't tell you."

"Are you okay, though?"

"Remember that party I told you about? With those missionary kids from Utah?"

"You mean when you were in—"

"Don't say where it was."

"Why not?"

"Just . . . don't."

She's worried about surveillance. She thinks the cops might be listening in.

"I know they're after me," she says. "I saw the police at my house. That's why I left."

"So you're just going to . . . run?"

"Why not?"

"What about your parents? They're going crazy."

"They should know me better than that."

The funny thing is, during my last conversation with Suze's mother, she seemed less panicked and more resigned, like she knew Suze had run, and she knew she'd manage somehow.

"I just wish I could see you," I tell her.

"You will."

"Suze, I don't even know where you are."

"You know where I'm headed, though."

"How'm I supposed to—oh." That's when it comes to me. That story about those missionary kids. It happened in Mexico. What was the name of the town? San Something Something. That must be where she's heading.

"Listen," she says, "I should go. Say hi to the girls for me? And DeShawn too. Don't tell them where I'm going though. Not yet. The less you all know the better. Nikki, do you hate me?"

"What? Of course not."

"You're not mad?"

"No."

"Nikki, you know you can't lie to me. What is it? What aren't you telling me?"

San Miguel de Allende. That's the name of the town. Suze spent a winter there with her parents, who were both writing books at the time. She went to a Spanish language school and they had home-made corn tortillas delivered to their house every morning. If I say nothing right now, that's where she'll go. She'll be safe and anonymous and I can meet up with her sometime in the future. Maybe next summer, when I'm sure the police aren't tracking me. I'll head to San Miguel de Allende and ask around for the tall americana with the light brown hair.

When I catch my reflection in the mirror, I'm surprised by how tired I look, how spent. I'm only seventeen. *Why do I look so old?* I guess, in a way, I've been on the run, too, for the past three years. That's what it feels like, anyway. You tell yourself if you just bury the memories, you can be free of them. Time will work its healing magic and you can escape.

But some escapes aren't meant to be. It's not fair. But if I've learned anything over the past three years it's that fair has nothing to do with it.

"Suze," I say, "there's something I need to tell you."

FRIDAY

MARCUS

"What time is it?" my mother asks.

It's Friday morning and I'm sitting in the passenger seat of my mother's Volkswagen, which is parked on Main Street in "downtown" Jonesville. My mother's knuckles whiten as she grips the steering wheel.

"It's thirteen past eight," I tell her.

Across Main Street is the police station, the only modern building in this area of Jonesville, the original village center. Everything else—and by everything, I mean the library and the Presbyterian church, because that's all there is—is whitewashed colonial. The police station looks out of place, the cutesy mash-up of brick and stone evoking a Lego set—one of the lamer collections, "Suburban Utility Building." You half-expect a little Lego police officer to come waddling through the front door pulling an ad-hoc Lego wagon with a Lego duck in it. Never before has Jonesville seemed so small.

"You're sure about this, Marcus?" my mother asks.

I am. And this is in large part down to the fact that, when my own conviction was flagging last night (after I failed to write the perfect exculpatory article), I asked myself the simple question: *What would DeShawn do?*

"Are you *absolutely* sure?"

"Yes, Mom."

There's no other way. And if our situation were reversed, DeShawn would do the same for me.

A silver BMW pulls up in front of the police station across the street. A few seconds later, a squat, middle-aged white guy with a mop of gray hair heaves himself out.

"That's him," my mother says. "That's Richard."

Richard's now my lawyer. My mother went to high school with him, and they spoke over the phone last night after she frantically called and emailed everyone she could think of in search of advice. Because that's what you do when your son tells you he's an accessory to murder.

Richard sees my mother, waves, and walks over, black leather briefcase in hand. I know I shouldn't judge someone on his looks, but Richard does not inspire confidence. He looks like a movie cliché of a low-rent lawyer, an ambulance chaser, a guy who'll leave out some critical detail and accidentally land his client—me—in the electric chair. I feel sick. The urge to flee nearly overwhelms me. No wonder Suze ran. I get it now, on a visceral level. When you feel the weight of the law closing in on you— and for some reason, the sight of Richard is what does it for me—all you want to do is run. But that's not what I'm doing today. Today I'm doing what DeShawn would do. I loop my finger through the door's latch and pull just enough to free it. Hearing the click, my mother turns to me, ragged with despair. When Richard raps his knuckles on her car window, armed with a friendly smile that strains his fleshy cheeks, she jumps.

"It'll be okay," I lie.

I open my door and wait for Richard on the sidewalk. I've already told him everything over the phone, but we go through it again, detail by detail. It's bright and cold, the reddening leaves of the maple tree in front of the church lending the proceedings an almost poignant beauty. *Such a glorious day to throw your life away*. Richard, dressed in a gray wool coat, keeps shrugging his shoulders to keep warm. I zip up my hoodie and pull the hood over my head.

Richard shakes his head and pulls my hood down. "Don't go in there looking like a criminal," he says.

I didn't realize the look was in my repertoire.

"I just want to reiterate that you are under no obligation to do this," Richard says. "You're not a suspect. You haven't been brought in for questioning. My advice, as I said earlier, is to stay home and let this play out without you."

My mother's eyes sadden. Deep down, she wishes we could take Richard's advice. I can only imagine what it must be like for her to watch me hand myself over to the police. No matter the circumstances, I know that it must violate some deep-seated maternal instinct. It wouldn't surprise me in the least if she tried to bundle me into her trench coat and carry me out of there.

"I'm not letting DeShawn go down," I tell him. "I'm the *only* witness."

"You're about to become an accessory," Richard needlessly reminds me.

"I know," I say, "but I have to do it."

I say this for my mother's benefit, not Richard's. I don't care what Richard thinks. We went through the whole thing last night. I know what I'm risking by coming forward, but if I don't, they'll lay everything at DeShawn's feet. I hope Suze Tilman makes it out of the country and disappears for good. Because even though I'm going in there to tell them she's the one who killed Tarkin Shaw, I hope they never find her.

The three of us make our way across the street to the police station, my phone vibrating incessantly in my pocket. Elena, begging for the real story, begging for the chance to publish it before the police make their statement. It's eighteen past eight. Forty-two minutes before her 9 a.m. deadline. But, according to Richard, I shouldn't say anything unless he's there with me. So, I'm sorry, Elena, but you won't be riding this story out of Jonesville. You'll have to cover it just like the rest of the press, *after* the police release their statement. Here's a headline for you:

"Jonesville Police Fail to Pin
White Kid's Murder on Black Kid"

When we get to the entrance, my mother rushes to the glass door ahead of me and grips the handle, stricken. Inside, two male uniformed police officers stand on either side of a woman in a jean jacket. I can't see her face. She has short brown hair and she clasps her hands behind her back. When she turns around to let the two uniformed officers lead her away, I recognize her immediately.

"Holy shit!" I blurt.

She spots me outside and shakes her head, as if to shoo me away before anyone sees me. Then the officers walk her down a hallway and out of sight.

"Who's that?" Richard asks.

"Suze Tilman," I say.

My mother grabs my arm. "I thought she ran away. Didn't you say she ran away?" She pulls me from the door as if it has the power to suck me straight through. "Marcus, does this mean . . . ?"

"I don't know what it means."

"Well, at the very least, we should wait this out," she says. "Right, Richard? Shouldn't we wait to hear what she has to say?"

"That would be my advice."

"Marcus, come on." My mother tugs at my arm. "Let's go home. Let's go home before anyone sees us."

FROM THE JONESVILLE *BUGLE*:

Teen Arrested for Murder of Tarkin Shaw
by Elena DePiero

The Jonesville police have made an arrest in connection with the death of local teen, Tarkin Shaw. Shaw, 17, was found in his home on September 12th, an apparent victim of an overdose of Rohypnol. Sources confirm that Suze Tilman, 17, of Jonesville, confessed earlier today to administering the Rohypnol without Shaw's knowledge or consent. Tilman had been wanted for questioning in connection with the teen's death when she disappeared from her family's home on Roberts Road. She was reportedly en route to Mexico when a friend informed her that the police had arrested another minor in connection with Shaw's murder. According to sources close to Tilman, she returned to clear the minor's name. She has admitted to acting alone in Shaw's death.

Though much remains unexplained about this case, a picture is beginning to emerge. On September 13th of this year, 57 pornographic images of Tilman appeared on a pornography website, reportedly without her knowledge or consent. The police would not confirm whether the existence of these photographs was being treated as a possible motive for the murder of Tarkin Shaw.

Lydia Moreau, a close friend of Tilman's, had this to say: "Suze Tilman is *not* a murderer. If she gave [Tarkin Shaw] those drugs—and I'm not saying she did, by the way—it was only because he did *the exact same thing* to her. She shouldn't be arrested for it. She should be congratulated for fighting back. Tarkin Shaw is a rapist."

Shaw was previously accused of rape by a fellow classmate at Jonesville High. But the alleged victim later recanted her story and no charges were filed.

Shaw's father, Darren Shaw, 47, had this to say: "Tark didn't need to drug girls or blackmail anybody. That's ridiculous. Everybody loved him. He could have had any girl he wanted."

Shaw's mother, Nicole Shaw, 45, added: "It's bad enough we've lost our son. Now people are attacking his character when he's not around to defend himself."

Ms. Tilman and her parents could not be reached for comment.

Bugle staff writer, Marcus Daubney, contributed to this article.

ONE WEEK LATER

DESHAWN

There's no juvenile facility for girls awaiting trial for the crime of murder, so Suze is sent to MCI-Framingham, a regular adult women's prison. I can't call or visit because I'm not on "the list." I gave my number to Suze's parents and asked them to pass it along to her, which they promised to do. But it's been a week since she was sent there, and I still haven't heard from her. I spend a lot of time on the MCI-Framingham website, studying its guidelines and visitation rules, hoping I'll be put on "the list" at some point. I haven't touched my soldering iron. Terence's leg is still broken. I gave up on that fire truck, too. I messaged the woman to apologize and suggested another modeler. Nothing that used to matter to me matters anymore. My parents keep trying to convince me that I should be happy I'm free. My mom still can't believe the "corrupt and racist criminal justice system" didn't find a way to pin the whole thing on me. She has thirty-four new gray hairs and they all came out at once because of me, right on the top of her head.

I got lucky. I keep telling myself that. I'm lucky. Yes, Mom, I'm lucky I'm not in jail. I'm lucky because Nikki told Suze I was arrested and Suze came back to clear my name. I'm lucky the fingerprints didn't stick. Scaletti and Dagmoor weren't supposed to take them because I wasn't actually resisting arrest. They also weren't supposed to question me without a parent or guardian present. They got overeager and their mistake is my good fortune. And whenever I catch Kiara sneaking glances at me, looking both scared and relieved at the same time, I do feel grateful that I got away with it. I know how much it would have hurt her to see me sent away to prison. So, yes, maybe I *am* lucky. But I'm not happy.

Marcus comes over every day after school to keep me company. He knows better than to try to cheer me up, though, or to tell me I'm lucky. He just sits there working on his articles while I study the MCI-Framingham website.

Marcus told me what happened between Suze and Shaw the night we stole his stuff, how she had sex with him to avoid being raped. That's what was going through Suze's mind that night at the pond, when she wanted me to help her forget. I think she wanted to replace that memory with something better. I hope it worked. I hope our one night together was enough to take the sting out of what she went through with Shaw. When I try to imagine how scared she must have been and how violated she must have felt, I can barely hang onto the idea. I don't know how she found the will. I couldn't have done it. Girls are tougher than boys. Maybe they have to be.

Marcus stops typing suddenly and looks at me. "You okay?"

When I shake my head, he closes his laptop, scoots his chair over, and pulls me into a hug. Normally when I feel this bad, I just want to be alone, to sit with my soldering iron and fix something. But I'm glad Marcus is here now, because I think I'm going to cry. I haven't cried since I was little, and I'm not sure I know how to do it anymore.

"I'm so sorry, buddy," Marcus says. "I know how much she means to you."

"Yeah?"

"Yeah," he says. "She means something to me too."

As it turns out, I do know how to cry.

A FULL TWO weeks after Suze is sent to MCI-Framingham, I get a call from her father telling me I'm on the list.

"She had some very nice things to say about you, DeShawn," her father tells me. "I think she'd really like to see you."

I'm so excited I can barely speak. I stammer out a *thank you*, then rush down to the basement to restudy the MCI-Framingham website's rules for visitors, which is completely unnecessary because I already have it memorized. Here's the hitch. Because I'm a minor, I have to bring a parent or guardian with me. There are no exceptions to this rule. My mother is out of the question. She's one hundred percent convinced my "friendship or whatever it is with that girl" is bad news and something she's hoping I'll outgrow. She's still raw from my overnight stay in juvie. I think she considers it a personal failing on her part, which is wrong. It was a personal failing on my part. So, on Saturday, while she takes Kiara to a friend's birthday party at The Trampoline Zone, I approach my dad instead. He's in the kitchen making a peanut butter and banana sandwich.

"Hey, can I have one of those, too?" I ask.

"Don't tell your mother," he says. "I'm not supposed to be snacking."

While he makes me one, I tell him about being put on Suze's visitor list and about how much it would mean to her if I could visit.

"It's not even a juvenile center," I tell him. "She's in there with adult prisoners."

I'm about to go on, but my dad wilts right away, doesn't even resist, just immediately goes limp. In his way, my dad is just as protective as my mom. The difference is my mom will stick to a plan, or dogma, or any rule she's invented out of stubbornness, but my dad can be persuaded. He bends. He screws the cap on the peanut butter jar, wipes his hands on the dishtowel, and says, "If you're gonna be a fool, be a fool for love."

I knew he'd get it.

ON THE DRIVE to MCI-Framingham, he tells me the story of how he pursued my mother back when he was in college. He was younger than her by eight years and she had no interest in him at all. She was a workaholic law clerk with a judge in Boston and he was a junior at Emerson studying communications. My mother had zero time for his undergraduate ass. But my dad hung in there, showing up at bars he couldn't afford to drink at, buying her expensive cocktails he could barely pronounce.

"I knew she was the one," he says. "Just had to wait her out."

I've heard this story before. And I know that my mom is not the kind of person who can be persuaded. If she fell for my dad, it wasn't because he was persistent. It was because she finally saw something in him, some hint of the man he'd become one day. Maybe he just had to grow up a little. At any rate, she took her own sweet time and eventually decided that Bartholomew Hill was the one for her.

"When you know, you know," I say, because it's what he always says about it.

"Exactly."

"So how come she can't understand how I feel about Suze? Why does she hate her so much?"

"She doesn't hate her, DeShawn. Your mother's incapable of hatred."

He's being naïve here. My mother may not actually hate Suze, but she is capable of hatred. She definitely hates the Jonesville police. Not dislikes, not disapproves of, hates.

"She's just trying to protect you," he says. "That's a parent's first job. And this girl really landed you in it. You have to admit that."

"It wasn't her fault, though."

"I'm not saying she wasn't a victim too, De-Shawn. But a boy is dead."

"He died from his own rape drugs, though. I feel like that should count for something."

My dad still has trouble grasping all the hideous particulars of this thing. Sometimes I forget that my parents have had less time than I've had to get used to the idea. The prospect of a boy drugging a girl, then taking nude pictures of her and blackmailing her with them is so far out of their zone, they can't make sense of it. They're still playing catch-up. In their day, kids didn't do this to each other. To be fair, I had trouble grasping it when Suze first told me about it, too. But I've had no choice but to make space for it.

"Give your mother some time," he says. "She'll come around."

"You gonna tell her about this visit?"

"Hell no. And neither are you."

FROM A DISTANCE, MCI-Framingham looks majestic, like a citadel or a college library—red brick and marble, with gables. On top is a crown of gray haze that, from a certain distance, looks like a ring of gypsy moth nests. As we get closer, I realize it's razor wire. Once you see that, it doesn't look like a college library anymore. It looks like what it is: a prison.

My father and I have to sign in, empty our pockets, and get patted down, which he does not like one bit. My stay in juvie is still fresh with him, too. I was only there overnight, but he's not going to get past it anytime soon.

As we stand stiffly in the waiting room, he takes in the rough crowd also waiting their turn, and I know exactly what he's thinking: If my mother ever finds out about this, we're both dead. When a guard escorts me to the visitor's room alone, I have to remind my dad that it'll be okay, that I'm not actually going to jail myself. I think he's regretting this whole visit.

The visitor's room is split down the middle by a grid of Perspex windows, visitors on one side, inmates in forest-green scrubs on the other. They speak to each other through gray telephone handsets that look like they come from the 1950s.

"Sit here," the guard says. "Don't touch the glass."

There's no chair, just a round, metal disk that sticks out of the partition. Everything in there is attached to something else, as if the entire room were one seamless object. I guess it's so no one can throw anything. I straddle my little disk and gaze through the Perspex, but I can't see much because of the dividers, which create a little cubby space for us.

When Suze finally arrives, I don't recognize her at first. She looks skinny. She's practically swimming inside her forest-green scrubs. Her hair is short now and matted to her head. She has purple half-circles under her eyes, and the acid-green light from the fluorescents make her look sickly. Despite all that, she's still beautiful, like a charcoal drawing of herself. She sits down, grabs the phone, and waits for me to do the same. "Hi," she says, without smiling.

"Hi," I say. "Are you—"

"Please don't ask me if I'm okay. I spent most of my last visit comforting my parents. It gets exhausting."

"You shouldn't even be here."

"Don't. Please. I'm way past that. I'm here. Facts are facts. The sooner you get to acceptance the better. On the bright side," she chuckles, "killing a guy for doing what he did to me actually goes over pretty well in here." She laughs again, but there's no joy in it. I think it's a pose she's trying out, maybe something she needs to survive now.

I realize I've barely said anything, but I'm afraid if I open my mouth I'll either start blubbering, or blurt out *I love you.*

"I'm sorry I didn't put you on the list sooner," she says. "It's taken a bit to adjust. And I wanted to wait until I had some news."

My stomach clenches. For two weeks now, I've been obsessing over numbers. Five years, ten years, twenty years. Life.

"Duncan says the police made some mistakes," she says.

"Duncan?"

"My lawyer."

"Is he good?"

"He's a shark all right, which I guess is what you want. He's smarter than the Jonesville police anyway. They questioned me without my parents present."

"They did that to me, too!"

"Well, they're not supposed to. We're minors. Duncan's trying to get the confession thrown out."

I lean forward, excitedly, like I could dive through the Perspex and whisk her away with me right now.

"He only said that to make an impression," she says, dampening my optimism. "He wants the DA to know we're going to fight. The truth is, they don't even need my confession. My fingerprints are on the beer bottle and on the box where Tarkin kept his drugs. There's enough evidence to prove what I did."

"But what about *why* you did it?"

"If I tell them that, it's just as good as having that confession out there. Duncan doesn't want that right now. He's still working out a strategy. He said the DA's being a hard-ass because he's friends with Tarkin's father."

Marcus warned me about this. The Shaws are "connected" he said. And connected people have a different kind of justice.

"Listen, DeShawn." Her face darkens and I know she's about to tell me something even worse. But I don't think I can take anything else. I want to go back to the part about her confession being thrown out. I want to know more about her lawyer's "strategy." But Suze has something else on her mind. "I don't want you to wait around for—"

"Don't finish that sentence," I blurt out. She sighs heavily. I shake my head at her, trying to cancel the very thought she's having, to cast it from her beautiful head. "I don't care how long it takes. I'm gonna be here."

But my words don't have the effect I was hoping.

"Don't you realize what that does to me?" she says. "The responsibility it puts on me? Don't do that to me, DeShawn." Her face crumples as she tries to hold back her own tears.

"When I came to you that night, before all of this, that night at the pond . . ."

I nod hungrily. *Yes. Tell me more about the night at the pond. Let's go back there. Let's talk about how we joined our bodies together under the stars. Let's talk about that misshapen W watching over us. Let's go there. Let's stay there forever.*

"I know it was a big deal for you," she says. And it was for me too, but—"

Oh God.

Her head drops. She's not even looking at me any more. She drops the phone to the table.

"Suze!"

"Quiet down!" a guard orders.

I lower my voice and say her name over and over into the handset but she can't hear me. Her shoulders start shaking slightly and I know she's crying. My left hand balls into a fist and I can feel my fingernails digging into my palm. I feel so helpless. It's how I felt in the cafeteria at school when everyone was looking at those pictures. When they wouldn't stop no matter what I did. When I was powerless to make the bad things go away. She keeps on crying and I feel like I'm going to explode.

Then, with a force of will I've never witnessed in anyone before, she shuts it all down. She sits up, wipes her face, grabs the phone again and, with a fragile composure, she says, "Don't do that to me, DeShawn. Don't let this ruin you."

There's a part of me that knows what she's asking. She's asking me to grow up. Now. Not gradually like you're supposed to, but suddenly, all at once, like she's had to. There's another part of me that doesn't want to acknowledge what she's asking because I don't think I can do it. I love her. I do. It's not a crush. It's not lust. It's love. And I think, if circumstances were different, *If this goddamn*

Perspex wasn't between us, if things had gone differently that night at Tarkin Shaw's house, she might fall in love with me too. It felt like love that night at the pond. How can I *not* wait for her? How can I not visit her every possible chance? I can't fathom it. But she can, I guess because she's been forced to. She's not being cold or heartless. She's being kind and decent, and unbelievably mature. And that only makes me love her more. So I lie, which does not come naturally to me. I say, "Okay, Suze. I won't wait for you. Don't worry about that. I'll be okay."

Then we just look at each other through this goddamn Perspex and don't say anything for a long time. I think she knows I'm lying, but she doesn't call me on it. Maybe she appreciates that, at the very least, I'm not asking her to reassure me that everything's okay. She shouldn't have to do that. Because it's not okay. And maybe it never will be.

ANI / LYDIA

What are you doing right now?

Watching *Orange Is the New Black*.

Oh God, I can't watch that anymore.

I know. It's too real.

So listen, my dad's friend is a criminal defense lawyer and you know what he said? He said sometimes the best defense is the bastard had it coming. That's a quote.

Really?

He said if the victim is a TOTAL dirtbag it creates sympathy for the accused.

Well he was a TOTAL dirtbag.

Yeah but we need to prove that.

How?

Um, the pictures?

Suze said they're not using that.

No the other ones. The ones of Izzy Rigoletto, Amber Lanes, etc.

Oh, right.

Especially Amber Laynes. They basically Prove that he blackmailed her into changing her story.

Yeah, but what does that have to do with Suze?

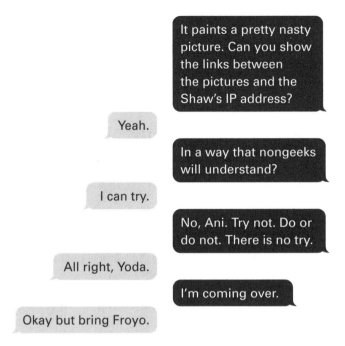

It paints a pretty nasty picture. Can you show the links between the pictures and the Shaw's IP address?

Yeah.

In a way that nongeeks will understand?

I can try.

No, Ani. Try not. Do or do not. There is no try.

All right, Yoda.

I'm coming over.

Okay but bring Froyo.

MARCUS

"This is utter *fucking* bullshit, Marcus! Call me!!!!"

Elena, in her usual charming mood. That's just the latest in a string of colorfully worded messages she's left on my cell. I don't dare actually pick up the phone, because, as she so tactfully pointed out, I suck at lying. Elena's excited because the case against Suze Tilman has taken an unexpected turn. She's mad because she doesn't know why. She's mad at *me*, because she suspects I do. She's right about that. I do know. I know the whole story. It's a tale of deceit and corruption and it goes something like this:

> On Saturday, October 10th, Essex County District Attorney, Timothy Cochrane, was enjoying a gin and tonic at the Abingdale Hunt Club in Waverly, Massachusetts, with some of the area's wealthiest denizens. A frequent guest at Abingdale, though not a member himself, Cochrane is rumored to have raised significant amounts of

money for his reelection campaign from Abingdale's members. Though it is unclear who exactly was present at the Abingdale Hunt Club bar on October 10th, one witness, who insists on anonymity, saw the following: sometime after 3 p.m., Duncan Heath, attorney for Suze Tilman, the 17-year-old currently awaiting trial at MCI-Framingham for the murder of Tarkin Shaw, arrived at the bar and asked to speak with the district attorney in private. Heath had with him a 9x12 inch manila envelope, which he was seen handing to Cochrane in an anteroom near the bar.

Inside that envelope were 143 photographs of nude teenage girls, including 57 photographs of his client, Suze Tilman. The photographs had been posted on a variety of websites without the minors' consent. Two Jonesville High students, Anamika Chakrabarti and Lydia Moreau, were able to demonstrate that they had been posted from an IP address belonging to the Shaws.

The next day, the district attorney arrived at the Cedar Vale home of Darren and Nicole Shaw to discuss the case against Suze Tilman. A longtime friend of Darren Shaw, Cochrane had been in regular contact with the Shaws throughout the process. On this particular visit, however, the district attorney brought with him the photographs linked to their IP address. Though Tilman's confession had previously been quashed because of mishandling by the Jonesville police, Cochrane explained to the Shaws that she was now prepared to testify that she did, in fact, drug their son. Her motivation for doing so was to "neutralize" him so that she could obtain and destroy the nude photographs he had of her. According to Tilman, Shaw took the photographs without her consent after sneaking Rohypnol into a cup of soda she was drinking at a party. He then used the photographs to blackmail her into a sexual relationship. The district attorney informed the Shaws that if the case against Tilman went to trial, her lawyer, Duncan Heath, was prepared to introduce these details in her defense. Heath was also prepared to introduce the photographs of the other underage girls in order to establish that their son had engaged in a pattern of sexual abuse, blackmail, and nonconsensual child pornography.

Three days later, the charges against Suze Tilman were dropped.

Okay, to be fair, I have no idea what Timothy Cochrane was drinking at the Abingdale Hunt Club bar. He seems like a gin and tonic guy to me. But he was definitely there. That detail comes from Elena, who has been busy hitting up every source, dirtbag, and ex-boyfriend she can think of in an attempt to figure out why the charges against Suze Tilman have suddenly been dropped. Elena went to high school with one of the waiters at Abingdale. Waiters at country clubs are fantastic sources, especially if you're covering local politics. And this particular waiter witnessed the handoff of that 9x12 inch envelope. So far, that juicy detail is all Elena's got.

The rest of the story is mine, cobbled together from the scraps I've been able to worm out of Nikki, Ani, and Lydia, all of whom have been beavering away behind the scenes on Suze's behalf. Here are some headlines to go with the story:

"DA Halts Prosecution on Behalf of Rich Donor"

"Dead Rapist's Reputation Scrubbed by Unscrupulous DA"

"Unequal Justice, A Tale of Sexual Violence and Payola"

I could go on, but there's no point, because this masterpiece of exposure—this wallop of truth leveled directly at power—will never be published. At least, not by me. Add it to the list of promising journalistic breakthroughs suffocated at birth. Maybe Elena will be able to get her hands on enough hard evidence to push it over the edge. But I doubt it, because the whole dirty business is sheltered under the protective blanket of a nondisclosure agreement. That was the deal Suze's lawyer worked out with the DA. She signs away her right to say anything about Tarkin's misdeeds, and she walks free.

To cover his tracks, the DA laid the blame for the sudden shift in the prosecution's case on the overzealous Jonesville police who took Suze's confession without her parents present. He claimed that Suze made the confession "under pressure," therefore he had no choice but to throw it out. Tarkin Shaw's death was ruled an accident. A self-inflicted accident.

To put the matter firmly to rest, the Shaws hired the PR firm of Andrus, Mann, and Bartley to disseminate this press release:

> Tarkin Shaw held himself to a very high standard, both as a student and athlete. His pursuit of excellence occasionally resulted in high levels of stress, which interfered with his sleep. In order to maintain his rigorous schedule of training and studying, he occasionally used Rohypnol as a sleep aid. He apparently took the wrong dosage on the night that he died.

That gets published. That piece of self-serving bullroar gets printed on page three of the *Bugle*, right underneath an item about the revamp of the Jonesville Community Pool. It's not on page one, because that would make too big a splash. The Shaws' goal apparently was to get their version of the story out there without drawing too much attention to it. So, if you did manage to see it, you could feel sorry for poor Tarkin Shaw, dead before his time. Dead because he tried too hard. He was too excellent. His standards were too high. What a hero. What a god among men. And the real story, the one about the DA's dirty dealings on behalf of the Shaws (undoubtedly paid for by a generous campaign contribution), simply disappears.

Elena's right about one thing: It is utter fucking bullshit.

In honor of said bullshit, I've added a new Post-it above my desk, right next to the one about journalism's first obligation being to truth. It reads:

The truth is rarely pure and never simple.
—Oscar Wilde

NIKKI

The big day happens on a Friday. After school, Ani and Lydia meet me at Suze's house to sit on her front steps and wait. Suze's mom said she wasn't sure how long the whole process would take, but we don't care. We want to be there when Suze gets home. Even if it's after midnight.

"She's not going to eat that, you know," Ani says, pointing to the homemade chocolate cake Lydia has brought for the occasion.

"It's *organic* chocolate," Lydia explains.

Ani peels the cellophane back and carefully picks off a gummy bear.

"Stop that," Lydia says. She puts the little yellow bear back in place, then moves the cake away from Ani. "I was going to decorate it with make-believe roofies."

"Oh my God, Lydia," Ani says.

"Relax. I changed my mind."

"She'll love it," I say. "Whether she eats it or not, she'll love it."

"I still can't believe she's actually coming home," Lydia says. "Like, we did that. We totally helped."

Lydia's right. It was the dirt on Tarkin that won her that deal. And we were the ones who dug it up. Well, Ani, mostly. But it was Lydia's idea and I wrote the cover letter to Suze's lawyer explaining where the pictures came from. Score one for the Shield.

When the Tilmans' powder-blue Kia turns onto Roberts Road about an hour later, Ani and Lydia rise from the steps, but I'm too scared to look. I have this sudden dread that Suze won't be inside, that there'll be some mix-up, the DA will change his mind, the Shaws will work some deal to keep her in prison despite that nondisclosure agreement. Maybe I'm just not used to things working out right. But when the car pulls into the driveway, I can see the shape of Suze in the back seat. Lydia squeals and runs to the car, followed by Ani. When Suze gets out of the back seat, they engulf her. She's so skinny she disappears between them. I make my way over and wait for Ani and Lydia to release her. Suze's face is wet. She's been crying.

"Is this real?" she says to me.

I run my hands through her choppy short hair. "As real as it gets."

As we make our way to the front door, DeShawn and Marcus speed around the corner on their bikes. Apparently, Mr. Tilman called DeShawn on the way home from MCI-Framingham, at Suze's request. They park their bikes in the driveway, then approach us nervously, as if we're guarding a forbidden treasure. I let go of Suze's hand and she runs to DeShawn, then kisses him softly on the lips.

"Get a room, right?" Marcus mutters to me.

We all crowd into the Tilmans' small kitchen, which was decorated once in the early '80s and never changed—cobalt blue Formica counters and a peeling floral border up near the popcorn ceiling. Suze's mom—who insists everyone call her Deborah, even though we never do—rushes around the kitchen, pulling together a smorgasbord of foods you don't usually find in the same meal: falafel, German weisswurst, ricotta cheese pie. Suze's father opens a bottle of German wine. It's supposed to be a celebration, but the mood is subdued. After a while, Suze takes me upstairs to talk in private.

Her poky little bedroom is painted the color of Pepto Bismol. They didn't change anything when they moved in. It's a temporary residence, like all of their homes. The wooden dressers are scuffed and splintery and the drawers stick when you try to open them. Suze flops onto the rusty canopy bed with a loud squeak.

I kick my sneakers off and sit cross-legged on the bed. "You're not regretting coming home, are you? You could be in Mexico right now."

She inches over and rests her head in my lap.

"Home," she says, glancing around the room. She's lived here for over six months, and she still has clothes spilling out of a vintage blue-gray American Tourister suitcase. "You know what my dad always says? He says *we're* home. Wherever we are, that's home."

"I like your dad."

"You don't think he's an utter weirdo?"

"Well, yeah. But you know me. I like weirdos."

"Like DeShawn?" she asks hopefully, looking up at me and blinking her big brown eyes.

"I'll get used to him."

Beneath the loose floorboards I can hear the low rumble of chatter downstairs, some laughter, the clink of forks on plates. Marcus is telling Suze's father about his work at the *Bugle*. Lydia is showing DeShawn some of her boxing moves in the living room.

"He's definitely won Lydia over," I say.

She flops onto her back again and pulls me down next to her. There's a yellow-brown water stain on the ceiling. "You know what's weird?" she says.

"Besides everything?"

"Yeah, besides that. I think what bothers me the most is the silence."

She's talking about that NDA and the fact that, for the rest of her life, she'll be the girl who took those pictures and sent them to Tarkin. Her boyfriend. For all eternity.

"Am I being selfish?" she asks.

"No," I say. "It bothers me, too."

LATER, AFTER WE'VE eaten Lydia's gummy bear

cake (even Suze had a piece) and gone for a second round at the ricotta cheese pie, Suze's dad yawns hugely and we take that as our cue to leave. Lydia's tipsy from the German wine, so Ani guides her to her own car, while Marcus and DeShawn head to their bikes in the driveway.

"Hey, Marcus," I say, walking to my car. "Do you have a minute?"

Hearing this, DeShawn tells Marcus he'll ride home on his own. "See you at school, Nikki," he says, swinging his leg over his bike.

School. After everything that's happened, it feels inane to have to go back to high school. It feels like we should have graduated already, that the experience we've all endured should substitute for whatever we have left to learn. *I'm supposed to care about my SAT scores right now?*

Marcus walks his bike over to my car. "You all right?" he says. "You've been quiet." A breeze picks up and blows his brown hair into his face. He's due for a haircut. But it looks good on him.

"I've been thinking," I say.

He drops the kickstand, then leans against my car. "Should I be worried?"

"Probably."

"All right, then. Worry me."

I lean next to him and cross my arms. In my gut and in my soul, I know that Suze did the right thing by making that deal and signing that NDA. I would have done it too. In no moral universe does it make sense for Suze to sacrifice her freedom for the privilege of telling a judge or jury what Tarkin Shaw did to her. Her silence is a terrible price, but she's right to pay it.

"I'm listening," Marcus sings.

"I want to tell my story."

"What story?"

"That one."

He looks at me, confused. Then he realizes what I'm saying.

"Can you help me with that?" I ask him.

He looks scared, the same way he was at Dunkin's when I told him what Suze did with Tarkin in that trophy room. I think I upended his world with that story. I might upend it again. And my own along with it.

"Look, I know I can just post it myself somewhere," I tell him. "But—"

"You want it legitimized."

"I want it *published*, Marcus. In a newspaper."

"People will attack you," he says.

"I don't care."

"They won't believe you. They'll call you a liar."

"I already feel like a liar. I've been lying for three years."

"You're sure about this?"

"You can't write anything about Suze and Tarkin, though. It can only be about me and Tarkin."

He swallows nervously. "Are there any witnesses? Any corroborating evidence?"

I shake my head. Tarkin and I were alone in Jayce Conway's parents' room when it happened. What evidence would there be?

"The Shaws are powerful," he says.

"Obviously."

"They'll push back."

"Are you trying to talk me out of this?"

"Maybe."

"Why? Are you worried they'll come after you? Because if you don't want to write it, I can find someone else. Maybe that colleague of yours."

"No!" he blurts out. "I just—I don't want you to get hurt." His pale cheeks redden, and he looks away to cover the fact.

I think I've been reading Marcus wrong. He's not an arrogant loudmouth. Well, he's not *just* that. He's other things, too. He's brave. And I think he's more sensitive than he likes to let on.

"I'd really like it to be you," I tell him.

"Why?"

"Because I trust you. Don't act surprised."

"Okay," he says sighing. "I'll do it. Where should we go? Dunkin's?"

"No." The thought of telling him face-to-face horrifies me. "Go home. I'll tell you over the phone."

MARCUS

It takes Nikki three hours to get through her story. She has to stop twice, hang up, and take a break. Each time she comes back to the phone, she sounds hoarser, more fragile. It may have happened three years ago, but it's still raw. It's hard for me to imagine what it must have been like to carry that secret around all this time. I think Nikki feels guilty, as if her silence allowed Shaw to continue. She may have been his first, but she wasn't his last.

But in a way, we were all silent about Tarkin Shaw. And I don't exclude myself from this category, either. I knew what he was, even before the Amber Laynes story. I heard the rumors. I heard him call Tamara Kasowitz a "disease-ridden whore" outside the cafeteria one day, to the explosive laughter of his idiot friends. It happened right in front of me and I didn't say a word. I shook my head and thought of a great insult, but I never *said* it. Shaw and his friends saw me hearing it and doing nothing, just like they saw everyone else doing nothing. Of course that emboldened them. Their immunity was reinforced every day. When Tony Petrof whacked Kendra Peaks on the butt after art class, I kept my mouth shut and let it go.

Me. This mouth. When you have a mouth like mine and you don't use it, you may just be a bystander, but you're not an innocent one.

I stay up most of the night writing Nikki's story because I have to get it right. I'm taking down a dead kid, a sacred cow. Nikki's right. The Shaws and their powerful friends will probably come after me for it. So if I'm going down, I want it to be for a perfect piece of journalism. At 5:47 a.m., I send Nikki the final draft and she texts back:

It's perfect. Thank you.

Now comes the hard part.

There's not a chance in hell that Schnell will publish this in the *Bugle*. For one thing, I can't prove Nikki's claims. It happened three years ago, and the only other person who could corroborate her story (A) wouldn't, and (B) is dead. For another, Schnell's too much of a wimp to risk angering the Shaws and their well-connected friends. Whatever passion he once had for journalism sputtered out a long time ago. He's a salary man now. He's not interested in making waves.

When I show up at the *Bugle* office on Saturday, he's there, slumped over his keyboard and joylessly banging away on something—a spreadsheet, probably, a budget, something to worsen his mood. Elena's there too, ensconced in her cubicle, swinging her chair side to side while *mm-hmm*-ing with someone on her cell phone who's clearly boring her. She puts them on mute so she can say, "How's your girlfriend?"

"Which one?" I say. Elena's been teasing me about both Suze *and* Nikki. I knock on the glass of Schnell's door. He gives me the one-minute finger.

"I know you know something," Elena says.

"You're the one with a mole at the hunt club," I remind her. "Is that him on the phone?"

"Here's what I don't get, though," she says. "We all know Cochrane's a money-grubbing piece of shit, but he's not a cheap one. And the Tilmans can barely rub two nickels together. So it wasn't a bribe. It wasn't cash in that envelope."

"I don't know what envelope you're talking about, Elena. I'm not a member of that club. I wasn't there."

"Why won't the Tilmans speak to the press? The girl gets off scot-free and she has nothing to say? Even the Shaws sent out that press release."

"The Shaws must care what people think of them."

"The Tilmans don't?"

"I seriously doubt it. Suze doesn't, anyway. I think she wants to put the whole thing behind her. Go back to her anonymous life."

"Anonymous. Good one. Why'd she skip town?"

"Wanderlust."

"Oh, come on."

375

"No, seriously. According to her friends, she skips town all the time. The Tilmans are basically nomadic."

"She confessed to roofying him."

"Under pressure."

"Does she seem like the type to be pressured?"

"Maybe," I lie. If anyone could stand up to police pressure, it's Suze Tilman. "I'm only just now getting to know the girl. But according to her friends, she's a bit of an enigma."

"Did Petronzio tell you that? Are you two a thing now?"

Schnell taps on the glass and waves me into his office.

"You should stay away from Italian-American girls," Elena tells me. "They're trouble."

"Tell me something I don't already know."

Schnell's office smells like cheap coffee, bad breath, and despair. He gestures for me to sit in one of his extremely uncomfortable wooden chairs, but I prefer to stand. He slumps into his own chair and downs an IBS pill with a can of Diet Coke.

"Good news," I tell him. "I've reconsidered the blog."

He eyeballs me suspiciously, assuming there's an angle, some way this could actually be bad news.

"No, seriously," I say. "I've been thinking about it and you're right. I do have something to say. And I'm well-positioned to cover the beat at school. There's actually a lot going on there."

"They want a mix. Hard news. Sports. Plenty of sports, Marcus."

"I can do sports."

"Features, profiles, lifestyle."

"Not a problem. I'm a versatile writer with a variety of interests."

"Yeah, yeah."

"There is one condition, though. I want total editorial control."

"No."

"My byline. My choice."

"Not gonna happen."

"No running it by corporate or business affairs first."

"That's a non-starter."

"Those are my terms."

"Denied. Everything gets run by me."

"Okay, what's Kik?"

"Pardon?"

"It's a mobile app. What does *on fleek* mean?"

"On what?"

"*Bae, thirsty, dead?*"

Schnell goes limp.

"Look, I know what this thing is supposed to be," I tell him. "By teens, for teens, about teens. And if it comes out with a goddamn corporate seal of approval, you know how many teens are going to read it? None. See how much VitaminWater that sells."

"Why are you doing this to me, Marcus?"

"Hey, don't blame me. I'm just trying to keep this newspaper afloat." I wink at him.

What comes back to me? Daggers. Flying straight out of his dead, seen-too-much eyes, aimed right at my freshly scrubbed, stubble-free face. He hates me so much right now. And I don't blame him. If I were Schnell, I'd hate me too. But Schnell is a tired man. He doesn't want to fight. He wants to make "corporate" happy. He wants to keep his job, so he can continue to pay his mortgage and live his sad life.

"They want it three times a week," he says, totally resigned to my terms.

"Twice," I say. "I need time to do regular news too."

"Fine. And you have to moderate the comments section yourself. Corporate doesn't want to get involved."

"With pleasure."

I have no intention of moderating anything. To my mind, there is no space more degenerate than a comments section.

The post goes live on Sunday morning.

FROM *TEEN BEAT* (NOT A BLOG):

Jonesville High Senior Speaks Out
by Marcus Daubney

From the moment he arrived at Jonesville High, Tarkin Shaw was a force to contend with. Already 6'3" and 217 pounds at age 14, he was courted by the Jonesville High wrestling coach and was the first freshman ever to make the varsity squad. As the youngest member, he was severely hazed, but, by all accounts, he never complained about it. Tarkin Shaw wanted to be a wrestling star. He became much more than that.

Shaw made a name for himself off of the wrestling mat too. He was a "stud," a "legend," a "player." He was also trailed by rumors of sexual assault. His aggressive sexual exploits were an open secret among his classmates and something he often bragged about in public. According to one of his victims, "It wasn't just about scoring with girls. It was about humiliating them afterward. Making them feel like dirt. That's how he bigged himself up. And kids loved him for it. Especially guys."

Despite such overt sexual aggression, previous attempts to expose Shaw's behavior proved unsuccessful. When it comes to sexual assault, victims are often unwilling to come forward and identify themselves. The fear of retribution is too strong.

#

Three years ago, Nikki Petronzio, 14 at the time, attended a party at an older teen's house in Jonesville. Tarkin Shaw, also 14, was at the same party. They had known each other since kindergarten. According to Petronzio, Shaw was "anxious to impress the varsity wrestlers by drinking as much as they did." At one point, three of the varsity wrestlers challenged Shaw to dive off the top of a staircase into a pile of sofa cushions they'd hastily arranged on the floor below. Concerned for Shaw's safety, Petronzio led him away into an upstairs bedroom. Her plan was to keep Shaw there while she called her parents to pick them both up. "We shouldn't have been at this party at all," Petronzio recounts. "We were way too young for this stuff."

When she realized her phone was still in her jacket downstairs, she asked Shaw for his, but he refused to give it to her. Outside the door, some older boys were shouting at Shaw to "nail her." When he tried to kiss her, Petronzio gently pushed him away, explaining that he was too drunk. Petronzio herself was sober.

According to Petronzio, her refusal angered Shaw. He insisted he wasn't drunk and that he could handle his beer. He tried to kiss her again. When she attempted to move away from him, he grabbed her by the shoulders and pinned her to the bed.

Petronzio tried to scream, but Shaw covered her mouth with his own, an experience she described as "suffocating." The more she struggled to get out from under him, the more angry and violent he became, digging his fingers into her shoulders and tearing at her clothes. "I felt like I was in a vice," Petronzio says. "I couldn't breathe. He was covering my nose too. I could hear the horrible, choked-off sounds I was making, thinking 'This is the last thing I'll ever know, the sound of my own death.'"

When Shaw finally removed his mouth from Petronzio's, she gasped for air. It was at that moment that she realized Shaw's fingers were inside of her. She started crying, which angered Shaw. He rolled off of her and vomited on the floor. Petronzio fled the room and ran home.

She told no one what happened, not even her parents.

In the days and weeks that followed, Petronzio remained silent about the incident. "I couldn't believe what happened," she says. "He was my friend. I've known him since kindergarten. We used to play in a paddling pool together. How could he do this to me?"

Shaw did not remain silent. He told fellow students a different version of events. In Shaw's version, it was Petronzio who initiated sexual contact with him, and it was Shaw who rejected her. For the rest of freshman year, Shaw and his fellow wrestlers taunted, threatened, and made crude sexual remarks to Petronzio, including threats of rape. On numerous occasions, Shaw's teammates grabbed her, snapped her bra strap, and slapped her buttocks. She says of the experience: "I felt like I was under constant attack, like they were preying on me. It was terrifying. They were everywhere. I couldn't get away."

In the three years since that incident, multiple allegations of sexual misconduct have been made against Shaw and other members of the Jonesville High wrestling team. Though some of these allegations are as yet unsubstantiated, in at least one case, a police report was filed. Amber Laynes accused Tarkin Shaw of rape at a party at Shaw's house on April 4th of last year. She later recanted her story. However, it is widely believed that she did so under pressure from Shaw's influential family.

"Sometimes I wonder what would have happened if I'd gone to the police that night," Petronzio says. "Could I have stopped him? Would that have prevented him from becoming what he became?"

We may never know the answer to that question. What Shaw became, however, is not in dispute. He became a sexual bully. He never made any attempt to hide the fact that he enjoyed sexual conquest and humiliation. In fact, he built his reputation on it. He is survived by 17 teammates, many of whom spent the last week making rape and death threats against Petronzio and her friends.

"They've created a climate of fear," Petronzio says. "If you challenge them, they threaten you. That's how they've always operated. And nobody does anything about it. They say, 'Oh, it's just a joke,' or, 'Boys will be boys.' They're allowed to say and do whatever they want."

Petronzio says that her silence for the past three years has been a source of regret. She wishes she'd spoken up earlier about what Shaw did to her. She believes other students at Jonesville High have similar stories.

"People think I'm a snob," she says. "Or a mean girl. But the truth is, I was so humiliated my freshman year, I basically lost the ability to trust anyone. It's not just the act itself, it's the aftermath, the constant harassment. I just want every girl at Jonesville High to know that this is not okay. You don't have to put up with it. I'm strong enough now to tell my story. And I'm truly sorry I didn't speak up sooner."

If you have a story you want to share, please contact me at *Marcus.Daubney@TheBugle Jonesville.com*. All sources will be kept anonymous except where identification is expressly permitted.

Whoever you are, you are not alone.

NIKKI

On Monday morning, the girls and I meet up early in the school parking lot and huddle around Ani's car. The article has been live since yesterday afternoon, but I haven't gone online and I don't intend to. I haven't even turned on my phone. I'm going analog for the rest of the day. Possibly for the rest of my life.

"Maybe we should cut school," Ani suggests. "Head to the beach?"

The first bell hasn't rung yet, so only a few kids are trickling in. We could make a clean getaway before any teachers spot us, cruise to Wingaersheek, spend the day on my rock.

Suze puts her arm around me. "Whatever you want, Nikki. Whatever you decide."

It's not just about me, though. The knives will be out for her, too. Never mind that the only reason she got off so easy is because of the Shaws' influence. Never mind that it was in service of Tarkin's reputation. Nobody will know that, because she's not allowed to talk about it. All they'll know is that she confessed to killing Tarkin Shaw and now she's

385

free, *somehow*. She'll spend the rest of her days at Jonesville High under a fog of suspicion.

Over by the soccer field, DeShawn and Marcus lock up their bikes, then run over to join us.

"Don't tell me about the comments," I tell Marcus. I can tell from the look in his eye that he's read them. "Are there a lot, though?"

"Do you really want to know?"

That means there are tons.

When I told Marcus my story, I was shaking the whole time. I don't think I would have gotten through it in person. Doing it over the phone made it easier. He waited me out, made no judgments, then asked all the right questions. Most importantly, he didn't ask the wrong ones. He didn't ask why I let myself be alone with Tarkin. Or why I let him sit so close to me on that bed. He didn't ask why I never reported it. All the questions I've asked myself over the years. Instead, he asked how I ever managed to be alone with a boy after that, how I'm not always afraid. I told him I *am* always afraid. I just try to hide it.

The first bell rings. We still have five minutes until we have to be in homeroom, and I can feel the tug of Wingaersheek Beach. But I suppose I have to face school eventually. At some point, I have to walk those halls and face those disapproving eyes. I have to be that freshman girl all over again. Only now, people will know the real story, whether they believe it or not.

"You're not having second thoughts, are you?" Marcus asks me.

Second, third, fourth, fifth. I'm thinking about what's going to happen when my parents read this. I'm having all the thoughts it's possible to have right now. What Tarkin said about me freshman year was a disgusting lie, but the truth is every bit as ugly. To be overpowered like that, to be smothered. To be reduced to a quivering receptacle, a *thing*. All so he could prove himself to some older boys. I didn't even count. I could have been anybody. There's nothing about that story that I want to share with the world. If I could undo it, I would.

I'm telling it because I want to stop them. Not Tarkin. It's too late for that. But his friends, and all the guys who take their cues from them, the way Tarkin took his cues from those older boys at that party. Mason Shaw and Sean Princely. Russ Minichek and Tony "Mad Dog" Petrof. Hell, even Principal Everett, who kowtows to them and their rich, influential parents. I want to stop *them*. Maybe this one article won't be enough. Maybe nothing is enough. But I have to try. Because I know what happens when you surrender to silence. You don't forget. You don't get peace. The secret you're keeping gets louder and louder until it's all you can hear. And I can't live with that anymore.

"No," I tell Marcus. "I'm good."

"Nikki," DeShawn says, "I hope I'm not being presumptuous or anything, but"—he unzips his backpack and pulls out a little package wrapped in tissue paper and tied with twine— "Suze and I were talking the other day, and I made this for you."

Inside the paper is a small, blue-and-gold shield with a starburst pattern on the front and a tiny handle on the back.

"It's pewter," he says. "And the handle there is a pin, so you can wear it if you want."

"You made this?"

Lydia and Ani huddle in for a closer look.

"I based it on the movie," he says. "Not the comic book. I hope that's okay."

"Is that what I think it is?" Ani asks.

It's Wonder Woman's shield.

"Put it on," Suze says. She takes it from me and pins it to my shirt, then opens her jean jacket and reveals an identical one pinned to her sweatshirt. DeShawn removes two more from his backpack and hands them to Ani and Lydia.

"I've been spending a lot of time in my workshop," he explains.

"I can vouch for that," Marcus says.

"Is this your way of sucking up to us?" Lydia asks, as she puts hers on.

"No. I've always liked Wonder Woman," he says. "She's crazy strong, but she's all about love."

Suze shoots him a shy, smitten look and he giggles and looks down. Jesus. *Smitten*. I never thought I'd use the words *smitten* and *Suze* in the same sentence.

When we all have our pins on, Suze and Lydia take my hands.

"Shall we?" Suze says. "I mean, now that we've got these shields to protect us."

I guess there's no point in postponing the inevitable. As we make our way across the parking lot in a tight huddle, Marcus tells me that he's already been contacted by four girls with stories of their own. Two of them are anonymous. But the other two, Sybil Camire and Star Gelling, are willing to go on the record with their names.

"I think this is the just the beginning," he says. "I think there'll be more."

I don't know how to feel about that. I can't say it surprises me. I've always known there were more of us out there. But as we near the entrance to the school, all I can think about is getting through this day. I try to draw strength from this little pewter shield, and from the circle of friends it represents. But the more I think about it, the more I realize I'll never be safe. No one is. And when you realize just how vulnerable and unsafe you are, it feels scary at first. And then it feels like something else. It feels like freedom.

"Hey, DeShawn," Lydia says. "Can you make a little sword to go with this shield?"

"I can make anything," he says.

"The Godkiller sword," Marcus says. "Isn't that what they called it?"

"Yeah," Ani says, "to kill Ares, the god of war."

But if I remember correctly, it wasn't the sword that had all the power. It was Wonder Woman herself. The sword was just a decoy.

Dave Abate and Richie O'Hearn rush through the entrance, like they can't put enough distance between themselves and us. Martina Landry and her clutch of cheerleader pals hang back to give us a wide berth.

"Shields up," Lydia says.

I hold the door open and take a deep breath. This motley assortment of troublemakers and misfits are my Shield. And now there are six of us, instead of four, so I guess the Shield is bigger. But it won't protect me. It won't protect any of us.

That's not even its purpose. I realize that now, and it's why I suddenly feel so free. The purpose of the Shield is to give us strength, to remind us who we are and where we belong. To say these are our people, our family, our home. No matter where we are. And no matter what happens.

"All right," I say as I step inside to face the inevitable one more time. "Let's go kill some gods."

The end.

ACKNOWLEDGMENTS

I would like to thank my brilliant and insightful editor, Jennifer Baumgardner, who understands these characters on a deep level and who came up with the title. Her edit notes were positively inspired. Larissa Melo Pienkowski, a fellow North Shore girl, was instrumental in aligning my memories of the area with the current reality of teens growing up there today. Thanks also to Hannah Goodwin, my ace copy editor, who wisely protected me from my worst instincts, to Kait Heacock for helping me understand publicity, and to Drew Stevens and Erin Wade for making this book look so great.

My agent, Jill Grinberg, has been a tireless champion of this book and has guided me through multiple drafts with her talented team, especially Denise Page, Sylvie Epstein, and Sophie Wazlowski. I would never survive the wilderness of publishing without them.

My friend, Ernest Stone, offered crucial insight into criminal matters and provided the wonderful phrase, "Sometimes the best defense is the bastard had it coming." I'd also like to thank Tracy Dudevoir for useful information about the criminal justice system in Massachusetts. Any mistakes are mine and mine alone.

As always, Andrew Woffinden has been a bottomless well of support and encouragement, as well as a living, breathing reminder of how beautiful men can be—which was incredibly important through the long years of researching toxic masculinity.

And finally, I want to thank my high school Shield: Lisa DeAngelis, Janis Jendrasek Linehan, and Janine Raby. We got up to some shit, but we had each other's backs.